QUEST PANDORA

QUEST PANDORA

DERRICK JOHN WIGGINS

authorHOUSE®

AuthorHouse™
1663 Liberty Drive
Bloomington, IN 47403
www.authorhouse.com
Phone: 1-800-839-8640

Published by AuthorHouse 5/1/2013

ISBN: 978-1-4817-3474-5 (sc)
ISBN: 978-1-4817-3472-1 (hc)
ISBN: 978-1-4817-3473-8 (e)

Library of Congress Control Number: 2013905546

For unto everyone that hath shall be given, and he shall have abundance:

Matthew 25:29

Put your future in good hands—your own.

FOREWORD

HOW DO YOU BEAT AN EVIL that can't be undone?

The gods didn't want man to throw his life away, no matter how much evil tormented him, but rather go on letting himself be tormented anew.

To that end, the gods gave man hope. In truth, it's the most evil of evils because it prolongs man's torment.

Friedrich Nietzsche

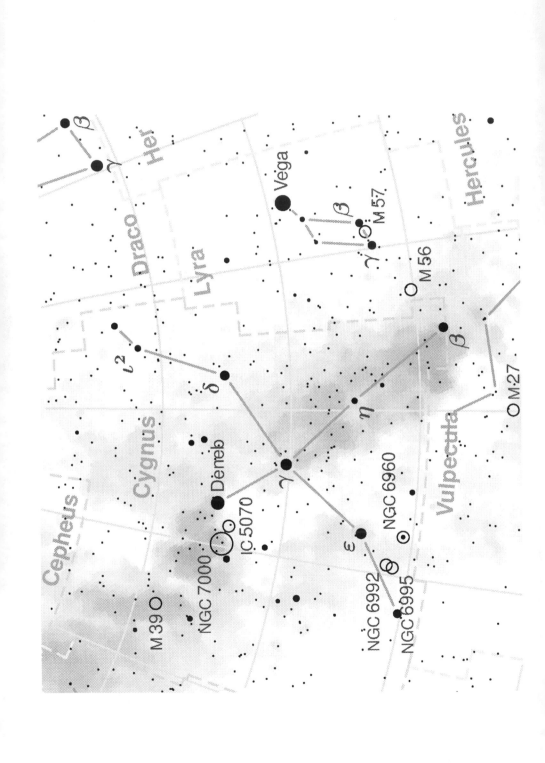

CHAPTER 1

ALASKA, THE DENALI NATIONAL PARK PRESERVE was what it was called now. The name had gone through some changes. First it was called Mount McKinley National Park in 1917. Then it was called Denali National Monument in 1978.

He knew all of the names and studied the place well. He had to; it was what he did all his life. He always researched his environments anywhere he traveled, slept, or worked. Today was a workday.

He speculated, how did Mr. Burrows see him make the move toward him? Was he getting old at this? No, he was only thirty years old. Was he getting sloppy? Yes, he was getting careless.

He'd been doing this job for ten years and trained for it five years earlier than that. He'd been doing this his whole life; *don't get shoddy now.* His superiors taught him better.

Maybe a grizzly bear or wolf will do his job for him? He laughed. Highly unlikely, he figured, given the circumstances that these animals, though vicious and huge, stayed away from humans, and it was the middle of the day. It brought him back to the reality that he was going to have to see this one through.

He ran over another honeydew grassy hill hoping to see Burrows. *Nothing yet.* There were only more rolling lush hills with miles of a tea green tundra.

He was surprised how fast he could sprint in his heavy black snorkel parka. Yes, he was still conditioned. He had to concentrate on his tracking.

His hunting skills were impeccable. His occupation at hunting humans might sound insane to most, but one had to look at it through his eyes. He saw the target as not human but more like a vermin. Think about it, he considered. *What do I do when I need pest control? What do I do to prevent diseases?* A pest to the fabric of his organization had to be dealt with so the disease won't spread. Believe, he assumed, it works and has worked many times.

He had been on dozens of missions before. For ten years he specialized in baiting, camouflaging, flushing, scouting, and trapping humans in the wilderness and civilized situations alike. He named his human hunts either big game or predator.

This hunt today was big game. It was big game because the individual being hunted wasn't skilled enough to escape. He may fight back, but with only futile results of his demise.

A predator hunt was skilled in what he was skilled in. The only edge he had was they usually didn't know he was coming.

The predator hunts were agents expelled from the association— rogue, awol, individuals of that nature.

This institute was run like the mafia; there was no getting out, this was his life. They told all the agents of this in the beginning.

He wondered, if he was to quit, was there an agent better than he, on the hunt for him? No time to think about that right now; he had a wild rabbit to catch and the farmers, his superiors, were nervous.

He could see his exhaust in front of him smoothing out now. He was in his rhythm and warm in the ten degree weather.

When he ran to the top of the next hill, he stopped for a second and checked his bearings.

The hills ended about a mile ahead of him, as far as he could see. In all directions there was nothing but flat gray grass that seemed to go on endlessly. The powder blue sky with white long clouds scattered everywhere would have been a spectacular view if he cared.

He smiled, not because of the view, but because he spotted his rabbit, Mr. Burrows. "Get it," he whispered, "rabbit—burrows."

He pulled his SIG Sauer P226 9mm from his jacket and took aim. He seemingly could have hit him from this distance, about a mile away.

He watched at the tip end of the black gun, Burrows run from his cover of the hills across the level grass. He moved his gun past Burrows to study his direction of flight.

Then he saw it. The small forest was about two or three miles east of Burrows' position. The many slender cylindrical evergreen trees called white spruce were spread wide from each other.

It didn't make a good hiding place, but used right and with the right skills, could lift your chance of survival, just a little. He knew Burrows lacked that skill. *Just in case, though, why wait to find out?*

He only had about eight more hills to run over. Then he'd have a clearer shot, and judging his speed over Burrows, he'd get him probably before his chances were raised.

He put away his gun and sprinted ahead.

The first two hills were easy; he jetted over them in about twenty seconds. The next few were taller and more evenly spaced out. They were harder to run over, but he pushed on.

He jogged six miles every other day when he wasn't on a mission. This is nothing, he kept thinking. The only strain he felt was adrenalin; the thrill of the hunt, and he was excited.

Every time he made it to the top of a hill he could feel himself closing in on his prey. He was sure Burrows felt it, too, death creeping upon him as he reached the crest of another hill.

He saw the rabbit glancing back as it sprinted.

Three more hills to go. Two. One.

He felt like shooting him from atop the final hill. The clear high open shot was tempting, but using his better judgment he thought against it. It was a sure kill, but to shoot on the flat ground in a direct line, of course the chances were greater for a hit on the first shot. A straight line from point A to B, mathematically always reach his destination quicker.

When he reached the hill's end, he pulled his handgun out again.

Strange, he pondered; the man hadn't made it far, he guessed about a little more than a half mile and about two miles from the forest. He knew the guy was overweight, but he wasn't that fat. He felt he himself was just that fit and Burrows wasn't used to this sort of exercise. He smirked, his bad luck.

Aiming, he fired his pistol. In the distance he watched the man drop.

Damn, he was going to have to shoot him again, he realized. He aimed at his head, but the bullet hit him in the back. He saw feathers flutter up in the air from the rear of the man's coat before he fell. From this distance the velocity of the bullet arched from the effect of gravity. It apparently didn't go deep enough because Burrows was struggling to get up. He might have miscalculated his ratio of miles. Burrows could have been a mile away. This flat, almost endless terrain sometimes can play tricks on the eye.

He jogged toward his injured target; he had to get this over with. This was still a civilian park, and a ranger could pop out anywhere at any time. Also someone might have heard the loud bang from the firearm. Hopefully not; he felt the gun didn't give off an echo though the mountains were just far enough away.

As he trotted, the ground was slushy beneath his feet, and his rabbit left no tracks. Like his rabbit's, his own footprints disappeared. His boots slipped ankle-high under the tall grass. Marsh mixed with frozen dirty snow sloshed about, slowing his trot a bit. Now he knew why Burrows didn't move as fast as he thought. After running over all those hills he had to make it past this almost unseen swamp before entering the forest.

Moving his pace to a walk, he found Burrows crawling through the muddy shrubs.

Burrows, who wore a dark blue snorkel jacket, tried to crawl as fast as he could, but just kept stumbling in the mud face-first, turning his entire wardrobe black and soggy.

He noticed, Burrows, realizing he was walking beside him, stopped and turned on his side huffing and puffing, his breath shooting out like steam on a nineteenth century locomotive.

"What ... I." Burrows coughed spitting up blood onto the mud. "What I leave ... behind will be woven." He hacked some more. "... will be woven into the lives of others." He breathed in deeply, trying to catch his wind.

Standing over Burrows, he aimed his gun at the man's head. The gun felt funny in his gloved hand as a cold wind whipped around him, making his thick pants flutter. Maybe he felt the cold now because the pursuit was over—no more adrenalin fix.

"A taste for truth ..." Burrows rambled on, "... at any cost is a passion—"

He shot him in the head. The bullet made a quarter size hole in Burrows's temple, shutting him up indefinitely. He lay there still on his side in the mud as if he were asleep. Blood poured out of the hole to gush slowly down the right side of his mudded face.

The *truth* is common people need not know about it; they couldn't handle it, he contemplated. Just like Burrows here. It was amazing he got this far. Burrows, throwing the hot coffee into his face back at the base, was a daring move, but it only bought him time.

He dropped his 9mm onto the grass next to the body. Bending down, opening the lapel of the coat, he searched through the inner pockets. The gray flash drive was in the left pouch. He took it out, smirked, then held it in the air probing it.

What truths were on here for the world to see? He didn't even know. He didn't care. His job was to track and retrieve.

He stuffed the thumb drive into his right pocket. He was superstitious about putting things in the same pocket as a dead man.

He walked out of the marsh from where he had came, leaving his gun behind. Taking into account, he considered, if detectives find the body, they won't have to search far to find out whom the weapon belonged to. That would be considering the elements or animals don't get to the remains first. The weapon was registered to a state trooper who reported it was stolen two days earlier. Who knows maybe authorities will see it as a suicide.

He shivered, not because of the act he just committed, but because of the cold. It was ten degrees, but the wind made it feel as if it was ten below. He jogged over the hills again back to the highly secure military base FG2.

To the public, FG2 was known as CRC, Cyberspace Regulations Center. The place was supposed to keep the Internet safe from major hackers of government-owned firms, domestically and globally. Part of it did; most of it didn't.

If someone was to investigate, they would find that the place was funded by S&T, Under Secretary for Science and Technology. The center, to him known as FG2, Fort Greely II, was also funded by and an extension of Fort Greely a army launch site for anti-ballistic missiles. *Now what did that have to do with cyberspace?* Nothing, he pondered.

Think about something else other than the cold, he kept deliberating. The late Burrows got a pretty good jump on him for him to jog all this way back to the center, a couple of miles to be exact. Burrows had some kind of sixth sense when he moved toward him in the cafeteria.

Burrows usually had lunch around one o'clock when everybody else was finished, then stepped outside for his lone afternoon walk. He was going to grab Burrows at that time, and make it look like he was shot in front of the facility.

The center weeks earlier had some threats made by some new far left-wing Green Party radicals. They claimed the CRC was just put together to spy on citizens' home computers. They alleged CRC hired the best hackers in the world, and was funded by the S&T, which was funded by Homeland Security.

They had been right. CRC was also funded by his directors, something the Green Party he assumed didn't know.

His superiors then formulated a plan on how Mr. Burrows was going to die. Green Party revenge.

Burrows must have figured someone was after him, the way he jumped at him. He had to give the guy a little credit. He did manage to chase him for miles out here in the cold.

He did for a minute wonder why his directors wanted this thumb drive so badly. He didn't know if it was stolen or did Burrows own it. It didn't matter, and he didn't care; all he knew, he was on a mission most people seldom traveled.

Most missions he took, if he had to tell anybody about them, he'd have to kill them. His name was secret, as were his benefactors.

As he continued back to the facility, he reached into his left pocket and took out a small old salt bottle, one he stole from a diner before taking the job. He poured some salt into his gloved hand, then threw the salt over his shoulder. Stuffing the bottle back into his pocket, he felt for another small object. Though he could hardly feel the soft rabbit's foot in his thick gloved hand, he imagined it. Just the idea that he knew the charm was there brought him comfort. He sighed; another operation well done.

CHAPTER 2

NZINGHA CHELSEA stood next to many full-glass ceiling to floor windows on the sixtieth floor, the last floor of the East Impending Tower. Her eyes closed, she faced a window already knowing the Rhodes State Office Tower, LeVeque Tower, and Scioto River were there. She closed her eyes with her head up and hands behind her back as if she were smelling the sweet air. She wasn't; she was meditating in deep thought.

She couldn't deny that she felt a little prevailing, though through her actions many people thought of her as modest. Her twin glass cylindrical towers were the tallest in all of Ohio and her black Carolina Herrera pants suit she wore today was custom made. Anyone in her position would feel this way—commanding.

She stood in the large conference room with prestige as if she owned Ohio, as if she owned the world. Without a doubt she was the richest self-made woman on the globe, and she had done it through technology.

Antimatter-propelled police vehicles in Columbus glided about below her. Police automobiles floating three feet off the ground, void of wheels, were now in every major city in the United States. It had taken two years to do this.

Many American scientists considered her company physicists geniuses when they unlocked the problem in the physics of antiparticles annihilated with matter giving off energy for centuries. Now Columbus, Cleveland, and Cincinnati's electric power grids were replaced by Chelsea Energy.

Scientists at the DOE, United States Department of Energy, said they were some kind of baryogenesis masterminds. Along with the Central Intelligence Agency, the DOE wanted to interrogate her people, but Chelsea allowed no such thing. She owned the largest law firm in America, and she was prepared for a vicious battle for privacy.

The government knew this and backed away for now. The United States Government had many tricks up their sleeves, like the renowned Patriot Act bill. Chelsea Industries, for now, was proven to be no terrorist, and side transactions like working exclusively with the DOE slowed government action toward the company.

Other things jumbled her thoughts as she waited in the large white round conference room. This was the largest meeting room in the building and the least visited.

A huge white donut-like table sat in the center with twenty-three green rolling chairs evenly spaced out around it. The room's clean white floor sparkled and ceiling alike. Above and equal to the size of the table a huge round mirror reflected the image below, causing an illusion of a hole in the ceiling.

Usually her assistants and executive managers were here first, waiting on her, but today was different. She wanted to ponder on the battlefield before the battle. Like an ancient maiden warrior, she cased the landscape alone before the great crusade.

Opening her eyes to look out the window, she noticed she was even higher than the late afternoon sun as it raced toward the west horizon. She truly felt domineering, just this day.

This important meeting was classified from most of her staff. The last time she had a meeting here, three years earlier, was about her antimatter energy. She had secret discussions on how to release it to the public, the press, the world. Today she was repeating the same thing.

Then, to talk about classified, brings back memories of a man, a few years ago, named Maddox Mathews, a.k.a. Mathew Mathews, a.k.a. maybe FBI agent, a.k.a. probably CIA. The spy who managed to get close to her worked for an advertising company called Alona.

Alona in which was still a part of the Chelsea Company claimed to be totally flabbergasted about the situation and apologized many times that they hired such a man. Till this day she didn't know if she fully believed them or not.

Then, on the subject of believing, several years ago, she wondered if what her stepfather told her was the truth. She asked him, "did you have anything to do with an assassin within my company killing industrialists in competitive corporations of Chelsea, resulting in my takeovers?"

Her stepfather told her, "yes, a hired gun within my company was sent to the States to infiltrate your firm."

There were rumors; the purpose was to make her company grow rapidly. The motive on why this individual wanted her to grow was unclear. Someone wanted to spread her technology quicker—maybe—but why? *Nigerian authorities with his personal investigators were inspecting the matter.*

Her stepfather claimed no hand in the incident and was shocked as she was when he heard of such things. *He'd been investigating for two years and had come up with nothing.* She wondered at first if she should believe her stepfather. She speculated if the conspirator was he himself. It would have been his motive to push his only daughter's endeavors.

She confided in him, for she'd known him all her life since infancy. He was the father and mother she never had, her mentor, her only family.

She'd known some women in his life in her teenage years, but he never stayed with them, never married. He was married to his business.

Through the years she felt she swiftly excelled more academically than he, but she never detected him for a hypocrite—ever. She cherished her stepfather, Xavier, the only man she ever loved.

Bring your focus on this meeting. Chelsea closed her eyes again. In five minutes the doors of this conference room were going to burst open with executives ready to discuss how to market her new project, PE.

The executive board agreed to call the product they were about to sell, Elf, after the attributes of the mythological Germanic beings similarities. Early and modern folklore about elves had changed from time to time but there was something constant about them.

Project Elf, mimicked the fable elves that were known as young, beautiful, beings with magical powers that kept them young almost indefinitely. The nanomedicine, PE, Project Elf, did the same to humans—like elves it advertised to keep you young, beautiful, and disease free. In reality injecting this product it was guaranteed the individual lived to be in the least the hundreds.

Chelsea Company scientists had mastered regenerating damaged cells using advanced drug delivery systems. They had found the secret to constructing cell repairing molecular machines, revolutionizing the medical field and paving their way toward a significant impact on the world economy.

The press had called the discovery, if true, the elixir of life. *This meeting, to date was most important.*

A secretary opened the door and stuck her head inside.

"Ms. Chelsea, I think everyone is here," she said toward Chelsea's back. "Should I escort them in or do you need more time?"

Chelsea, opening her eyes, spun around and gave a half smile. She clapped her hands, rubbed them, then spoke, "Carmela, let's get this started."

Chelsea observed Carmela's visage enlighten as if to say, *okay, let's do this; the moment of truth is here.* Chelsea watched her dip out of the room. *She looked cute in her black skirt suit.*

The businessmen filled the room, pouring in like a charcoal and navy blur of suits. The smell of cologne and aftershave replenished her nostrils. She welcomed it all, the masculine scene. She grinned inside; outwardly she showed the guys her serious game face.

After everyone shook hands and greeted each other they occupied eleven chairs around the table. Five executives sat on Chelsea's left and five on her right.

"A blind man knows he cannot see," Chelsea spoke out, glancing at everyone, "and is glad to be led; but he who is blind in understanding is the worst blindness of all. He believes he sees the best and scorns the guide." She folded her hands. "Gentlemen, let's hope the bind of understanding, the world, doesn't disparage us."

Looking at several different faces, she watched some of them grin.

"To open this conference, we first begin with our motto," Chelsea continued speaking. "Never put off till tomorrow what you can do today. This brings us to step up Project Elf. I know our first attentions are financial. Not only will this increase our shareholder values, we'll reinvent the medical world."

Executive Vice President Bruce Tolliver was an old, small, wrinkled man with box-like glasses bigger than his head. Chelsea knew he'd speak first; he always did.

At seventy-five years young, he had the most experience in the business world, had worked on Wall Street as a broker for eleven years and been through many corporations. She definitely put him in her book as the shrewdest at the table, and why he was VP.

"This product you're releasing will shake the very foundations of society." Tolliver's high pitched voice sounded throughout the room. "I fear for you again, my dear lady. I know you're strong, but the world is stronger."

"I'm willing to be the sacrificial lamb on this one," Chelsea said. "When you see the mountain of money that'll be put into our pockets, you might throw me at the wolves personally yourselves."

Some of the members laughed as Tolliver gave a mischievous but vague expression.

"How advanced is this product?" Robert Gibson asked. "When do you think it'll be ready for the market?"

Gibson, the CCO, Chief Commercial Officer, was thirty years old, the age of most of the C-level executives. His pudgy features didn't fit his small round eyeglasses as he smirked at Chelsea for an answer.

"As soon as the board agrees to give the green light it'll happen quickly," Chelsea said. "Not like before."

"So it's assumed PE is ready to go?" Todd Harvey asked, who sat next to Chelsea. Harvey, the CDO, Chief Design Officer, was the most serious guy on the board.

"So much for surprises, *Todd*." Chelsea smiled and the fellas laughed again.

"Cutting to the chase," Tolliver asked Chelsea, "what figure are we looking at in shares?"

"They'll soar from 35 to 75 dollars a share."

Instantly everyone mumbled under their breath. Chelsea heard whispers of, "How can this be? Is this a sure deal?"

"I'm curious." The CMO, Benjamin Vasquez, spoke. "I never actually sat down to really comprehend this Project Elf. Can you explain to the board or me per-se in laymen's terms? In my sake, in kindergarten terms, about what this project is?"

The guys nodded in agreement toward Vasquez's inquiry.

"Yes," Chelsea said, glancing at the Chief Marketing Officer, then glimpsed at everyone else. "PE basically is nanotech-based drugs. We've invented nanomachines that can enter human cells and sense the differences from healthy ones to damaged ones and make modifications to the structure. They'll work cell by cell; whole organs can be repaired. Your arm can be amputated and we can grow you a new—"

"Like, autotomy," Vasquez said, interrupting Chelsea and squinting his eyes with his hand over his mouth.

"Such as lizards," she responded. "PE will cure DNA damage, like cancer and viruses. In laymen's terms, cell repairing machines."

"Cell repairing machines," Tolliver repeated and gazed at Chelsea. "We must be cautious in selling this to the market. We could be meddling in things the world isn't ready for. Legislators will talk about the reverse effect of this invention, like using it as a weapon to kill our foreign or domestic enemies. Or the enemy could get their hands on the technology and detonate this nano-stuff over a city, causing an unstoppable mechanical virus to kill millions."

The gentlemen mumbled among themselves apprehensively.

"Tolliver, sir, you drive a hard bargain," Chelsea spoke. "Its only design is to cure, not destroy. Nothing in the structure has reverse effects. The capability of that happening was never thought up."

"Well, we haven't thought it up, but …" Tolliver said, then demanded, "I'd like to look over the paperwork again on this project."

"Yes, sir," Chelsea replied. She picked up a white phone connected to the table and pressed line one. "Carmela, you can bring them in."

As Carmela came into the room placing hundred page pamphlets in front of each of the executives, Chelsea introduced CFO Harold Miller.

"Our Financial Officer and my personal adviser will also tell us where we stand on the project," Chelsea said and bowed for him to speak.

He stood and passed brochures out that he had in front of him. "This is a first draft proposal on how financially we're going to promote the product. Like, in how many days it's going to take for distribution. If the board gives the go-ahead, there are legal obligations to sign, bi-laws to abide by …"

After everyone sipped many glasses of water, the meeting lasted an hour.

CMS, C Medical Systems, a biomedical engineering company, had called during the meeting through two-way video conferencing. The company was the only entity allowed to disturb the meeting, and for good reason.

They were supposed to merge with this company and it couldn't have been a better time. CMS dealt in artificial limbs and heart transplants. With her new technology, she felt CMS knew when to quit. If you can't beat 'em join 'em, she guessed was their slogan, and they agreed in favor of her board for the green light.

The merger with this company was years away. A new era was about to be born, and CMS didn't want to be left out of the loop.

Chelsea smiled today, for she truly felt officious.

In closing the assembly, they scanned through the official procedures promising to take it home for more scrutiny.

They all agreed the scientists who worked together on the project should be compensated and the technology should be spread in every hospital, not just for the affluent.

Like many corporations, humble beginnings and sensible ideas will soon fall between the cracks from greed and vanity, Chelsea theorized, as everyone filed out of the conference room. She had faith in her company that it had not become as countless others.

Sitting, alone again, she buried her face in her hands, closed her eyes, and rubbed them.

She became aware that someone was still in the room or did someone come in to clean? Opening her eyes and turning toward the door, she found her intrusion. Chief Executive of the designing department, Aaron Lerman, leaned by the doorway with his arms folded.

He strolled in the room toward Chelsea and sat next to her. Her eyes followed him. He smiled.

"You know of all the meetings," he spoke, "and we had a lot of meetings, I've never seen you this nervous."

Though Aaron didn't ask a question, Chelsea still felt as so. She grew a slow smile before she responded, "Is that nervousness you see or fatigue?"

"Maybe a little of both," he said, staring into her bloodshot eyes.

Handsome and groomed short black hair fit flawlessly on his oval head. His eyebrows almost met in the center of his brow in a sexy way. She stared at him, almost not comprehending what he was saying.

"You must be a little besieged," Aaron stated more than asked. "Anyone would, considering every country is on the verge of going to war with America, the misusage of your inventions, and the government keeping a close eye on you."

Chelsea folded her hands in front of her face, resting her elbows on the table, and placed her small chin on her thumbs. She sighed and blinked at him a couple of times before she spoke. "What war? Since we gave them the Vc technology, the government has put a tighter grip on North Korea and the Middle East. China is even afraid of us. Russia, a little upset we keep policing the world more than ever, but what are they going to do?"

"Nothing, we're way ahead in the game of technology. The U.S. is even building a city on the moon."

"And they couldn't have done that without our Vc, speed of light technology."

"Isn't that something, huh?" he said, still not asking a question. "Something we've created could change the world so drastically."

"It has its corks, too."

"Yeah, it certainly does. I remember that government prototype speed of light vehicle punching a hole in United Airlines 144, causing it to crash—no survivors."

"Yeah, followed by the bogus story the FAA gave to the press."

Chelsea huffed and so did Aaron. She sat back in her chair, placing her hands on her lap, and crossed her legs. So did Aaron, almost simultaneously.

She grinned at Aaron, watching him do as she did. She hadn't smirked at a man for over two years. It felt cozy.

In the past two years of her life most of her executive associates had told her she looked stressed. She hadn't seen it that way, though. She felt she was just busy as her life always was. A little more hectic a year or two didn't make or break her.

Little did people know about Vc, the vacuum c project vehicles ever existing. No one except for the VP of her company, Aaron, the DOE, and certain individuals of government knew about her treaty.

When her corporation admitted creating the vacuum c technology and gave it to the DOE, some secret bureaucrats and power brokers visited her in finalizing vindicating her company from the 2011 assassination hoopla.

Two years earlier someone in her company or herself could have faced charges of sanctioning murders. A chief security guard in her company had assassinated top executives of opposing businesses, forcing acquisitions to better her corporation. Though these happenings were beyond her knowledge, the press still saw her involvement. After the security guard's death in an explosion, the Chelsea Enterprise board dealt with the bureaucrats who had put the story far behind the company, belittling it to a suspicion.

Then there was Aaron. She liked Aaron. She stared into his light brown eyes as they spoke. Maddox the spy had light brown eyes, she reminisced.

Never mix business with pleasure. Look at what it did to me before.

Aaron liked what she liked. They spoke about her floating squad cars distribution in New York, Los Angeles, and Ohio. They both giggled as they talked about the news reporting a man who stole one of the cars and tried to drive it into the ocean. Later, after the man was pulled out of the water, he said he wanted to know if the science fiction vehicle could drive across the sea. *The fool probably would never comprehend the science of the car.*

The mechanism controlling what made the car float three feet off ground always stayed at that ratio. So driving it into the sea the car would only detect the ocean floor, full with sea water, then give out.

The same if he was to drive it off a cliff. He might think the mechanism controlling the gravitation might save him from the fall. As soon as the car fell off the cliff; the relation to the ground would be canceled and he'd fall to his death. If the mechanism somehow survived the fall, it would start all over again, then float, but not before the crash. Hopefully no one had tried it.

With the lights off in the room, Aaron and Chelsea laughed out loud, talking about the automobile as the sun washed in colors of red, orange, and purple. They talked until the sun disappeared into the horizon, giving the white walls a flat blue appearance.

Who could she talk to about such things? She'd known Aaron about ten years. He had many lady friends, and at thirty-eight years old, never settled down.

Remember the cardinal rule, Chelsea kept thinking. *Never mix business with pleasure—but who could I talk to about such things?* Not counting her fake-kissing-relationship with a spy, she hadn't felt the affection of a man in years.

She speculated about courting Aaron for a second. She reminisced on her empty love life, recollecting on her demanding livelihood as a commercialist with no marriage in sight. She wondered, at her soon to be age of forty, was she going to die alone?

Chelsea felt she wasn't as stressed as Aaron figured, but she was concerned about her desires. Her drive in life was capitalistic and scientific, but she liked a little pleasure, too.

CHAPTER 3

MATTHEW ROGER HARRIS didn't believe in hope, like many of his friends who were optimistic about Taffy getting better. He felt he was either doomed or fortunate in health. He was either prosperous or condemned in life from his actions of cause and effect.

Taffy, a pipe smoker all his life now had to deal with the effect.

He'd either do something or he didn't; he'd never sit back and wait on hope. Things he didn't hope for usually happen more frequently than things he did hope for. He despised hope.

He loathed seeing Taffy this way. Jeremy Taffy a year earlier was diagnosed with small-cell carcinoma; in short, lung cancer. In the last few months the prognosis moved from a limited stage to an extensive stage. He didn't quite understand the diagnosis, but was sure the extensive stage wasn't good. The doctors gave Taffy eight to thirteen months to live. Of course, being the stubborn man Taffy was, he didn't believe the doctors. In Taffy's heart, or somewhere deep inside his brain, Harris knew that Taffy knew he was going to die.

It was Harris's harsh reality of being doomed or fortunate. He despised hope. He'd never say he hoped Taffy would get better.

Matthew Roger Harris had gone by many aliases in his time with The Company. The world knew him as Matthew R. Hellems. Only Taffy was supposed to know his true birth identity. It was one way The Company protected their deep cover field agents.

He was a military brat whose parents were killed in Vietnam. He was seven years old when his parents died and nine when he met Taffy.

He couldn't remember what he was doing on that day, but understood from an officer he'd never see his parents again. Later in his young life Taffy explained to him that his father, a lieutenant, died in the Easter Offensive, and mother, a part of the Army Nurse Corps, died in that same year from a disease called multiple myeloma.

Jeremy Taffy had became the man he loved as a father, his mentor and first and last boss he had ever known. Now it had come to this—cancer.

Taffy had traveled across the entire State of Pennsylvania from Beaver Falls to camp in Pennsylvania Hospital that sat in Center City, Philadelphia. He'd lived there for five months and got on most of the male doctors' nerves and propositioned all of the female nurses and physicians alike.

How dear he, Harris thought and laughed. This hospital had some of the best doctors in the United States, was on the top ten list for finest hospitals in America, and being that he was about eighty years young, he still had no shame in his game.

Harris presumed he should be himself; he was dying anyway. Damn, Harris chewed over, he hated to see Taffy this way. The man was a legend in the Central Intelligence Agency and Federal Bureau of Investigation. He was a champion at the caliber of General George Custer or George S. Patton and a man of true astuteness. Taffy was the best director the CIA and FBI ever had.

Walking down the halls of the hospital reminded him of a five star hotel more than a medical center. The nurses, therapists, and assistants walked around calmly and confidently, not like some inner-city assistants. The place was indeed luxurious, right up Taffy's ally, he deserved it, Harris felt.

Harris had seen Taffy twenty times since he crashed this joint, but this time he heard in Taffy's voice that he really wanted to see him. He hoped this wasn't going to be the time where his mentor was going to whisper in his ear his last death wish. Harris felt he wasn't ready for this, and his use of the word *hope* was just a metaphor. Harris smiled to himself, correcting himself.

He glanced at his watch, seeing that he had about three hours to talk to his stepfather. The visiting hours were from 11 to 8PM. He tried to get here sooner, but the traffic was murder.

Knocking on the door to room twelve, he slowly opened it and straightened the sleeves on his maroon shirt. He distinguish Taffy had to know he was coming to the room. Every time he came an orderly had already paged his stepfather.

There Taffy was, on his Craftmatic electric adjustable bed, sitting on top of a purple plush comforter. He was wrapped in a colorful luxury 100 percent Turkish cotton bathrobe.

Typing away on a laptop on his lap, he looked up and squinted at Harris. Taffy pushed his spectacles onto his bearded face from leaning his head down and staring at the computer screen.

"Traffic," Harris blurred out and shrugged, spreading his arms wide.

"Well," Taffy began in his deep voice. "While you were in some *traffic*, I was looking further into my research. Did you know, nowadays the environment itself is one of the leading causes of cancer and asthma?"

"Been so for some years now," Harris responded. He stood next to Taffy with his arms folded. "Don't know if it's number one yet over heart disease, but I'm sure it's up there."

"I was going to say that. It's the food we eat, the air we breathe, and do you know what's contaminating these things?" Before Harris could answer, Taffy spoke, "Huge greedy corporations." Taffy shook his head, stared back at the screen, and sighed.

Okay, Harris contemplated, now I know this wasn't the important thing he called me for. He knew enough better Taffy was giving him small talk before a more somber tête-à-tête.

Taffy looked good for an elder gentlemen, especially considering he was diagnosed with cancer. The chemotherapy didn't seem to have affected him yet, but he did look a bit pale and fatigued.

"Well, my dear boy," Taffy began. "I know you don't believe in the actual existence of extraterrestrials."

Harris sighed.

"Though knowing all the secrets of this government," Taffy continued,

"I know you've come to the conclusion that we and ally regimes are doing this to scare the world into a one world bureaucracy."

Harris scrunch his face.

"Wait a minute, because I know what you're going to say already. We've done it in the past, like the creation of the World Bank."

"Look, sir," Harris spoke as if he'd repeated it time and again. "I don't want to make you upset again; you need your rest. Like, your health is more important right now."

"Ahh, my health!" Taffy said, startling Harris. "This is important. Stop thinking for me. Stop having pity for an old broken man.

"I pitied him in his blindness, but can I talk, I see. Perhaps there's someone close by who pities me," Taffy and Harris finished the last part of the proverb in harmony.

"Yes," Harris said. "I know, you've taught me that statement your whole life."

"And you're still not hearing me."

"Things are different now, sir."

"I've been following a lead *vigorously* for eight months," Taffy said, looking at Harris hard.

It was his way of saying the argument was over, Harris knew. He was a serious man almost all the time and seemed to never crack a smile.

"A contact of mine," Taffy continued, "offered me a deal of a lifetime. He said some above the law important people of our government have tapped into something extraordinary."

Harris stood at attention and listened to Taffy.

"This connection claims to have proof that a secret lab in Nigeria was holding genuine exobiology DNA. You see, it all started in Africa."

Harris watched Taffy wait for him to take in what was said. Harris continued to give him a straight face.

"My contact says they call it Pandora."

Harris started to pace the room before replying, "You're really serious about this thing, huh?" He didn't ask him a question, but more said it as if for a fact he already knew the answer. Instead, he asked, "Who's this contact? You never mentioned him before."

"That's just it," Taffy whispered now. "All the time I've been talking to the old crank, I've never believed him, until this." Taffy turned the laptop around so Harris could see the screen.

The *New York Daily News* web page was open to the technology section. Taffy gave Harris a few minutes to read a small article titled *Green Party Revenge on CRC Technician.* It talked about a worldwide anti-hackers company called Cyberspace Regulations Center based in Alaska that fell to a tragedy.

> *Authorities have already captured a suspect in the brutal murder of Anthony Burrows, a project manager of the company for ten years.*
>
> *Some Green Party activists had talked out against the CRC organization, claiming they were illegally spying on civilian home computers.*
>
> *The man who shot Burrows had a past criminal record and was rejected many times from officially joining the GPUS. The suspect said he did it so the Green Party would respect him. Doctors labeled the man emotionally unstable. Law enforcement had in question, did this man actually steal a policeman's pistol, chase Burrows, and gun him down?*
>
> *"Strange," detectives stated. "This unstable man ransacked Burrows's office and home as if in search of something other than money. The case is pending.*
>
> *Anthony Burrows, a prestigious man in the CRC, will be missed by many.*

"Short article," Harris blurred out. "I assume Anthony Burrows was your contact? So what does this all mean?"

"You assume correct, my dear boy. This means everything." Taffy put his hand out for Harris to sit in a chair near the bed, and he sat facing his stepdad.

"You know, for years I've been chasing Pandora," Taffy spoke. "Since my retirement I wanted to look into this … this wonder if we're truly alone out here in the vast universe. I'm convinced we're not, for it would be an awful lot of wasted space. Nothing is more dishonorable than an old man stricken with years who has no other evidence of him having lived except his age.

"I've researched Pandora and have come up with dead leads. You and I know the in's and out's of these cloak-and-dagger societies. This Pandora is hidden from them, and they're trying to figure it out. The U.S. government in all their existence and unlimited access to the world have never witnessed a true exobiology being. They've only produced made-up rubbish.

"Anthony Burrows was the closest I came to discovering substantial evidence that Pandora is real, and I'm not crazy. Then poof, just like that, Burrows is murdered. Just a coincidence, huh? No, my son; I say convenient. We know how these secret governments work. I need you again on this one. The most savage controversies in this world are matters as to which there's no good evidence either way. I need evidence."

"Sir, I've made an official retirement from the world of clandestine societies," Harris said, "from your advice, no doubt."

"Grant an old man a final wish," Taffy babbled out, not looking at Harris, but at his laptop. Harris also looked away from Taffy and stared at the brown wall in front of him.

I didn't want to come here for this, Harris gulped. He knew he wasn't ready for this, but the inevitable was here. He wanted to cry, but held it inside.

I'm done with the CIA, never to return again, he shouted mentally. Now this.

Hell, of course he was going to grant the old man his wish, and Taffy already knew he would. He had never let Taffy down, and he never will. Taffy knew he'd do the job promptly and thoroughly, because he had been the best. Nobody had that skill. If anybody, he knew he could bring him back that proof if it exists, or uncover the sham.

"I found long ago," Harris said, "there's no success in arguing with a tired old man."

Taffy closed his laptop and lay back on his already propped bed. He sighed as if a great weight had lifted from his chest.

"Tired, and old, yes," Taffy whispered.

There was a knock on the door.

"Please, come in," Taffy shouted.

A pretty and young nurse entered in all white dress, apron, and cap. Her smile brightened her appearance more, Harris observed.

"Oh, I didn't know you had company," she said. "Just came to check on you."

"Not a problem, my dear," Taffy said, leaning to look around Harris, who blocked her shapely figure from where he sat. "We're almost finished here. You come back and check on me in a minute, darling."

"Okay, sure, Mr. J. T." the young lady responded. She glanced at Harris, still grinning, and closed the door.

"J. T." Harris mimicked the lady.

A smile finally formed on the groomed gray and black bearded lips of Taffy, a rare sight, Harris detected.

"I like the sound of it," Taffy said. "My wives used to call me JT."

"Interesting," Harris spoke. "They must have been the ones during my college years."

"I want you to know, son." Taffy turned serious quickly. "I appreciate you doing this."

Harris smirked, then mused, hey, we only have known each other for a lifetime. "So, where does this start, because I totally don't have any old connections anymore, no funds. Spent all my money on another cruise out to Barbados. While you were enjoying the life of luxury in here I was out there wasting it on women like that." Harris nudged toward the door.

"I see you've picked up my humor over the years," Taffy said without cracking a grin. "You'll be my eyes and ears in Alaska, my boy. That's where we'll start. Your first assignment, ask questions about Mr. Burrows. Someone there will ask you for my last name. Everything will be paid for, at no expense. I'm afraid we haven't much time."

Harris knew what Taffy meant when he said we haven't much time. Taffy knew he was dying; he'd just rather not talk about it. Who would?

He had an obligation now. Damn, Harris brood, what did he get himself into? He'd retired for two years, from the SOF, Special Ops Force, a special unit that worked out of the CIA. Over the years he grew tired of the lies and clandestine nerve-racking missions that had lasted since the Reagan era. At forty-eight years old, he felt it was all spiritual healing from here on—still young for most retirees.

This off the record mission Taffy was putting me on was probably going to be a wild goose chase anyway.

Harris deliberated. He already knew for a fact, no government or any human had found any sign of life of any kind beyond the Earth. He knew the conspiracies of governments, especially the United States, England, and other European nations, throwing the fear of an impending alien attack to continue bringing the world under a one world control. We're utterly alone in the vast universe.

This trumped-up scenario escalated since the discovery of Vc, the speed of light vehicles, some two years ago. He welcomed the idea. *Humans needed to be controlled or else there would be chaos. Ancient civilizations talked about it all the time.*

Though, there's a flip side to all this, Harris considered. Just because there's absence of evidence, doesn't mean that the evidence is absent. Evidence of absence simply means he can't prove that something doesn't exist. It would be safe to assume that if a certain event had occurred, evidence of it would have been discovered already by qualified investigators. Harris supposed the argument could go on forever. Strange universe we live in.

Hey, this was for a dying man's wish anyway; how could he say no? The man was his only immediate surviving family.

Taffy had mentioned this operation before, but he never paid attention. Okay, Harris contemplated, what exactly is this Pandora?

CHAPTER 4

IT WAS ONLY A PARTY, Chelsea envisaged. She despised parties, but the executive board kept insisting. They kept saying it was good for business to endorse Elf in this way. She didn't down the promoting; she just didn't want to show up at the festivity. They said it would be considerate of her to show her face in front of the other companies supporting Elf—her very own creation. Yeah, she pouted, that would be the formal thing to do, she guessed.

Kaleem Nastafar, the speaker for Chelsea Enterprises, had held a press conference about the technology a week earlier. Kaleem, explained how the nanomedicine worked, then the press had a bombardment of questions which opened up into days of coverage on national television. The publicity had brought her here today at the Greater Columbus Convention Center ballroom.

The Battelle Grand was colossal. The ceiling went up fifty feet with a lighting system that lit up like a sky of brilliant green stars. The ceiling to floor windows were covered by massive olive curtains. A mezzanine, though closed, stretched halfway across the fifty thousand square foot main area.

Thirty-five round elegantly dressed white-clothed tables were spread out across the floor. Huge tables with food of all kind and a bar sat across the room opposite of the low balcony.

Set up on the walls around the box-shaped amphitheater were screens showing reruns of Kaleem answering reporters' questions. In another segment a person in a business suit explained Project Elf in yet more detail. Eight projectors illustrated Kaleem on these screens and two displayed many commercials for PE in repetition.

The place was crowded with a sea of blue business suits and multi-hued evening gowns. Though hundreds of individuals were in conversation, the place didn't sound boisterous. Occasional laughter was heard as they hummed like mammoth swarms of bees.

Most sat at tables eating and some gathered in groups around the room or in front of the projecting screens. Waiters in black buzzed like flies around the tables and groups serving trays of hot food, cocktails, and hors d'oeuvres.

Chelsea sat at a table with Aaron, her escort, VP Bruce Tolliver, and his wife. Joining them around the table was the CEO, Michael Rosenbluth of CMS, a biomedical engineering company, and Joseph Vasella Rudolf, the CEO of a Switzerland pharmaceutical company called Locarux. They also brought their wives, making the table full.

Billion dollar snakes, Chelsea perceived, as she frowned at the new faces before her. Locarux and CMS had been charged with fraud by the Department of Justice and Interpol many times over the course of fifteen years. *Always somehow they seemed to have settled the dispute with the DOJ. Maybe now would be a good time to learn their manipulative ways, just in case I get into a bit of a jam.*

Chelsea smirked at them.

They were here today, though, to learn her ways, Chelsea knew. They wanted the secret ingredients to Elf, and they were willing to pay big to get it. They knew it was the threshold into the future. Snakes, Chelsea chewed over again.

There were a lot of politicians around the room from about ten states across the country, some Democrats and some Republicans. Last, Chelsea couldn't forget her Green Party acquaintance, Co-Chair John Carroll, and his supporters who filled half the room.

The tables full of food had caviar, lobster, filets of wild duck, chopped truffles, artichoke puree, and champagne. White cloths on everyone's laps who sat and the ting of forks and knives ringing around the place completed this evening etiquette business cocktail party.

Aaron had told her several times that she looked beautiful tonight in her one piece nylon blue dress. Chelsea wasn't use to her exposed shoulders and top round part of her cleavage, or the dress revealing the sides of her hourglass midriff. Despite the fact that the dress kept her cool, she still more welcomed the comfort of a business suit.

"Charming that among us carnivores of world industries, we have a vegan." Rudolf spoke in a strong Swedish emphasis. He raised an eyebrow as he ate a piece of meat from his platter.

Obviously his statement was directed toward me, Chelsea presumed, as she ate some string beans from her dish.

"I'd consider myself more a insectivorous, such as a Venus Flytrap," Chelsea said and sneered at the white pimp stripe-suited tycoon.

"My kind of flower," Rudolf quickly responded with a grin. The sixty-year-old man was lightly elbowed by his twenty-eight-year-old wife.

Chelsea knew their age; she had looked them up on the Internet. Rudolf was a well-built guy for his age, clean-cut, and fine managed slick black hair with silver highlights.

He let out an energetic laugh. "Ah, honey," Rudolf said, "we have to be polite to Ms. Chelsea for she may lead us into a bright future."

"Yes," Aaron said, cutting in and touching Chelsea on the thigh in a gesture to say, *I know you're agitated, I'll retort.* "A future that could take us to vacationing on the moon and beyond." Aaron smiled.

"Of course," Rudolf said and gave a polite grin. "Oh, the beauty of what science can come up with today. It could bring entire industries back into the stone age."

Chelsea alleged these big moguls one day soon were going to have to bend to her technology, whether they liked it or not.

"I see, Ms. Chelsea," Michael Rosenbluth spoke, breaking into the conversation. "You seem to flow with the wind when it comes to loyalties. Today it's the GPUS, yesterday the Democrats, and at one point the GOP."

"Mr. Rosenbluth," Chelsea said, staring into his brown eyes. "If you're trying to say I'm spineless—"

"No, no, I'm not …" Rosenbluth spoke, recoiling his statement, and gestured with his hands in the same way.

"No," Chelsea replied. "I already see what you're insinuating and I have to clarify. I flow with what's in the best interest for me and the country. In this diverse land, the truth doesn't always fall on the side of the Democrat or Green Party. Truth is truth, and there's nothing wishy-washy about that."

Rosenbluth's long face gave a smile. "Point taken," he said. "So I suppose your *truths* lie with the GPUS today?"

Chelsea answered him with a smile full of dimples.

"Well, no matter what you think we think of you," Rudolf said, "I must say this science of yours is indeed with no question, extraordinary."

Chelsea gave a stern nod accepting Rudolf's compliment, and his wife smirked in a way saying, *those accolades are rare.*

"The speaker of your company did well in delivering the understanding of this nanomedicine," Rudolf continued. "I'd very much like to meet …"

A commotion at the entrance hall turned everyone's head simultaneously from what Rudolf was saying. Chelsea strained and stretched her head around to see what was going on, and as everyone else did, she witnessed a glimpse of action across a crowd of people and tables. About five or six individuals in white shirts wrestled with a couple of persons in suits.

Before a multitude of black and blue three-piece suits obscured her view, she saw a peek of what one of the t-shirt characters were wearing, *Conservative and proud of it.*

Two security men rushed past her table, then someone shouted, "Down with socialism!" The men in white, Chelsea supposed.

The crowd of people who belonged to the hall hum of conversations, like red dye dropping into clear water dissipating slowly, developed into a whisper as they became aware of the situation.

Everyone heard shouts of, "Too late! Police State! Too late! Police …" The chants faded away as the apparent assailants were escorted out the hall by security.

Murmurs of confusion for a few minutes echoed throughout as the crowd tried to understand what just happened. Gradually, within a timeframe of five minutes the place hummed again with laughter here and there, assuring things seemed to be flowing habitually.

John Carroll in his blue suit always looked ten years younger than his age of fifty-eight, Chelsea noticed. Carroll, clean cut, had semi-spiked but neatly trimmed dark blond hair, acted as if he just graduated from college.

Disregarding everyone at the table, he walked up to Chelsea and they shook hands.

Chelsea gave him a warm smile; she knew it was just like him to ignore the industrialists. She always felt he was more of a down to earth person—more with the people— grass roots, and unmistakably why he was elected so fast to be a Co-Chair of the GPUS.

"I know nothing like this would rattle your cage, Nzingha," Carroll spoke with the energy of a twenty-year-old. "Just a bunch of far-right conservative fanatics trying to crash the party, claiming your corporation is working with the government in a conspiracy to take over the world, again."

Carroll and Chelsea chuckled.

"Don't worry," he said, "my constituents and I took care of it, at no expense." He glanced at her company at the table.

"Thanks, John," Chelsea said. "I'd ask you to join us but the table is a bit full right now."

"I ate already," he said, tapping his stomach. "It looks like you're handling yourself just fine." He glimpsed at her plate of half eaten green beans then again at her company. "Well, it's always a pleasure to see *you*, and I do hope we chat before you leave."

"Of course, I owe you for your bravery at the front door."

Carroll winked at her and disappeared into the crowd.

Chelsea's mind raced in many scenarios. As the paranoid person she was, she wondered why she was talking to these fraudsters. She didn't need them and they knew it.

The youth of Carroll brought her to feel more connected with the masses. It made her feel young, look young. If he could do it reaching almost sixty, she had no qualms in doing the same.

Glimpsing at Vice President Tolliver brought her back to the reality at hand. Her board of directors really wanted this. It was their method of working with the manner of the world.

She'd never encountered extremists this close since the start of her business. Considered an activist herself some seventeen years earlier, she had forgotten the thrill. She wondered was the government still harassing her, like creating a false anti-Chelsea Company group to stir up trouble just for the media to spread controversy. Hard right conservative groups to informants, the government knew best how to destroy her integrity, and she knew they were watching her closely whether she had a deal with them or not.

The last state of affair was her escort. Trying for a moment to take her mind away from the talons of toil and espionage woes, she wondered about Aaron. He looked handsome today in his gray suit and tie.

She let him do most of the talking at the table with the entrepreneurs. He knew she despised them, so he answered most of their curious inquiries.

Chelsea recognized Aaron was physically attracted to her; most men were. Men claimed her exotic features were enticing and her dark marble jade eyes only exaggerated her attractiveness. She wondered if Aaron, through time, could learn to like her, love her even—much harder to love her individuality than her appearance.

Time was moving fast and her love life, which was void, was moving at a snail's pace. Never mix business with pleasure was her motto, but some ideologies, she began to speculate, were soon going to have to be thrown out the window.

CHAPTER 5

WHOEVER WISHES TO KEEP A SECRET *must hide the fact that he possesses one.* Where he was going, without a doubt, was top secret, but to the public, a government-owned global anti-hackers facility. Sent on a mercenary mission by Taffy, three people, and three people only had given him clearance.

The first two folks, CIA agents Brian Glyn and Sara Sanders, had asked him many questions before he won their consent and assistance. It didn't take long to induce them, for they were his co-workers before he retired. He also hadn't figured two years into retirement was a long time.

Sara, whom Harris felt was more of a friend than Brian, asked him easy questions. "Are you coming back after all these years? What sparked your curiosity in the Vc Project?" He simply explained it wasn't his idea at all and that Taffy, who was bedridden, wanted the information.

Taffy had him make up a story that his dying wish was to know the Vc Lunar Project was a success. This wasn't far from the truth, Harris thought; just the wrong project.

Brian asked him the harder, smugger questions. "Don't know when to quit, huh," Brian said smirking. "You should tell the old man not to worry, the new project is in good hands. Mistakes are far and few nowadays."

Harris wanted to punch Brian in the face, but *nowadays* he kind of needed his help to pull off Taffy's real intentions. Then again, he had to excuse Brian. The past years he worked with him it was always his nature to down the veterans. Stinking, arrogant, novice, Harris reflected and smirked back at him.

Then to the most important individual who also welcomed him on this operation, the head of the base, General Anthony J. Powell. Not only was he an old hand of clandestine procedures such as this, he was a dear buddy of Taffy and welcomed Harris along with open arms in a letter.

You want back in, son, because we got a place for you, was Powell's last words on the memo. Enough said, Harris concluded.

The ivory unmarked Airbus A330 airliner gracefully dropped just below cloud cover, descending to twenty-thousand feet.

Harris felt the plane vibrate into a slight plunge as the captain announced over the intercom, "We'll soon arrive at Denali, Ak, e.t.a. forty-five minutes."

Harris was well rested and stared at some notes in a folder that sat on his lap. Before reading the Vc Lunar Project file stamped in red *highly confidential,* he glanced at his surroundings.

Flying coach in a three hundred and thirty-five passenger airliner, eighty-six seats were taken. Including himself, the passengers, some in suits but most casually dressed, were generally scientists. He also counted four lieutenants and five captains of the United States Army, grouped together in the center of the economy class seats. He distinguished who they were from their navy-green uniforms and insignias.

Everyone, had to first fly out to Texas for however long that took, considering where they lived, then they took this plane to the CRC facility. This last-stretch seven-hour trip from Texas to Alaska put most people aboard asleep.

The scientists and researchers sat scattered about in three row seats, some by themselves and some bunched together, a few in conversation.

Harris sat by himself in the third seat away from the window, somewhere he figured on the left side middle of the plane. He slept on his first flight and most of this one, but devoted the last hour in scrutinizing this Vc project.

He already learned the Vc Lunar Project, quoted by the US Army as a test research project, was no test. A small six mile wide human colony was already established on the moon, and now he was going to witness another flight out. The facility he was headed to wasn't really called the CRC, but an extension of an anti-ballistic missile base called Fort Greely.

The time he had left to examine his files, he learned these specially and carefully picked scientists were flown out here every weekday with the exception of the army officers and himself today.

The base was a lot smaller than Fort Greely. Named FG2, Fort Greely II, was a hundred and twenty miles from the original base and tucked next to Mount McKinley.

He sat back and crossed his legs in wonder. Wearing a brown shirt and black slacks, he smiled and thought, *no disguises today*. Usually on most of his missions he was always undercover, a spy, an informant. He liked the feeling now of presenting himself as himself.

Hell, he was after all retired and kind of off the record just checking things out for an old friend, better yet a mentor, a father figure.

HARRIS and crew arrived at the base at nine o'clock at night. It was late May here in Alaska, the largest state, and the sun still held its ground above. Adjusting his watch to Alaska time, he knew the sun was going to burn for a good five more hours before setting into a twilight sky. He probably wasn't going to have to get used to the sunshine and forty degree weather because he was going to be inside most of his time.

The place appeared like a college campus with one airstrip, nowhere near the size of its hub. It didn't need to; the crafts here needed no runway.

Mount McKinley loomed over the site, its wide snow-filled slopes and crevasses went up forever disappearing into low clouds. The mountain simulated a rugged but serene gateway into the heavens. It was a magnificent sight, Harris perceived.

Harris's first day at the base he didn't do or see much. Everyone introduced themselves, then went their separate ways into their dormitories for some shuteye.

The second day, the day of the launch, he did everything. He only had a day or two to get to know the researchers or personnel to ask questions about the Anthony Burrows murder.

Most of the place reminded him of a hi-tech computer research center. Hidden and deep within the bowels of this semi-fortress were places much harder to roam.

He managed to speak to six scientists who were C level employees assigned to the most restricted part of the base, and as usual were soon going to witness the launch. He knew it would be a good place to start considering Burrows was a C level employee.

Harris, a visitor, had breakfast in a home style lounge and ate waffles and eggs where others ate pancakes. Of the six people he sat with, he asked simple questions just to stir up the incident for a moment. He started by small-talking the bunch, getting into discussions of Alaskan weather and wildlife. Then he moved on to more serious matters.

"Who would ever think some Green Party nut would travel all this way and murder one of your best scientists." Harris edged Paul, more than asked him a question.

"So he was murdered alone? Nobody saw anything?" he asked Rogers.

"I would think a well guarded facility such as this would be hard for anyone to attempt any kind of murder, especially from a outsider," he spoke to Josephine.

Their responses were vague. "We don't know all the details on that terrible day," Paul spoke. "Stuff like that could take months and even years to find out what really happened."

"Yeah, those Green Party bastards have been harassing us for some time now, through their letter-threatening and phone calls," Rogers said.

"Ah, we really don't know what happened," Josephine said, agitated. "We have to leave it up to the authorities to solve."

Harris wanted to retort in a blitz of inquiries, but decided for the better to back off for now. Their dialogue gradually slid back into interest in the environment and the task at hand, the departure of an interesting device.

NOON soon led everyone to the C level part of the institution, the core of the establishment. The entire perimeter of the base was surrounded by hundreds of acres of green grassy hills. Forty small bizarre maze-looking architectural buildings were spread out in a flawless circle around fourteen large beautifully designed structures.

The smaller buildings had five or six floors while the larger ones had ten to fifteen. Of the larger buildings, four were surrounded by all the buildings; the level C section. The building he was in was the only launch site; the other three buildings exact duplicates were decoys.

The buildings' exteriors were ugly, Harris noticed. They simulated white, spherical, windowless, huge nuclear reactor power plants. The interior of the building looked comely in a futuristic way. It reminded him of the inside of the Pantheon dome in Rome, just a lot bigger, shinier, and slicker.

The researchers, army officers, and Harris stood ten flights up on an open twelve foot extended platform with rail that followed the complete massive circular circumference of the building. They overlooked an enormous white round stage at a colossal shuttle. Spaceship was a better word for it, Harris professed.

The countdown for the launch was five minutes away and, though he didn't show it, he was excited. He knew about these vessels, but this was going to be the first time he saw one with his own eyes.

On the ground floor, built into the wall across from the shuttle and them behind huge glass windows, was the control room. Peering inside, Harris saw about fifteen people in lab coats moving around frantically getting ready for the takeoff. He was briefed in there just hours ago at a calmer moment on how it all worked.

The moon, father of stimulating mythology, had embossed calendars and influenced artist throughout the time of man. Colonizing the lunar surface had been dreams to the ancients.

The technicians and researchers learned as well as he that the moon's façade was more of an beige to fawn color, and moon quakes were more frequent than previously thought. The main mission to the moon was to mine its rich iron and abstract ice water from the shadows of huge craters.

The creators of this operation felt they hadn't affected the environment because they made the iron on the moon and didn't truck it back to earth. The same for the water; it was kept on the moon.

The surprising thing to most of the scientists about the moon's water and regolith was that it seemed more purified then earth's resources. For example, plant growth on the moon's regolith in an oxidized atmosphere grew faster and wilder; remarkable, Harris thought.

Now on the Sea of Tranquility with a perimeter of six miles, an American colony sprung. Looking at monitors in the control room, Harris witnessed the gray balloon structures of the moon base called Andromeda.

The MD's, Moon Dwellers, a name given to the colonists by scientists, cleaned up many Russian, American, and Japanese failed Luna missions on the surface. They also were preparing to make another larger colony called Mytikas on the Ocean of Storms site.

To most of the world this Vc technology wasn't supposed to exist yet. The government felt it should be disclosed maybe in eight years. The MSS of China and MIS of the United Kingdom, knew about the moon base, but not exactly how the United States got there.

The vessel about to be catapulted to the moon in a minute and counting was also a remarkable discovery. The craft appeared to be two in one.

The main body of it favored a two hundred foot long and three hundred foot tall white metal angel fish. The second formation of the ship, the center bulk of it, mirrored an indigo orb, its radius about the same size as the vessel. The metal on this part of the ship was so glossy Harris couldn't tell if it was violet or just dark blue.

Two huge silver Space Shuttle-like engines obtruded out the back of the ship. Absent of landing gear, it hovered eight feet off the platform.

The futuristic Space Shuttle called Zeus conducted eighteen missions to the moon and back. The payload for Zeus today were five MD's and solar panel equipment.

Harris knew the Vc shuttle was going to make it to the moon in one second flat. He also knew it didn't need those huge engines; it was only so it could move through space slowly when the crew wanted to.

All this reminded him of the discovery of the Vc technology, from the Chelsea Company, two years earlier. It was his last mission with the CIA. He went in as an informant, disguising himself as a businessman to find out the intentions of the company and acquire its technologies before they might give it to another country. That mission, of course, was successful.

Harris had met many pretty women in his day and rated the CEO of the Chelsea Company in his top dozen. Infiltrating the company, he acquired a simple relationship with her, but it was a scam—occupational for the government's interest. Women to him were a dime a dozen, though he did want to settle down one day. He even bet that sucker Brian of the CIA that she'd fall all over him for a relationship.

Milky brown skin tone, tall, strong-build, short wavy hair, and light-brown eyes fit perfectly with his square head; he felt he was handsome enough to find any women when he was ready to settle down. At forty-eight and forsaken of any true relationship, Harris began to wonder where his years were really headed. Was he going to become an attractive, unemotional hermit all his life?

In his peripheral vision he spotted Josephine staring at him. *Was she looking at me for my good looks? Hmm*, Harris sighed, *she didn't look bad either. She had a cute face, flowing straight silky black hair just past her shoulders, and was seemingly in her mid-forties.*

He glanced at her as the countdown began at ten seconds, sounding from a speaker system. She eased her way toward him. This'll be interesting, Harris felt, and smiled more inside than at her.

"Nine, eight, seven," the automated voice on the speaker talked.

"Follow me to the women's bathroom right after the launch," Josephine whispered. She came to stand a foot away from Harris, making sure no one else heard her, and stared straight ahead at the ship.

They weren't rendezvousing for any romantic interest, Harris figured as much. It was probably going to have something to do with his Mr. Burrows questions earlier. Playing along, he looked forward and slightly nodded.

"Five, four," the countdown continued. The ceiling quickly slid open in a spiral style, opening into a hole wide enough for the vessel to fit. Sunshine and a clear blue sky washed the entire arena.

"Three, two, one," the robotic voice spoke, and before it could say liftoff, the shuttle disappeared.

From the sudden rush of air replaced by the massive missing ship, there was a loud pop or better yet burst like a gigantic balloon exploding. Air rushed in from behind, almost knocking everyone over the banister. Harris watched as the people in front held onto the handrail and women with long hair watched it flutter forward as if huge fans were turned on behind them for a few seconds.

Interesting ordeal, Harris deemed. He never experienced anything like it. It felt as if huge air conditioners had just blasted him from behind.

In the corner of Harris's eye he watched Josephine with two other women depart out a back door to the right. Everyone else withdrew through a door on the left. He recognized the door on the left led to the control room. He understood everyone wanted to see the five astronauts depart Zeus safely on the moon.

Following the women out the right door led him into a white hallway lavatory area. Harris observed the two women recede into the ladies room laughing and chatting away about what they just experienced. Tailing Josephine, he stopped right before she went into the restroom and she turned to face him.

"What's Jeremy's last name?" she asked.

"Taffy," Harris answered, and she slapped something small and smooth in his hand.

"Don't look at it; wait until you go to the bathroom," she whispered. "There're no cameras here; it's the only place I could talk. Listen carefully because I'm only going to say this once."

She looked around, over his shoulder and behind hers down the hall.

"Anthony knew about someone named Jeremy Taffy some days before he died and begged me to give that thing I gave you to him," she said, continuing to look around nervously. "Anthony said if he was to get in trouble behind what he was researching to give it to the first person who started asking questions. That is who wasn't a detective and knew Jeremy's true last name. Anthony had some kind of pact with Jeremy. He gave me that thing I gave you in a just in case he died scenario. I told him I wanted nothing to do with what he was doing, which is prying in on government cover-ups.

"This secret department is a prison enough to work in. I don't need the drama, and I've already signed many confidentiality agreements as did he."

She heard laughter in the bathroom, stopped talking for a second, looked around, then into Harris's eyes. "If whatever I gave you isn't enough, then I can't help you. I hope you know what you're doing because I'm risking my life with this transaction. After we come out of the bathroom, you don't know me. It would be my hope that we never speak again, about anything."

"Then I presume this information should be sufficient?" Harris asked.

Josephine gave him a callous stare and went into the ladies room.

Harris entered the men's bathroom and walked to the mirrors and sinks. He looked around, under the stalls, making sure he was alone; he was.

Opening his hand, he found in his palm a three inch glass vial. Inside was a long piece of paper curled up like a Chinese fortune cookie. He raised the vial to eye level to get a clearer look at the paper inside. Something was written on it. He comprehended a sentence that he couldn't make out fully unless he opened the vial.

Preempt prophecy and pro— was part of the sentence, then the paper curved inward. Probing it for a minute, he knew he was never going to grasp it immediately, also someone might burst into the bathroom. He put it into his pocket, turned on the water, and washed his hands.

So far this was all interesting—Taffy's crave for the proof of aliens, Burrows murder, and secret riddles. This was all up Harris's alley and he welcomed it. He knew many secrets of the world, and this one, if cracked, would be a doozy.

He didn't believe in extraterrestrials, but figured why not pursue the investigation of it. Maybe he could put to rest once and for all that they, in his lifetime, didn't exist, but in the future, who knows. Then either Taffy or himself could rest on proof or no proof about the little green suckers from Mars.

CHAPTER 6

QUEBEC CITY WAS A LOT QUIETER than Montreal, and that's why Harris liked it here. A matter of fact, Canada in a whole was a lot calmer than all of the United States, and that's why he moved out here for the past two years. What better place to retire than a city with hardly any crime. There hadn't been a murder in Quebec for at least a year.

On the plateau of the Les Rivieres borough, Harris's humble abode sat. Though he couldn't view the La Citadelle or Chateau Frontenac Hotel that dominated the city skyline, he was comfortable enough blending in among these French-speaking citizens.

His two-story white house fit on a block with many other similar houses; he welcomed blending in with the affable neighborhood.

Most bachelor pads were messy, Harris believed, but his wasn't because he was rarely home. He figured retirement meant vacation time to roam out and about, and he wanted an early start. After Taffy's call, that all ended. Sitting on one of his two white couches in his immaculate living room, Taffy and he for a half hour tried understanding the riddle he'd brought back from Alaska.

His laptop rested on a small well-polished wooden table in the middle of the room where Taffy's live face shown in the upper left corner of the thirteen inch screen. June 5, 2 P.M. read on the bottom right hand. The webcam built into the laptop was set up so Taffy could see and hear him.

"You've told me the story in many ways already," Harris said, rubbing his eyes. "How Cronus ate his children to save his throne. You named all the children he ate. I still don't see what Burrows is trying to tell us. Maybe we should take a break for a minute?"

"Maybe you're right," Taffy agreed, with grief.

This myth of gods eating babies was making him hungry, and he hadn't eaten since breakfast, Harris thought.

"Let's start over," Harris said and groaned. "Maybe we should look at what he's asking in more light of what's going on today."

Harris stood, walked five steps into the kitchen, and glanced again at the tiny slip of paper.

What did Cronus do to preempt prophecy and protect the throne?

He opened his in-the-wall refrigerator and took out a carton of orange juice. He took a glass from his black cupboard, walked back into the living room, and plopped back onto the couch in front of his computer.

"So who was the young lady who handed you this riddle?" Taffy asked. "Did she seem legitimate? Did she ask for my last name?"

"I believe she was legit," Harris responded. "She didn't seem to want to talk to me … possibly scared. Yes, she knew to ask for your last name. Mr. Burrows must have talked about you to her and he trusted her. She wanted to keep the information she gave secret. Something is going on, I felt, legit or not."

Harris poured a full glass of orange juice and drank a swallow.

"Burrows and I made a pact just in case something like this happened. So how'd you like the shuttle?" Taffy asked, but Harris sensed he truly wasn't interested.

He watched Taffy inspect the riddle he'd written on his pad.

"It was an extraordinary experience; the thing disappeared before my eyes," Harris spoke. "The MD's made it to the moon with the supplies, so I'd say the technology works."

"Uh-huh," Taffy uttered, glancing at Harris, then back at his pad.

"The security there is unbelievable. Everything is kept covert."

"Really?"

"Really."

"No," Taffy said, correcting Harris that he wasn't talking about his Alaskan experience. "I think I just figured out our riddle."

"How so?" Harris asked and drank another swallow.

"I think you're right, my dear boy." Taffy smirked. "Sometimes the teacher must listen to the student." Taffy cleared his throat. "Burrows must have swallowed something important before he was killed, like what Cronus did to his children to try and stop the prophecy and protect his throne."

"But the prophecy went through anyway because he was tricked by Rhea with a rock Cronus thought was Zeus."

"That's the story I told you in depth, but this brainteaser isn't asking that. It's a simple question of what Cronus did to protect his throne. How did Burrows protect a secret he had? He ate it."

Harris sighed, drank the rest of his drink, and sat more back on the couch.

"Like you said, look at it in the light of today," Taffy spoke.

"So what are you thinking here? Because—"

"You're going to have to go in there, my dear boy, and perform an autopsy," Taffy said.

"And what if you're wrong about this and we find nothing?"

"I haven't been wrong yet."

Harris hated to admit Taffy might be right on this one. He wasn't convinced of aliens yet, but something fishy was going on. He was about to commit to possibly doing a half-ass autopsy on a body. The strangest thing that came over him was that he felt he was going to find something.

"How are we going to do this, sir?" Harris asked. "We don't have the authority nor consent of the family, and who's going to get a medical examiner to re-examine a body probably already examined?"

"We're the CIA," Taffy said. "We're above authority, veterans at it, for crying out loud."

"*Was*, and sir, I emphasize that strongly."

"Come on, all those years working for The Company has to amount for something. I'm putting everything on the line for this."

Harris shook his head and folded his arms. Taffy stared back at him with the gravest scrunched face.

Harris felt he was about to be catapulted into another webbed conspiracy; could be government, could be private organization. Something was going on, and an investigation was about to be launched. *Damn,* he sulked, *some kind of retirement. Humph.*

"**DETECTIVES**, now CIA," the medical examiner said as they walked through the morgue in the basement of Memorial Hermann Medical Center in Houston, TX. "You guys are lucky. Tomorrow is the last day for this cadaver's stay here." The examiner chuckled.

"Ain't he the lucky stiff," Harris said and giggled also.

Sara elbowed Harris in the side, looking at him intently.

They were all dressed in blue scrubs. The medical examiner named Jack wore more to his outfit and moved more fluently than his guest. Besides a mask, like his company, he wore gloves, cap, and gargles. Harris and Sara moved stiffly as they had to put the scrubs over their shirts and pants.

The area was gray with a long corridor of row upon row of aluminum-colored three by three foot shoe box morgue storage unit doors imbedded in the left wall. The white cement floors shined in the brilliance of ceiling lights that went on and on in sequence.

It was cold, like walking through a giant refrigerator, Harris detected. He was used to the chill of death, though he saw in is former co-worker's brown eyes, she wasn't. She would have never made it past the real smell of death, Harris believed; she was certainly a throw up victim. The smell here was only of antiseptics.

Usually Sara's mahogany and brown shoulder long straight hair would bounce around as she walked, but not now. She sauntered with her arms folded, staring straight ahead.

"Yup, the family is coming for this one finally. It's been about a month now," Jack spoke and turned into a room with a huge white clock hanging from the ceiling.

In this area supplies and equipment were jumbled together on three tin counters against three walls. In the center of the room on the aluminum coroner slab a bluish-gray body lay covered with a white sheet from the waist down.

The bearded heavy set cadaver had a small bullet wound on the right side of its cranium. Harris glimpsed at the toe tag, *Anthony Jesse Burrows*.

"Where do you want to investigate first?" Jack asked.

Harris watched Sara grimace as they approached the corpse.

Sara glanced at Harris, and he cleared his throat looking away from her and at the examiner before he spoke. "Preferably I want to know what's in the stomach. If something of significance is there, I'd like to extract it."

"Not a problem," the coroner said. "Would you like me to use an endoscopy before I cut?"

"Sure, let's see what we got."

Harris had called Sara two days earlier to set this all up. He had to tell her the truth about the whole operation to attain access to the things Taffy wanted. There was no other way.

The CIA were the only ones who could get just about anything in the world done. He had the connections, and now was the time to use them. If he wanted things done in a timely fashion and not probe this undertaking for years, he had to rely on the CIA. Taffy didn't have that long anyway.

Sara, as she stated, was on a boring, classified surveillance of certain citizens' assignment, decided it would be interesting helping him. Tracking down where Anthony Burrows's body was kept and flashing her credentials in front of Jack, the medical examiner, for Harris to get to this point was no sweat.

She told him she established Burrows's body had been shipped back to his home in Houston and explained to the coroner that this was a CIA investigation and that he was on a need to know basis.

Harris told her, he owed her a lot and didn't know how he was going to repay her. Sara smiled and said she was sure he'd come up with something.

Jack searched for the endoscopy on one of the counters. Finding it, he spread gel on the black five foot thin long snake tube.

"Because of rigor mortis," Jack spoke and put his mask over his face, "I'm going to enter the nostril cavity instead of the mouth."

Jack turned on huge powerful lights above the coroner's table.

Harris surveyed Sara glance at the clock above them and inspected the toe tag. He smirked as Sara looked everywhere but where the examiner was struggling, stuffing the tiny long hose up the cadaver's nose.

After two minutes the coroner waved for Harris or Sara to come closer. It was obvious; Harris came forward right away.

"I think I might have found something peculiar," Jack said. "Probably what you're looking for."

Jack moved his head away from the lens so Harris could peer in. As Jack held the otoscope-looking device steady, Harris right away noticed something familiar in the gray innards of the stomach; another glass vial. He noticed this one seemed smaller, but still contained a fortune cookie-like message.

Harris nodded at the medical examiner and he pulled the endoscopy from the corpse.

As the examiner went for his scalpel, Harris surveyed Sara pretend to scrutinize the equipment around the room.

"**HERE**, write this down," Harris spoke into his cell phone in a downtown Houston Hyatt Regency business plan room.

Harris sat on a brown well-made bed in the plush hotel room in front of a flat screen television. The anchor on *CNN* rambled on about Iran negotiating in recognizing Israel as a sovereign nation.

That was interesting, Harris deliberated, squinting at the screen. He knew some kind of secret deal had to have gone down among governments behind that move. If he was still at Langley, he would have known about it and why. The Agency's affairs weren't his issues anymore.

He turned the television sound up, not because he wanted to hear the program, but to drown out his conversation. Though he knew nobody was listening to him, he turned it up out of habit.

He waited for Taffy to get a pen and paper between coughing in his ear.

"Alright, go on," Taffy said, feebly.

"Folder Hephaestus, password Prometheus," Harris said into his Bluetooth, placing it in his ear and putting his phone down by his side. He unwrapped the tiny long scrolled message, and held it in front of his face. He read the rest of the note more fluently, slowly. "Location, basement, level B five-sixty dash six-twelve, East Impending Tower computer. Warning, don't open under any circumstances, emits emissions of B class star."

"For one thing, I already solved some of this riddle," Taffy said. "Besides the obvious passwords, locations, and warnings, I know what five-sixty, six-twelve stand for. It's verses from the *Theogony* by Hesiod, where he speaks about Pandora for the first time. We're going to have to get into that basement computer to know more."

"I'm starting to see obviously this all revolves around the Pandora myth," Harris said. "Maybe this has something to do with a secret device or weapon of some sort more than extraterrestrials. Think about it; Impending Towers, Chelsea Company, technology, star emissions."

"Hmm, maybe, but only something other than us can harness the power of a sun."

"Not necessarily; some three years ago you would have said light speed was impossible. A matter of fact, we're moving faster than that."

"You could be right again, my dear boy," Taffy said and coughed again. "This Chelsea Company could have stumbled on a weapon as powerful as the sun. Chelsea's experiences with the CIA and FBI aren't so splendid. An assassin from Chelsea already ousted a FBI agent some years ago, so if Burrows knew about something, they could have sanctioned his murder. I believe we've been through this before."

"You're right, sir, we could have stumbled onto something big here."

"What did Sara say about it?"

"I don't think the Agency has a clue. She wanted me to keep her posted. It was like my reimbursement to her for helping me examine Burrows."

"I'm going to transfer a few million into your account," Taffy spoke. "We have to get to work on this double time, at no expense."

"That said, I assume this is going to lead me back to my last case, the Chelsea Corporation."

"You assume right, my son, you assume right," Taffy said.

Harris let out a long sigh.

"What's wrong, son?" Taffy asked. "The time to use that old vacation Barbados passion is at hand." Taffy hacked again, more intensely this time.

"Sir, don't worry yourself none, get some rest," Harris responded. "I suppose I'll figure out some kind of approach on my way to Ohio."

"Look, stop worrying about my health," Taffy replied and coughed. "You're making me sicker with your pity."

Harris felt Taffy sensed the worry in his voice, and he was. Cruel old cranky bastard, Harris thought. He knew the way Taffy was was probably keeping him alive this long. He loved the guy, though.

CHAPTER 7

HE WAS HERE IN BRATENAHL AGAIN. The last time he was here, he came as an attempted murderous traitor. That's how Ms. Chelsea was going to perceive him.

He figured he could have infiltrated the Impending Towers and pinch the information he needed—he knew the building blueprint. Then again, he didn't have much knowledge about the basement of the towers besides the sewers. It would have been a tedious task. This might look like a lazy move, Harris guessed, but this time he was approaching her sincerely.

How great would it be if she just believed his story? He needed information from her because it was his boss's last dying wish. She'd indeed laugh in his face, but it was worth a try to come to her truthfully. Not as Maddox Mathews, his last alias, but as Matt R. Harris.

In hindsight he did save her life, he mused. His mission was to eliminate the target—creator of the technology. He reneged; he could have been killed for his insolence. Her company never sold the technology to a foreign country so he understood the Agency spared her and him. He put his own life in jeopardy to save hers, but he had a feeling today Chelsea was never going to understand.

He could kidnap her and force the basement information out of her through torture. No, he thought, those days were over. Somehow, he pondered, he was going to have to win back her trust. This was going to be a futile mission, but he had to try anyway.

He didn't have a blueprint of the two-story white million dollar home, but he was familiar with it. After flying to Ohio, checking himself into a downtown hotel, and booked it for a month he drove here. He sat in his rented car for about an hour deliberating. Leaving his car a couple of miles down the road and walking to the house, he continued thinking of a plan.

He sketched on how he was going to infiltrate the Chelsea estate security. He waited for the sun to sink a little and decided the roof was the easiest way to go. It was 8:30 and the setting sun gave the sky and house a hue of cornflower blue.

It was amazing how he managed to make it this far. He somehow bypassed the home security, or so he alleged. Moving cautiously through some scrubs on the eastside of the home, unseen he made it past visible dome cameras placed on the side of the building and grounds. Climbing a palm tree next to the house, he jumped onto the flat white roof, ran across, then climbed down using a gutter drain pipe into a yard where he began lurking.

The back yard had a spherical crimson brick floor. In the center was a round inglenook and surrounding it a three foot scarlet C shaped brick stoop. In front of the stoop were fifteen pallid marble steps leading to a veranda, and glass doors to Chelsea's bedroom. A garden with Greek-style white vases filled with purple and red Anemone flowers decorated the yard and porch.

At the foot of the steps Harris peeked up past the slits of tan draped curtains finding Chelsea asleep on her bed on top of the sheets. He crept up some steps to get a better look.

Nzingha Chelsea looked as ravishing as she did when he had first set eyes on her some years ago. She only wore a long white button shirt, exposing her petite shaped tan legs and feet. Her short hair had grown a little, Harris observed, or was it the way she was sleeping?

She appeared like a Barbie doll, so perfect, as she lay there in the lackluster light of the room. He felt like a peeping Tom or some kind of fiend, but she was beautiful.

An ultrasonic sound of a high frequency ping disrupted his ears, making him grab them. Some kind of ultra-bright flashing disco strobe light emitter from the roof blinded him.

For a second he felt disoriented and nauseous. Chelsea's alarm system must have gone off, he presumed. He knew this wasn't going to be that easy. *Wonderful defense mechanism.*

When the sound and light emitter died, he staggered, almost dropping to his knees becoming deaf and bind. Then he was hit with something else. The light and sound show he felt was his excuse for being punched in the face, blindsiding his peripheral vision from the right. He fell to the floor in a heap.

I'm getting too old for this was his first thought. Survival mode then kicked in and he felt he wasn't that old yet.

The guy who punched him was about six feet, muscular, and bald-headed. In black suit jacket looking thirty years old, clean-shaved, and shades, he stood over him, balling up his fist. Typical bodyguard, Harris figured.

On the floor Harris grabbed the man's legs and lifted him off his feet. Slamming the guardian on his back onto the floor, Harris landed on him.

The man went for his shoulder holster. Harris grabbed his wrist and they struggled with a black and silver Glock. Harris, winning the wrestling match for the handgun, was punched in the ribs by the bodyguard's free hand.

"Mr. Mathews, what's going on here?"

Harris, regaining his hearing, heard a familiar voice. Letting out a long sigh from the pain in his right side, he spoke loud for everyone to hear. "Okay! Easy! I'm going to let go and surrender."

Looking into the guard's dark shades, he still sensed an angry gaze. As Harris discerned the man stop struggling, he let go of his wrist and they both stood. Harris put his hands into the air and the bodyguard cocked his gun, pointing it at him.

"Give me one reason why I shouldn't have him shoot you where you stand, *Mr. Mathews*?" Chelsea asked.

There Chelsea stood above him on her veranda in front of her glass doors. She was now in black slacks with a scowl on her oval face.

"I can give you two," Harris said with a smirk. "One, I have highly important information that you're going to want to know about. Two, whether you like it or not, I kind of know you, and I know you're not a killer like me."

"You don't know me, *Mr. Mathews*," Chelsea said with a snarl. "But I do believe you're sincere when you say that you're a killer. Maybe we'll be able to resolve all this with some sincerity."

Harris glimpsed at the bodyguard, then at Chelsea. "It wouldn't be possible that I could talk to you alone?"

"Why? So you could get another chance?" Chelsea asked in an annoyed tone.

"Look, I spared your life and risked mine." Harris put his hands down, trying to explain as the guard continued pointing his gun at him. "If I wanted to kill you today, I could have. I was winning the fight with this dude—"

"*Winning?*" the bodyguard spoke. "Yeah, right."

It was obvious the guard deliberately made his voice deep, a sure sign of lying, Harris judged. He wondered if Chelsea detected it.

Harris looked the man in the face. "First of all, if he's such a guardian, how did I get this far, right to your bedroom doorstep? And I was winning that fight. Listen," Harris talked fast, "pat me down. I have a gun in my shoulder holster and one on my ankle." He looked at Chelsea. "Then can we talk?"

She nudged at the bodyguard and Harris put his hands again in the air. The guard, after searching him, retrieved a black Desert Eagle and Glock.

"Nice," the guard said, holding the Desert Eagle, weighing its weight.

Chelsea huffed, sighed, and crossed her arms. For a full minute she glared at Harris, causing both men to stand there stupidly.

"Come up, Mathews," Chelsea said with a frown. "I know you didn't come all this way to test my security."

Harris walked up the stairs, giving a smug glimpse at the bodyguard.

"Daniel, stand outside please," Chelsea continued as Harris reached the deck.

Harris put his hand out for her to go in first, but she rolled her eyes. After she disregarded his polite gesture, he stepped into her room.

Her large beige room walls matched her polished tiled tan floor. Four white abstract lanterns hung from a twenty foot ceiling illuminating a low queen size bed with white wool carpet underneath.

What stood out most was the eight by fifteen foot painting centered over her headboard. It was a brown and fawn colored oil painting of a female bust looking down thinking. The painting appeared unfinished, showing little detail of the shoulders. It had the appeal of Leonardo da Vinci, Harris discerned.

"Nice," Harris said, looking around. "I don't believe I've ever been in this room." He breathed in deeply, smelling the lilac scent of potpourri. Wow, he distinguished, Chelsea's bedroom.

"Thank goodness," Chelsea said, closing the glass door behind her, but didn't move the drape back into its place to where the bodyguard watched them from outside. "And perhaps your last." She moved past him to sit on the edge of her bed of ruffled silk brown sheets.

It was obvious she wasn't going to offer him a seat or drink or anything, so he quickly got his thoughts together.

"I see the temperature in here hasn't changed. It's cold," Harris said, rubbing the sleeves of his dark-gray suit jacket.

"Okay, Mr. Mathews, you have twenty minutes," Chelsea said and crossed her arms and legs.

He'd heard her say this once before, but this time he saw the enthusiasm in her eyes for him to leave, and she was counting down the minutes. Get it together, Harris mentally prearranged, and took a deep breath before he spoke.

"My real name is Matt and I've worked for the CIA," he explained, gazing into her eyes.

"Worked or still working?" Chelsea requested insipidly.

"Worked," Harris answered. "I'm retired now, two years. Look, to just get right down to it, I'm sorry for what I've done to you; it was just business. You're all about business. I knew you'd understand."

Chelsea tightened her lips.

"Today I'm trying to come to you as a friend," Harris spoke. "Look, my old man is dying and we need to know what's on a computer in the basement of Impending Towers. This has nothing to do with the CIA. It's personal."

Chelsea responded with a grimace and opened her mouth in awe. "You government guys kill me. It's not enough that I make deals with you, expecting you to leave me alone. No, you bring me the same agent, a familiar face who tried to form a personal relationship, then tried to murder me, to spew more lies. You're coming to me *personally*? You came to me personally last time, Mr. Mathews, I mean Mathew Mathews; oh, I'm sorry, Matt. Is that short for Matthew?"

Harris frowned. He comprehended, explaining this was going to take more time and work than twenty minutes.

"Just Matt," Harris answered flatly. "I don't know how to actually explain this, so I'm just going to upchuck it. There's a possible existing device that has the power to create a self-sustaining sun and we, my father and I, want to know if it exists and that's it. There's no CIA involved. We found some evidence leading to your towers. This could have nothing to do with you or it could have all to do with you."

"After what you've done to me, what do you expect me to do, help you?"

Chelsea smirked in an evil way, Harris observed.

"Look," Harris spoke, pleading this time. "All I'm asking right now is for you to take time to consider." He moved closer to her, trying through body language to show his sincerity. "I'm just trying to find out if such a device exists, nothing more."

"Yeah, right. It's never, and that's it. There's always a catch. Are you trying to play me as a fool or are you playing with my emotions? Which?"

"Neither. All I can give you is my word. This has nothing to do with any government agency. It's simply, personal."

"I don't have to think about it, Mr. Matt," Chelsea spoke. "The answer's no. The first time you wanted to know if a certain technology exists, now it seems you're back for more. I just wanted to hear your proposal of what it was this time. It doesn't sound worthy and your time with me is up, for good."

"Okay," Harris said, smirking, seeing she made up her mind. "Can you just think about it? Can you just tell me if an undisclosed computer exists in the basement of your towers? You can text me here."

He reached into his left suit jacket breast pocket. Simultaneously the glass door opened behind him and Daniel the bodyguard entered.

Chelsea put her hand up to stop the guard's advances as Harris handed her a business card. She snatched the card from his hand and threw it over her shoulder to land behind her on the bed.

Harris noticed Daniel wasn't alone this time as another guard stood by the doorway.

"Just do me a favor," Harris beseeched, "think about it? You have to believe me. This has nothing to do with the CIA."

Chelsea glanced back at a small blue digital hologram clock on a shelf near her bed. "Your time's up, Mr. Matt."

As security escorted him out the front door he pondered over his mission so far. It was going good until he hit this bump. The meeting with Chelsea didn't go well, but he figured so.

He had to move her up from his list of top dozen women he liked to the top five. Even with her hair discombobulated, apparently from when she was lying down, she was still more attractive than he previously remembered. Maybe it was the antagonism in her facial expressions that attracted him more. He had to shake those fantasies away and think more on his dying father.

The secret messages from a dead man had led him here to the footsteps of Chelsea's home. He believed he was going to have to tell his father his charisma hadn't work this time. He was going to have to try again at some point, he figured, and *hope* Chelsea will soften a little. He was soon perhaps going to have to believe in hope. *Argh!* He hated hope.

CHAPTER 8

HER CONCENTRATION PONDERED ON TWO THINGS.
One, the meeting at hand, the other, men. Her office investment meeting was going well, but her thoughts of an ideal man was not. *Men—let me specify*—Chelsea corrected her principles, *finding good men, was far more complicated than my finances.*

On the twenty-first floor in her large spherical lime-green office in the East Impending Tower she stood behind her desk.

Bamboo and Reed Palm plants decorated the room following the curvature of the windows. Their leaves and stems reached up at the ceiling toward an enormous round light in the center.

In front of her ivory desk sat her Chief Financial Adviser, Harold, and Chief Executive, Aaron. They both looked handsome in their blue three-piece suits, but through Chelsea's, eyes Aaron looked finer. His suit was more Persian blue, if that made any sense, she appraised.

"I want a full evaluation of my gold and diamond investments," she spoke. She slowly paced to and fro, rotating two silver Chinese designed Baoding balls in her right hand behind her back.

"Your China and Russian value of the rocks is rising," Harold responded, looking down at a folder with charts on his lap. "And the crises in Japan shouldn't affect your gold there."

"Watch our hedge funds in Germany," Chelsea said, pointing at Harold. "I want a meeting with you and our investment manager sometime next week about our mutual funds in that country."

"Yes, ma'am," Harold answered. He opened a black E-Keeper pad and with a pen jotted down on a tiny calendar what was just agreed. He also footnoted it on his cell phone.

"Aaron," Chelsea spoke, looking into his eyes. "I noticed the CEO of CMS, Mr. Rosenbluth, was interested in your magnetism at the party. Set up a meeting with him to begin our acquisition presentations."

"Sure thing," Aaron responded. "The press is going to be all over this one."

Chelsea answered with a smirk.

Dressed in her black pants suit, she wondered did Aaron still see her as seductively as he did at the party. When she was dressed like this, she figured he tended to see her as just his boss. She didn't see it that way. She was attracted to him most of the time and kept giving him a tantalizing stare every five minutes of the meeting, but he didn't catch on.

She then thought about Mathew—Matt, Mr. CIA man. Was he really coming to her sincerely, that he quit the agency and this was for his dying father? No, it was just another ploy to gather intelligence about her company, unquestionably trying to figure out what she was doing for company future events. He was trying to get into her head by using her past feelings for him.

On the other hand the government already knew what she was doing and she presumed they were already following her closely. *Maybe they were just making sure?*

Matt was a more handsome man than Aaron, and had a far better build. Matt didn't have to use his time to sneak into my room and tell his life story, but he did. Bull! He had some nerve coming to me seeking some kind of redemption.

Maybe she'll at least hear what he had to say, she thought but she wasn't going to call him. If he was so serious about gaining her trust he'll come after her again. *Keep your friends close, but your enemies closer.*

"Ms. Chelsea, is next Friday afternoon, alright?" Harold asked again.

Chelsea realized she was staring aimlessly out the window and into the clear blue sky watching some pigeons fly by. She glanced at Harold, comprehending that he could have asked her for the third time.

"… yes, Friday is good," Chelsea finally replied. If they only knew what she was thinking.

HE hated and loved surveillance work. He despised it because he didn't like waiting around. He was a predator, a killer. He wanted to shoot and get it over with. He cherished, though, the detective work, the actual thrill of the hunt.

This mission's surveillance post was downtown Columbus, OH on the sixth floor of the Courtyard Marriott in a king spa guest room.

Sprawled across the brown linen on his bed lay photos of Chelsea. One picture was of her walking into a building in New York and another walking into Impending Towers in Ohio. Other photos were of her in different positions at her desk or at a meeting. All the snapshots close-up and somewhat pixilated were taken from a distance, resembling paparazzi or some kind of fixated stalker photographs from an unknown window.

In an open suitcase by his side he pulled out a manila envelope. Opening the envelope, he took out some telephone transcripts. He glimpsed at the texts and numbers which were mostly business oriented about mergers, deals, and future planning on how to make more money with other companies. Some calls were to France, India, and South Korea.

The calls over the past month that bewildered him most were five out of the thousand. The five calls were to and fro from Nigeria. It sounded more personal than business. "How are you doing? How was your day today, sir?"

Was it a boyfriend overseas? he wondered. *But you wouldn't refer to your boyfriend as sir, now, would you? Chelsea, when speaking to this guy overseas always said, yes, sir, or no, sir. Maybe it was nothing; maybe it was just how she spoke to that specific person, at a company called Livenal.* It was something to look into later.

Right now he was waiting for a phone call from an informant in the Chelsea Company for more information. Staying on top of his immediate mission at hand, he had a new target. It was unclear on who to eradicate, for his handlers said the operation was going to be first strictly observation before annihilation. He didn't care how long or for what, just give him something to kill.

He inspected more photos in his briefcase of different executives of the Chelsea Company. Interesting, he ruminated, they were all male. He wondered why such a beautiful woman as Chelsea continually surrounded herself with men, when she seemingly could get as many men as she wanted at any time. *It looked chauvinistic, all her employees being male. Or did she think she was some kind of prima donna where all men served her? Hey, she knows best, she's the richest woman in the world,* he thought.

His cell phone rang and he answered it on the second ring.

"Yeah," he said in a low voice.

"There will be more expansion on the C.E. and PE projects, but nothing yet on Pandora," a nervous, fast talking voice said on the other end.

"Thank you," he answered. "I'll contact you again soon." He hung up the phone, wrapped it in some plan white paper from his briefcase, then tossed it into the garbage next to a wooden desk.

Following the codes, the Chelsea Company mole really said, there was going to be an expansion of C.E., Chelsea Energy. The PE project, Project Elf, the name of a nanomedicine invented by Chelsea, was soon about to go public—maybe. The biggest project, Pandora, was supposed to be some kind of device that had the power of the sun or suns. The existence of such a weapon still remains unknown.

All he knew was that his bureau had been watching the Chelsea Company since they discovered the Vc technology some years ago. So they knew the company's every move except for this Pandora, and now they called him to find out.

They also called him because they knew someone had been messing around with Anthony Burrows's body, a kill he'd already forgotten about. The flash drive he recovered from the body was empty, so his benefactors told him. They didn't have a clue why someone in the CIA would be snooping around the late Burrows. They assured him when they found out, he was going to be one of the first to know.

Of course, he presumed, this was all interconnected—secret information of Pandora that was supposed to be on the pen drive, the power of Pandora possibly hidden in the Chelsea Company. *Possibly, maybe, this device never existed and Burrows died in vain.* Whatever, he thought; it was all just a job to him.

What was he to do? *This wasn't a clear-cut kill mission. It wasn't a surveillance mission either; they had that already down pat. I basically could be chasing a ghost. They had been paying me for all this down time—peanuts to the Society. Oh well, they told me this was an important mission, so I'm on it.*

He rapped his knuckles on the desk in front of him. He felt he was summoning good spirits that lived in the tree that made the desk.

This was doubtlessly going to be his easiest mission yet. He put on black gloves from his case, checked the magazine in his Smith & Wesson 9mm, and shrugged. "But then you never know," he spoke softly.

CHAPTER 9

THIS WAS ONE FESTIVITY she felt was worth her precious time. Not many politicians and executives came to this fundraiser. Only a hand full of Democrats from New York and California came to the beneficial convention, to save the Amazonian rainforest.

CEO's of many companies she had dealt with were even fewer. She did, though, recognize and meet Warren Buffett of Berkshies Hathaway, a holding company, and William Gates of Microsoft.

Mr. Gates rambled on about his private philanthropy foundation, pitching it to her, promising the great asset she would be if she was to join. Her only response was that she'd look into it.

Chelsea wore a black Donna Karen, long-sleeve, silk-wrap dress. Aaron, her escort, John Carroll and his wife, with two more couples from the Green Party Co-Chairs; the dinner table was full.

Tonight about a hundred generally wealthy GPUS supporters in mostly black and blue tuxedos and multi-colored gowns filled the Ronald Reagan and International Trade Center Building on Pennsylvania Avenue in Washington, D.C..

The atrium's glass hundred and twenty-five foot skylight was an enormous sight as its terrazzo and marble shiny floor. A mammoth green banner hung over huge long stairs leading from the entrance to the banquet level.

Amazon Rainforest 28% of the World's Oxygen. Stop Deforestation Now!

Chelsea felt tonight was spectacular. Though there were only ten well dressed white tables with centered bushels of white roses in tall glass vases, everyone managed to eat.

As the night lingered on, some people stood and some sat in political and worldly conversations as an orchestra of thirty players played *Mozart's Divertimento in D Major* on a balcony.

"You've truly put us back on the map," John Carroll spoke, holding a wine glass full of red wine. "Your company simply advocating us, our supporters have already gone up at least fifty percent."

Chelsea, Carroll, and Aaron stood in a circle surrounded by others in dialogue, holding drinks.

"Who knows," Carroll continued, "more Green governors throughout the states, the presidency? Make me understand clearly. You dropped the two biggest political parties in United States history to rally with us?"

Chelsea was glad to respond to his inquiry for she had been through this before. She knew he liked her responses and wanted to hear it from her again. Or he could have been intrigued that a woman of her type knew such things.

"I've already explained it to you before," Chelsea said, smiling, showing her dimples. "I'm beginning to wonder if you just want to hear me speak."

"Maybe, indulge me?" Carroll asked and sipped his wine.

Aaron folded his arms and silently huffed, staring at Carroll. She detected Aaron's jealousy and liked it.

"I guess I'll explain it in another way," Chelsea clarified. "You Greens are almost like civil libertarian Democrats and your policies of your *Four Pillars* is what I would put on my front door."

"It should be the new constitution," Aaron said, jumping in.

"No, I wouldn't do that," Chelsea retorted. "That would destroy the grassroots democracy these Greens believe in." Chelsea looked Carroll in the eye when she said the statement and he smiled. She sensed Aaron didn't like that. "Global responsibilities, feminism, your future focuses; why wouldn't I want to support such things?" Chelsea declared more than asked.

"What do you mean, we're like libertarian Democrats?" Carroll asked. "You never said that before."

"Warrantless wiretapping, the Patriot Act, we all agree, I think, that it erodes the Bill of Rights."

"True, you might have a point, but overall we're nothing like Democrats."

"Of course not," Chelsea said. "I said almost like. I far like the deepness of your politics. If we could only channel it and present it to the masses better."

"I like your style, Nzingha, I like your style," Carroll said and raised his glass, giving a toast in the air, then drank a swallow.

BESIDES the steady drizzle of rain, the evening was perfect, Chelsea contemplated. Everyone had said their final goodbyes and dispersed.

Eleven o'clock; the night was still young, she pondered, as everyone leisurely filed out of the building. *Who knows, this could turn into a nightcap with Aaron if he played his cards right, or if I played mine.*

On the 14th Street side of the building some couples and groups were being picked up in a Bentley, Mercedes-Benz, and limousines. The short trip to their rented BMW reserved in front, Chelsea felt there was no need for an umbrella as Aaron escorted her.

Glancing up at the waving wet green banisters attached to lamppost with words about the event, she felt tonight was a great accomplishment. If they saved one acre of the forest, it would be time well spent.

In her peripheral sight she saw something that made her mind become jumbled. With all the floodlights about, it was unmistaken that not something, but someone, had startled her.

Mr. Matt, Mr. CIA man, stood next to a detailed dimgray statue of a man sitting up on his side in a bed with sheets covering its bottom parts, but exposing its muscular top build. An exposed boy also a part of the sculpture had one arm leaning on the man's shoulder knelt behind.

It's ironic, Chelsea thought, previewing the inscription on the gray base. *The voice of reason is more to be regarded than the bent of any present inclination.*

Chelsea interpreted as Harris trying to tell her to listen to *his* voice of reason. *Why come out of a building with a statue like this and not try to hear what he had to say?*

He stood there next to the sculpture in a beige raincoat made brown by the rain with no hat. With his arms crossed he had a stupid smirk on his face, eyeing her as she passed.

He obviously followed me here to D.C. to fish his cock and bull story about needing my help in favor of his dying father and leaving the CIA.

She stopped in front of Harris with wonder in her eyes, more than surprised.

Uncrossing his arms, he looked at her with the most serious face. "I'm practically begging you to reconsider," Harris said, his black short wavy hair and face soaked. "I need your help, Nzingha, and I'm willing to pay you if I have to. You know, like owe you something."

He's really desperate, Chelsea rationalized. Bold effort, she thought, but this time she had no idea what he was talking about when he fed her the story of a device that had the power of the sun.

For one thing, if she did have such a device, for damn sure she wasn't going to tell him about it, or anybody, if she could keep the secret long enough from the government. But then she'd never know, her father might have known about that assassin in her company and could know something about this.

She shook her head. *No, this Matt guy was crazy and had some nerve following me.*

"Look, we both know what I said before," Chelsea spoke, looking at Harris. "Following me stupidly isn't going to change my mind. I'm sorry, Agent Matt."

Harris stared at her for a second longer before he looked away toward the ground.

For a second, and a second only, Chelsea felt his dejection. She had to walk away from this scene. This was foolishness.

Aaron gently put his arm across her shoulders, helping her move from the helpless man.

"We have to go, you're getting wet," Aaron said. She sensed Aaron's grudge again as they walked to their car, and she reminded herself she liked it.

"I remember once, you said you believed in second chances," Harris shouted at Chelsea as she climbed into the car. "I believed you then and I believe you now."

She watched Harris lower his head and walk away as she closed her door. Thunder clapped in the distance as Aaron started the car and the rain came down harder, slamming onto the roof like pebbles.

"Wow, what was that about?" Aaron asked in wonder.

Ignoring Aaron's question for a second, she thought about the roles being played here. They were actually reversed to where Harris now seemed the victim in a weird way. Helplessness is a victim to us all, she considered. He did have a heart when he had a chance to finish his mission and kill her, he spared her. Her walking away like this and not even giving him a chance did seem a bit heartless, especially him claiming his father was dying. A life for a life echoed in her psyche.

As Aaron slowly pulled out of the parking spot, she realized he was still talking.

"... you know that guy because he sure was weir—"

"Stop the car!" Chelsea demanded.

"What? What happened? You forgot something?" he asked, puzzled.

"Yeah, my manners, maybe."

"Huh?"

Chelsea opened the door when the car jolted to a stop and walked back into the rain.

She spotted Harris easily, for there were only valets walking back into the building. He had his collar up and head hunched down as if that was going to save him from the weather. After walking around a large water fountain and creeping behind him, she pulled on his arm sleeve and he turned around with his hands in his pockets.

"I'm at the State Plaza Hotel; if you want to talk, just ask for me at reception," Chelsea said and watched the surprised face of Harris turn into a smile. It was a grin as if the sun had just broken through the clouds.

She smirked at him, about-faced, and rushed back to her ride.

AARON didn't like it one bit. After telling her story about the CIA informant, Aaron strongly insisted she not go through with the meeting. The entire ride to the hotel he argued with her about seeing this agent. She wondered was it jealousy or was he trying to protect her? It was probably a little of both.

She knew Aaron most likely thought she was going to do what she wanted to do anyway. Chelsea gave him her look of assurance that everything was going to be okay and that she had everything under control. He did remind her again that his room was right across the hall as was her protection.

Aaron asked her again, "Are you sure this is what you want to do?"

"I think so," she replied and gave him a nervous smile. "Don't worry, I'll be okay. I can take care of myself." She winked at him and went into her room.

Her bodyguards, after patting down Harris thoroughly, only retrieved his Desert Eagle.

Harris gave Aaron a stupid smile before walking into her suite. Aaron looked back with the most serious face as Chelsea shut her door. Men; ego thing, she thought.

She handed Harris a white towel from the bathroom and he patted his soaked head.

"Thanks," he replied. "Nice hotel room, spacious."

She didn't respond as they both sat in the living room. She sat in a single brown cushioned wooden chair and he sat on a orange pillowed couch across from her.

"I very well couldn't let you follow me all the way out here to D.C.," Chelsea began the reunion, "to send you back home crying." This was going to be all business, Chelsea contemplated, keep it business.

"Thanks," he responded.

"Talk to me," Chelsea said, sat back, and crossed her legs, still in her black dress. Her dress was long, so she knew he couldn't see her legs. "What are you talking about?"

He smiled. "Well, I'm going to need a little of your time. Twenty minutes just might not cut it."

"Talk, Matt," she said frustratingly. "You'll know when your time is up."

"A government scientist was murdered about a month ago who worked on one of your discoveries, the Vc technology. He left a note or riddle of some kind, guiding us—me and my stepfather—to the basement of your towers. Level B five-sixty, six-twelve, computer bank. Does that mean anything to you?"

Chelsea thought for a moment. "I do have a B level basement in the building and a computer there labeled five hundred and sixty. Five hundred and sixty is a serial number, a tracking number for our IT security of the building; using remote access if need be for repairs and such."

"What's the *such* part?"

"It's so we can monitor our employees in illegal business if need be throughout the system."

"And they say the CIA tries to get into people's business."

"What we do is perfectly legal, Mr. Matt. Our employees are fully aware of the scrutiny."

"Just Matt."

"Mr. Matt," Chelsea spoke defiantly.

"What about computer six hundred and twelve?" Harris asked, getting back to the heart of the conversation.

"There's no six hundred and twelve. The serial numbers start from eighty and end at five hundred and ninety."

Harris rubbed his chin. "Do you know anything about a device that has the power of the sun, or a B class star?"

"Before I answer that, I'm curious. How did this scientist who was murdered become an expert in my tower's basements?" Chelsea looked at Harris intriguingly.

"According to my stepfather," Harris spoke, "this man knew of information for years about technology beyond many people's comprehension. Your company has technology beyond comprehension. This man then one day points the finger at your towers, indicating a new device with the power of a star might be among us. C'mon, you put the pieces together."

"A B class star, huh?" Chelsea spoke softly.

"Yeah, it's a star that's—"

"I know," Chelsea cut him off. "Our sun is a G class star, the B class star that's supposed to be seventeen solar masses, also known as a blue supergiant; you're saying my company could wield that kind of power?"

He nodded answering, "Possible. Some years ago traveling at the speed of light was insane. Your company achieved that."

Chelsea uncrossed her legs and sat up straight in her chair. She folded her hands on her lap and sighed. This man isn't going anywhere, she thought. Maybe telling him the truth, he'll go away. The truth was, she had no such weapon or device that had the power of any such star—yet, though she had a feeling it was worth asking her stepfather of such things. On the other hand, somewhere deep in her feelings, if she knew anything about Harris it was that he was a serious guy.

"What makes you think if I had such a weapon," Chelsea asked, "I'd tell you?"

She watched Harris sigh and crease his brow as if in thought about her query before speaking. "If anything, I know you're an honest, obliging person. No nonsense, able. You're not a bullshitter, and I think you can tell if I was bullshitting."

"About quitting your job or your dying father?" Chelsea shook her head. "Perhaps I don't believe any of this."

He stared at her glossy-eyed with the most serious face as if to say, I have nothing left; you either believe it or you don't. For some reason, and it scared her deep inside, she knew he was telling the truth. *Damn,* she thought, *just my luck.*

"Let me think about it, Matt," she said, looking at his damp gray shirt. For some reason she didn't want to look into his seemingly truthful fawn eyes. "As you know, this is all sudden to me."

"Please," he said sincerely.

"I'll be free in Ohio Wednesday where we can continue this conversation or possible search."

She had to acknowledge, physically it felt good to see him again. *It was like one of those relationships where I know we would never become physical, but man, what was wrong with dreaming about it?* Back to her game face, she mulled, and gave Harris cold eyes when he departed.

Chelsea curiously wanted to know why she was entangled in this weird story, and what was this mysterious power she was supposed to possess? From her vantage many things were answered already.

Her company's creation of Chelsea Energy, antimatter capability, had powered Ohio and could power other cities for decades. The usage of nanotechnology and ambient intelligence was now prevalent because of her corporation. Light speed and trips to the moon would have been null if deals weren't made between Chelsea Enterprises and the DOE— her nanomedicine, Project Elf now going public. She had nothing more to hide.

Who was Matt or this scientist who was killed to tell me my company was hiding a covert power more powerful than our sun? If this was some kind of government trick, well, they were tricking themselves, Chelsea thought, growing annoyed.

She folded her arms and sighed, still sitting in her chair alone in the room. Wednesday was in four days. Let's see where this goes, she thought, and find this mystery that didn't exist. *Let's see how far Matt is going to take his story, in the name of his so-called dying father.*

She picked up the phone on the table in front of her and dialed the suite across the hall. *Aaron will be happy to hear it's over, for the moment.*

CHAPTER 10

FOR THE FIRST TIME, Harris was presented with a tour of the Chelsea Tower's basements and he didn't have to spy to achieve it.

Level B-F was two floors submerged under the center of both buildings. Cooling systems kept the temperature here at sixty-five, perfect for the data center. Ideal for Chelsea, Harris figured. He wondered did she frequently come down here. He thought better not to ask. He made it this far, don't jack it up.

After trailing Chelsea through a maze of corridors, they sat in a room next to the server room. She explained the many backup procedures from the constant monitoring of telecommunication systems in the data center to the extensive backup methods of the server room. She didn't allow him in those rooms for their attention was computer 560.

The room they commandeered was identical to the data center, but smaller. The black and white designed place surrounded them in racks of telecommunication equipment.

"This room is less frequent than most," Chelsea began. "It's nothing but old backup data dating some sixteen years ago."

"About when your company got its start," Harris said assertively, more than asking.

Chelsea gave him a smirk and typed in the password to start the computer.

Harris glanced at Chelsea, observing her today, black business suit and blue shirt. Reminiscing some days earlier on her short sleek seal brown hair, wet from the rain, made her exhilarating. Stay focused, he thought. Don't let your inner feelings creep into your head.

"Okay, where do we start?" she asked.

"I suppose we're looking for a file or folder."

"A file or folder labeled, maybe, six hundred and twelve?"

"So you were paying attention that day?"

Chelsea didn't respond; she just moved the cursor about, searching for a folder among hundreds. As she moved through the records in the document files, she moved past a folder that caught his eye.

"Wait!" he shouted. "Go back. Can I see that folder?" He pointed at a folder that read *Hephaestus*.

Moving back to the folder, she clicked on it. To their surprise a warning popped up.

RESTRICTED, PASSWORD

A window appeared on the bottom to type in the secret code.

"Interesting," Chelsea said, scrunching her face. "That never happened before. But then I've never seen this folder before, or what I could remember or paid attention to. I could ask the executive who used to control things down here." Chelsea spoke as if she was talking to herself.

"You won't have to," Harris said confidently. He knew he had to keep as many people out of the loop about what they were doing as possible. She was good at keeping secrets; he figured she'd approve. "I think I know the password. I want to keep as many people out of this as possible. At least until I know what this is."

Chelsea stared at him hard for a few seconds before asking, "You sure you're not working for the CIA?"

"Yes, I'm sure, I'm not," Harris responded. "I could tell the way you look at me, you don't believe me because of what I did in the past, and there's nothing I can do to change that. Assuming I'm telling you the truth and we find something, do you think this would be something right-away to share with everybody?"

Chelsea didn't reply and looked back at the screen.

"Try *Prometheus*."

She typed in the Titan's name. Again, restricted. Harris uttered a bunch of names and Chelsea typed them in.

"Hephaestus."

Restricted, the screen seemed to scream at him.

"Six, twelve."

Restricted.

"Most passwords you at least have to have six ciphers," Chelsea said, looking at him stupidly for making her type in the numbers six and twelve. She sighed. "We may never ..."

Her voice of doubt faded from him as he thought of calling Taffy. *Maybe I missed something in the riddle that Taffy might have already told me. Maybe I said something and Taffy could remember what I said.*

Then it hit him like a train, what Chelsea said. *That had to be it. Six ciphers.*

"Try six, twelve, five, sixty or the same set number in reverse. Like five, sixty, six, twelve."

Chelsea sighed again when 612, 560 came up restricted.

"I'm not going to be down here all day and neither are ..." Before Chelsea could finish her statement whispering her last word, "you," the folder opened. She had typed the number sets in backwards so fast she surprised herself.

"Of course, five, sixty, six, twelve," Harris said. "Hesiod speaks about Pandora for the first time." Harris now seemed to be talking to himself. "The riddle just had everything jumbled up."

"What?" Chelsea asked Harris.

"The guy I told you about who was murdered left behind a clue for us to follow. He wrote on a piece of paper, folder Hephaestus, password Prometheus, locale basement level B five-sixty, six twelve East Impending Tower computers."

Harris watched Chelsea ponder for a moment, then she added, "okay, we solved finding basement computer five-sixty, Hephaestus, and password, but this isn't under the East Tower."

Harris made a face of puzzlement and folded his arms. They stayed quiet for a few seconds, then Chelsea opened her mouth in awe. It was an expression, Harris thought, he would have liked to see more. Her surprised smile of dimples.

"But ten years ago this equipment was under the East Tower,"

Chelsea stated, staring at the screen that showed a file inside the Hephaestus folder.

Harris knew Chelsea could have said it better herself, but he said it. "And to complete this whole mystery, what file is inside of Hephaestus, but Prometheus."

"What is this you're bringing forth to me, Matt?" Chelsea looked at him with interest for the first time in two years. He also couldn't forget she said his name with true regard.

On the other hand she looked more perplexed than anything. He had thought she was hiding something before, but now he was starting to believe she truly had no idea about a device that had the power of a star.

"What is this, with these riddles, using Greek gods in connection with my company?" Chelsea asked.

"We're about to find out," Harris said, nodding at the screen.

Chelsea clicked on the PDF titled *Prometheus Confidential* and it opened showing five pages of scanned documents. They were handwritten pages on what resembled to Harris as antique ephemera paper.

Harris had seen the background on the paper before, in Chelsea's boat and her home. It was of an ancient globe map with the Lady Justice over it. He watched Chelsea's eyes broaden as he knew she knew what this all meant. After all, it was her symbol, her secret emblem.

"So you know what this is?" he asked.

"No." She glanced at him, then back at the screen. "I mean … somewhat, but overall … you have to believe me, I have no idea what this is."

"Now who's to believe who here?" Harris asked, rising a brow.

Chelsea narrowed her eyes, getting a better look at the scrolls and moved from page to page. "The paper symbol obviously I'm familiar with, but I can't remember ever hiding anything in a ten-year-old backup system." She moved the mouse to enlarge the PDF. "Well, let's take a closer look at the writing."

Enlarging the file to a hundred and forty percent, reading the neat script, Harris and Chelsea leaned toward the screen.

In finding this atlas one must first know the cartographer. Discovery and perception of the atlas you begin to comprehend the energy of Pandora's box.

We have stolen energy from the gods. Energy mapped in dna.

Destroyed once, yet the substance still lives in evidence. The Atlas, chart to the heavens, recipe to Pandora's Box.

The next page strictly talked about the cartographer, about how he orchestrated the entire project; how he was the genius who found a DNA code to unlock the energy men seek, and how he gathered the genetic and alternative engineers to achieve his objective.

The third page was written about the atlas, regarding how this chart was going to lead man into the next stage of evolution. It also talked about how the atlas was a guide to the heavens.

The fourth page described the energy and how it was beautiful yet deadly, peaceful, yet chaotic; light, yet dark like unto yin and yang.

The last page discussed preserving Pandora's Box and keeping the story a secret by creating the greatest story ever told, assorted with a touch of mendacity.

The last line on the fifth page bothered Harris.

Men will not believe in Pandora's Box. The greatest trick the Devil pulled was convincing the world he didn't exist, hence that deception is mine.

"I've no clue," Harris said with a scrunched face of incomprehension. "Can you print a copy?"

"Sure," Chelsea responded, squinting at the screen. Then her expression changed as if a light bulb brightened upon her head. "I think I know what some of this means."

Harris nodded at her to go on.

"I think I know what The Atlas is, chart to the heavens, The Atlas." She spoke as if she memorized or heard about the phrase before. "My father has this."

"Has what?"

"The Atlas."

"What do you mean?"

"My father has a glass display in the middle of his lobby," Chelsea explained. "In it is a scroll box. The inscription in front of the exhibit reads, *The Atlas, Chart To The Heavens.* That's been in plain sight for years. Anybody can see it when they enter the building."

"Hiding a clue in plain sight might be what this passage is trying to say," Harris explained. "Creating the greatest story ever told is like creating a great lie to cover a truth."

"Right," Chelsea responded. "Fabricating a story until you don't know what to believe."

"The description of the Atlas sounds a lot like your company," Harris spoke. "Like it said, it was a chart to lead man into the next stage of evolution."

Chelsea looked into his eyes for a few seconds. "I have a confession to make," she said and talked slowly. "Only some people in my close circle know. If you can, try and keep it to yourself. It's something I kept from the press for years and wish to keep it that way. I guess this is my test of revitalized trust between us." She took a deep breath and Harris made a facial gesture for her to continue. "Xavier Kcired is my stepfather whom you already know is the holder of Livenal."

Harris gazed at Chelsea with no expression of surprise, but more of bewilderment.

"Interesting," Harris spoke. "The CIA already knew in their investigation of you, but I never saw it as important at the time. I did always know your company and Livenal were interconnected from the start. I guess that would make sense. Xavier helped you in earlier organizations. At first I thought you got grants from the government to go to MIT. So *he* paved your way through school and gave you your first business break."

Chelsea nodded, smirking.

"So you truly know nothing about this Pandora and harnessing energy from stars."

"Well ..." Chelsea spoke in a matter a fact way. "These memoirs speaking about creating the greatest story ever told and the gathering of genetic engineers reminds me of an incredible story that floated around Livenal for as far back as I can remember." She took a couple of deep breaths, then continued. "My father and a crew some forty years ago went sailing off the coast of St. Helena Island and was supposed to have came in contact with an unidentified craft that was theoretically to have started Livenal's science division."

What a can of worms we've opened today, Harris thought. Maybe *his* stepfather wasn't crazy about the alien theory after all; his father leading him to Anthony Burrows' mysterious death, to leading him here with Chelsea, to now leading him to Livenal—Xavier Kcired, her father. He did remember Taffy talk of a secret lab in Nigeria where this all started.

His last mission to Nigeria he found an undisclosed laboratory in the Gotel Mounts. He never did find out what it was really for. A face was beginning to develop on this puzzle, and it looked like Livenal.

"I have a confession to make, too," Harris said, raising Chelsea's brow. "The story I told you about finding this solar device was actually a second theory my father and I had. Our first theory, or I should say *his* first idea, was that he wanted me to find proof that extraterrestrials exist." Harris chuckled. "Funny, until now I would have ruled that out entirely."

Harris wondered did he and Chelsea gawp at each other for a few seconds in bafflement or was it discomfort. Chelsea blinked at him a couple of times and, sure enough, he noticed, discomfort surfaced across her face. She looked away from him and at the screen.

"I see we both have opened a can of worms," Chelsea said. "I hope this doesn't mean we're engaged or anything?"

Harris smiled. "So, you think your father would like for me to pay a visit?"

"No," Chelsea said, and a smile grew on her face. "Absolutely not. He wouldn't approve of you at all. Listen, maybe we should keep as many people out of this as possible, at least until we know what this is." Chelsea gave him a look of *don't you agree* or was that a attitude of *back at you?*

CHAPTER 11

FIVE O'CLOCK, RUSH HOUR; everyone in the city was hurrying home, including the employees of Impending Towers. *I should be going home, too, but, no, one more meeting; a recap of the aggravation just dealt to me.*

On the elevator coming from the sixtieth floor and heading to her main office, she wanted to think about anything but the meeting at the moment. No one in the elevator, VP Tolliver, and Aaron looked at each other; they only stared at the elevator's marble white floor.

How was Matt going to probe or confiscate the Atlas in the Obelisk Building, in Nigeria, my father's building? I'd much rather think about that. It was more adventurous than this damn meeting. Yes, think about that, Chelsea kept assessing and maybe she won't be so angry. *Did I just curse?* Chelsea thought. *Yeah, I'm pissed.*

She had to admit to herself, and always questioned, did her father's UFO story have any validity? He told her at a young age that the world was full of strange things and strange stories. When she got older he brushed it aside as rumors for the greatness of his achievements.

"Let people believe in a great rumor and they'll think you're great; ah, let it ride," he would say, and she took the story for a hoax. She started to dream about the story some years ago, staging the events in her head as she thought they would go. Now she speculated how much of this hearsay was true, and if any of it was, wow.

Matt, this impatient man, wanted to go head-first into the tower. She told him the place was heavily guarded, but she knew that never stopped him in achieving his goals. She understood he was an expert at sneaking around, so this would be child's play to him. She told Harris in a few weeks she'd visit her father and get a chance to talk to him.

Harris didn't like the idea and suggested again that maybe it was best to keep everything on the low until he had everything figured out. The figuring out part meant sneaking into the Obelisk Building; not to steal the map but take pictures of. Besides, he said his father didn't have much time.

She guessed if she didn't alert her father's attention about Harris's whereabouts at the Obelisk Building; Harris will learn to trust her word that she'd stay quiet about this whole situation. When Harris finished taking snapshots of this map, and didn't pinch it, she'd trust his word he wasn't a thief for the CIA. She also told him that she wasn't going to get involved *yet* in his quest, but to keep her posted.

Harris's father being sick brought her attention back to the meeting and why she was vexed. She was now in her office seated behind her desk with Aaron and Tolliver sitting in front of her.

"The OECD representative seemed to be the only one somewhat on our side," Tolliver said in his whiny voice.

"And even he agreed in the end with the rest," Aaron spoke to Tolliver. "That the process of this is going to take some time. The red tape needs to be carefully unraveled."

Chelsea gave a weak smirk before speaking. "It's apparent Secretary Stossl of the Department of Health and Human Services believes Project Elf may have global implications and help lead this country into socialism."

"They only started talking about that when you mentioned transforming the world with cheap efficient universal health care," Aaron said. "You could practically take a pill and cure almost any known disease—amputees grow back limbs with one swallow of this solution."

"Utopian Dreamers, the media called our company," Tolliver spoke, and the room seemed to grow deadly silent. "A technology like this shouldn't be sold, but given away. It's a gift from heaven you have." Tolliver glanced at Chelsea, then stared at the wall. "But coming back to reality, of course we could make great profit selling inexpensive drugs, but be not surprised, this country doesn't work that way.

"They hire people to avoid meeting costs of medical treatment for policyholders to increase profit."

"But Tolliver," Chelsea said pleading. "We control this project, not them."

"Do we? They've already threatened you, and you don't even know it. China, Russia, and other countries, they said, will get this technology when it leaks out; PE could be dangerous and develop into a uncontainable disease.

"Economically, with the lack of universal health care in our system, PE will cripple every major health care company in the US. Do you think those power brokers will let that happen? People will flock in waves to get out of this country to get healed if we sell it to another nation.

"We already have deals pending with the DOE. Those deals are sanctioned strictly for the US. Our only ally is the World Health Organization who had backed us before, but what can they really do? I told you this will shake the very foundation of society. You're working way to fast for the world, my dear."

"We had discussions about this before with government organizations and won," Chelsea said. "Look at CAI now."

"Did we win? There are gag orders on your scientists so they won't talk to other nations or anybody for that matter. Look at CAI. CAI is now restricted to the US, M.E.G. your anti-matter project restricted to Ohio, oh, and restricted to just police cars. How many years did it take for us to do that? We're going to have to face the hard cold reality that our technology is for the rich."

"It sure seems they aim to keep it that way," Chelsea said, looking at Tolliver, then Aaron. "They're throwing our slogan in reverse, put off until tomorrow on what you could do today. Oh, except the rich."

Chelsea didn't like it, but knew Tolliver was right. She was always thinking revolutionary when she should have been thinking evolutionary. On her way to slowly change things, she thought she could maybe trick her friends and enemies into seeing things as she saw it.

She loved change, but in the real world the process was always protracted, perilous, life-threatening. As she thought before in the elevator, she'd much rather think about something else.

A dream she had last night haunted her again. She was running with some soldiers incased in some kind of futuristic armor firing guns and lasers at an enemy unseen in a jungle. One of her men lost his arm. It was blown off from return enemy fire.

She watched another combatant pour some kind of blue solution on his stump and his arm grew back like magic. The soldier with the new arm was handed his gun and he continued firing at the enemy.

Imagine having something like that in this world, a super solution, a super-soldier. Instead of curing diseases I would be aiding war efforts for not only the United States but the world. There would be war without end, if the planet wasn't on the brink of war now.

Her super solution which was made into a pill was also like a recent dream she had about the tree of life and pool of everlasting life. Humans had been wanting to live forever since the birth of conciseness. The world would kill for a formula like this. *Maybe Tolliver, but more so the legislators, were right; I was moving too fast.*

The rich of her time have no mercy for the poor, she theorized, and moaned. *To change this and help the masses, it was going to take a lot more than dignified planning.* Long-term-time and red tape seemed to be her enemy.

Her thoughts then dwelled on her father. Someone from Livenal ordered a top security guard within her company to assassinate competitive business executives. It forced some mergers; she figured all for the sole purpose of expanding her business more rapidly. It was like this silent but deadly arbitrator knew she'd have problems with distributing her technology.

Her father brought on her thoughts of Harris, trying his quest in the Obelisk Building. If Harris got caught on what he was about to do, she'd tell her father about the incident, after the fact, of course.

Xavier will explain everything about this Atlas as he had in the past about her rogue security guard. He'll eventually straighten everything out, Chelsea knew; he always did and always will. In her eyes, her father was incapable of lying to her. He never did before; why would he now? She loved him unconditionally.

CHAPTER 12

HARRIS FELT EXHILARATED to be in Nigeria. A semi-consent from Chelsea on the go-ahead in the picture-taking of a treasure map in the Obelisk Building—his team, stepfather and Ezequiel to get it done—why wouldn't he feel he was on top of the world.

Missions like this used to be his everyday job and what he was accustomed to, reconnaissance, surveillance, extract and obstruct if necessary.

Ezequiel Suarez lived on Victoria Island in a forty floor condominium on the thirtieth floor. Harris saw that he had a beautiful view of the condos that had recently sprung up around the area and the Lagos Island skyline.

Ezequiel said he preferred the Atlantic front over the city view; he loved the ocean over the steel skyscrapers. Harris still couldn't get over the view of the city skyline. For more than fifteen years Lagos had grown into a mega-metropolis on par with major cities of the world like New York and Tokyo.

Nigeria now ranked one of the fastest growing economies in the world, battling alongside for first with India and Singapore. They accomplished this with the aid of the Three Gods of Nigeria. Three enormous companies called Energ, Xur, and Livenal were rumored to have industrialized Nigeria, creating it to have the most advanced infrastructure of all Africa.

Now the freest country in Africa, The Three Gods expanded Nigeria's global trade with the United States, Japan, and Europe, generating the busiest ports on the continent. Nigeria's low tax rate, market-based economy was business-friendly, competitive, innovative, and least corrupt in Africa, making foreign investors flock to the nation.

Like father, like daughter, Harris thought, as he remembered long ago Chelsea say constantly that she ran a clean and respectable business—Xavier taught her well.

"So how exactly did you freeze the two cameras facing the display?" Harris asked Ezequiel.

"After surveying a few nights I followed the guards' break habits," Ezequiel answered, looking down at his white shirt. He was trying to get a brown source stain off the shirt about two buttons down. They just finished eating a meat pie twenty minutes earlier; he was still messing with the blemish, only making it worse with his fingers.

Ezequiel continued, "the one guard leaves the camera room for about fifteen, twenty minutes every morning around two o'clock. Ten minutes was all I needed to pause the two cameras facing the display.

"I manipulated the DVR with a special USB drive. The camera where it shows me entering the room I erased. That camera will continue to show a view without recording." Ezequiel presented a tiny black SD memory card in his black gloved hand. "They won't know anything until late morning when they check the monitors like they always do."

"How long will desk security take his break again?" Harris asked, checking the magazine in the .45 Ezequiel lent him.

Harris wore a black custom-made full scuba diving suit, gloves, and boots as he stood in the messy living room. He felt he was well prepared for this unclassified mission. In his utility belt and pouch on his side occupied a digital camera, night optical device, gas grenades, suction cups, electronic master keys, and spherical diamond-cutter. In Ezequiel's car they placed an electrical harness machine.

He took this stuff on all his highly classified jobs and now he was doing it for his x-boss, his stepdad.

"About ten, oh, fifteen minutes," Ezequiel responded, looking at his watch. "But I'd get out of there in about nine just in case. Remember, you'll enter the east side of the building, but you're to head to the south lobby."

"Got it," Harris said, tapping his watch. "Compass should work."

"Hope you still got what it takes, kid," Taffy said and coughed aggressively.

On Harris's laptop, by webcam upon a stack of newspapers, on the living room table Taffy's face was stuffed in a handkerchief.

"That's going to depend on how well I was trained," Harris spoke to the screen.

Taffy cleared his throat. "Then the assignment should be a success."

Harris smiled, but of course Taffy didn't.

"I gave a look see at the clues you sent me from the Impending Tower basement computer."

"And?" Harris asked.

"I'm still collating," Taffy answered, then coughed violently for a full minute. Gaining control after some wheezes, he continued. "I think this DNA these clues keep mentioning might have something to do with Livenal's cloning abilities. Answers to these riddles must be on that Atlas." He coughed viciously again.

"Want anymore Kunu before we're off?" Ezequiel offered, showing Harris his practically empty glass of the wheat color liquid. "We got about forty minutes."

"I don't know how you can keep drinking that stuff," Harris spoke. "For the job I'm about to do, I'll pass. Maybe, after."

"You sure we just shouldn't confiscate the map?" Taffy asked in a last minute desperate attempt to change Harris's mind.

"I'm sure," Harris responded. "I swore to preserve it. Like I told you before, if I throw my weight around, I might not get much cooperation from others, and we could blow ever finding this Pandora."

"What happened to the old days, huh? It's all about diplomacy now, huh?" Taffy asked with a scowl. "Ah, watch over this guy, Ezequiel. Good luck, son."

"Thanks, we'll be back in no time with perhaps more clarity," Harris said.

"You give me a call right away," Taffy demanded, then barked again louder.

"Don't worry, you just rest, okay?" Harris request considerately, but demandingly.

"Oh, you're giving orders now?" Taffy smirked. "Whatever." The screen went blank and showed a caption that read *Lost Signal*.

"A bit cranky again, I presume," Ezequiel said. "He seems to be losing weight. How's he doing?"

"Not good I think, but you'd never know it," Harris answered. "Come on, let's get this done."

Ezequiel and Harris moved with enthusiasm. They climbed in separate rented black Volkswagens and drove toward downtown Lagos Island, the Obelisk Building. It was 3:20 this warm, late in the month June morning; they had forty minutes to get into position.

Harris had known Ezequiel for eleven years. Ezequiel had helped him on many CIA missions in Sudan and Libya. Harris's cover was almost blown in Sudan. Ezequiel happened to be visiting a friend at the time and played along with his lead of deception. They had remained friends since.

He remembered like it was yesterday why he was sent to the region. It was to report back to the United States, if they should intervene in keeping the peace among the Sudan government and rebels in Darfur. If there was a sure sign of genocide, crimes against humanity, and crimes against humanitarian workers, he was to report it.

Not only did he discover there were atrocities from the government and rebels, both sides hated westerners and attacked UN peacekeepers. He almost died in that cesspool just to bring back information which the United States never used.

Thinking that he gained nothing out of the mission, in hindsight he did get something valuable; he obtained Ezequiel. *God works in mysterious ways.* Giving Ezequiel a substantial amount of money throughout the years, Harris personally hired him for his eyes and ears in the Sub-Saharan. It just so happened that he needed Ezequiel again, here, so close to his home in Nigeria.

HARRIS parked his car two blocks from Tinubu Square, where many Nigerians called the heart of Lagos. Across the street on the east side of the park stood the hundred story Obelisk Building, the tallest structure in Lagos. In fact at a whopping 450-metre the skyscraper was the tallest building on the African continent. The perfect obelisk tan-tinted glass-looking structure with gold pyramid gleaming capped top was truly a wonder, Harris perceived.

He hopped into Ezequiel's car and continued their drive toward what he considered the back of the building on Obe Street.

Ezequiel stopped the car on the corner of Obe and shut off the engine. He looked at his watch. Harris knew why he didn't drive onto Obe Street. Too many outside building cameras surveyed the block pointing toward the street.

Walking toward the structure wasn't going to be a problem. Starting at the corner of the building, the cameras had a blind spot and it continued if he hugged the wall all the way to the front doors. The cameras in the building, of course, he thought, will detect him once he entered the east lobby, but that wasn't his immediate destination.

"Okay, we got five minutes to explain this one more time," Ezequiel said and took a deep breath.

"You okay?" Harris asked. "You look more nervous than me."

"Well, I do hope you don't blow your cover. I just went in there some days ago, and today disguised as IT installation. You get busted, they'll definitely remember the suspicious IT person. They always do. I might even have to leave the country because of this—besides that, this could be my last payday."

"Ah, they never remember the IT guy. After all this, who knows, maybe I'll send you on one of my Barbados cruises."

Ezequiel chuckled, then turned serious looking again at his watch. "It's 3:46 now, so by 3:55 you should be over the tile above the display. The guard will take a fifteen minute break at four o'clock, but remember, he's come back in ten. I'll be staking out the perimeter right here for police activity. This place is twenty-four hours, so if any pedestrians decide to show up leaving or entering the building while you're still dangling above, this mission is trashed."

"Got you. My phone is strapped on my shoulder so if it starts vibrating I'll know an officer has spotted you."

"Right, if some officer deems me as suspicious, I'll leave, circle around and be right back here. By then, I hope you should be done."

Harris made a face like maybe.

"Hey, don't give me that look," Ezequiel said with worry in his voice.

Grabbing the harness machine, Harris abruptly left the car when he saw that the street was absolutely clear. He watched Ezequiel, who was surprised; shake his head because he left so suddenly.

Harris was multitasking while engaged in the conversation. He watched the streets for an opening. As soon as a couple and two guys who followed closely but separately behind moved away from Obe Street, he found that window of opportunity. He knew this contemporary city still had people moving about in the wee hours of the morning so he didn't have all day to wait on his four o'clock engagement. He knew Ezequiel understood.

Harris moved swiftly, hugging the wall. Passing the main lobby doors he moved, until he came to a clothing store that shared ground floor space with the building. Of the three stores that shared the ground floor, this one had the least cameras and didn't have a camera positioned at the entrance.

He went to work right away on the front door using his master key. The door opened in about five seconds and he entered, above a neon yellow sign read *Yeside*.

Ezequiel and he in disguises already surveyed the store some days ago and learned through observation about the flimsy alarm. The alarm system was in the same room as the adjacent vent leading to the main south lobby. Perfect, Harris thought.

He moved away from the large glass windows out of view of the bright street lights. Some of the store lights were still on, giving off a gray shadowy look to the place. That made him move faster. Speedy is my middle name, Harris contemplated.

He circled toward the back of the room against the clothes rack walls avoiding the cameras that focused more in the center and cash registers. Finding the manager's office in the back behind the registers, he opened the unlocked door, stepped inside, and closed it behind himself.

The first thing he had smashed, with a small hammer from his pouch, was the dome camera above him facing a safe. Though he wasn't here to steal money, he still needed the four foot safe as a stepping stool for the vent above it. He had about a minute before the alarm went off and alerted every NPF officer in the vicinity.

It took three swings of his tool to knock the white plastic eight by eight inch security box clear off the wall. It didn't hit the floor right away as red and black wires prevented it from doing so. Grabbing the dangling box, Harris pulled it fully out of the wall, snapping all the wires followed by pieces of plaster. He also pulled a five-outlet phone jack from its socket. One of them connected to the alarm system to contact the authorities, but not anymore, Harris figured, as he dropped the box and outlet to the floor.

It was 3:50 as he climbed on top of the safe and worked on unscrewing the four screws from the vent cover. The delayed minute for the alarm didn't go off. So far, so good, Harris pondered, as he removed the thin steel grid and laid it sideways in the shaft.

He dressed in his harness machine, securing the straps around his waist and shoulders, like suspenders. Another part of the machine locked around his pelvic area like a jockstrap. Throwing the two metal poles and electric motor into the vent first, he climbed in.

Trying to make as little noise as possible, he covered his eyes with his NVD, night vision goggles, and shimmied through the pitch black dusty vent. The metal poles of the harness mechanism attached to him by thin steel wires clanged about every now and then on the tight quarter walls. He prayed that the guard in the lobby didn't hear anything suspicious above him. Did he pray or did he hope? No time to think about that now; stay focused, he thought.

He was sweating everywhere when he came upon the part of the vent that split in two, going left and right. He knew to go left, but checked the compass on his watch anyway. "Left it is," he whispered, and moved on.

The left vent went up about twenty feet. Using his back against the wall and knees on the opposite side, he slid upward in a fetal position. Holding his harness equipment on his lap, he finally made it to the top, now drenched in sweat.

He welcomed the cool air on this level of the ventilation shaft and light emulating from a vent cover two yards away. Climbing out of the downward shaft, he situated himself at the grate.

Looking through the slits, he witnessed the bright ceiling lights of the south lobby. He glanced at his watch; 3:55. *Good timing so far.* He couldn't see the main desk, only a star constellation configured gold ceiling.

The other day, snooping around to get a feel of the place, he never noticed the ceiling when he entered the lobby for the first time. In the daytime everything looked different with the sun shining in. Now the ceiling was illuminated, viewing more details. Interesting, he construed.

No time to gloat, Harris thought, and unscrewed the vent in front of him with his screwdriver. Placing the detached dusty grid in the shaft, he slowly poked his head down to get a full view of the lobby.

Like he saw yesterday, huge brown and gray marble pillars and walls, elegant chestnut leather couches with tables in the center full with flowers, and a glossy granite silver floor reflected like a mirror. Hundreds of people with suits were going to flood this place in a few hours.

Harris looked toward the huge main brown reception desk, the second important aspect of his mission. Nobody was there; the guard had already left to take his break. It was four o'clock.

He searched and saw the first imperative phase of the mission directly below him a little to the right. The eight foot display case was thirty feet beneath him. The exhibit was centered in the lobby so if he was to head toward the elevators he had a clear view of it. Secrets hidden in plain sight, Harris reminisced.

The display was a gray five foot marble column with a flawless glass cube case on top of it. With every side of the cube three feet, a beautiful hand-crafted wooden scroll box sat inside the center.

Setting up the poles in the shaft securing them around the frame of the duct, he gave a strong tug on the wire connected to the motor. The motor was suppose to carry up to three hundred pounds; he was a hundred and eighty.

Placing his NVD on top of his head, he blinked a couple of times, adjusting his eyes to the lobby lights. Slowly climbing out of the vent, he dangled from the frame still holding on with one hand to get a good feel of the harness.

Then he let go and stayed suspended in mid-air about fifteen feet from his destination. Pressing a mechanism on his hip, he descended rapidly but smoothly toward the display. He could hear the gears above him whining as he moved closer and closer to his prize.

In a perched kneeling position, Harris's boots never touched the polished floor as he stopped his plunge. Hanging behind the glass case, he took out his spherical diamond-cutter and sliced a seamless one foot diameter round hole in the side that faced the elevators. Removing the glass with suction-cup and handle already attached to the diamond-cutter, he placed the two connecting pieces on top of the cube.

He looked around the empty lobby constantly in case he was surprisingly interrupted. Nothing; nobody was there, only the sound of his steady breathing. He glared at his treasure.

The oblong foot and a half by six inch auburn festooned box sat in the brilliance of a direct hanging light from above. If the display was to speak, it would say, "all attention on me," Harris envisioned. No time to revel, he thought. He stuck his hand into the artificial hole he made and opened the unlocked chest.

Inside, resting on rose-colored padding, was a leather scroll rolled up in two steel rollers. Commandeering the copper-colored scroll, he pulled it from its cavity and unraveled it on top of the cube next to the removed glass. The map opened up about two feet, uncovering images of a dragon, nude woman kneeling over a chest, a tree next to a waterfall, and Lady Justice. It was also full of Greek writings in paragraphs and triangular symbols.

No time to figure this out now, he alleged, and took out his digital camera and flashed away. Time, 4:05.

A WHITE Nissan Santra with blue stripe and the word *police* startled Ezequiel from his slouched position in his seat. *Damn* was the only word that popped into mind.

The Nissan cruised down Obe Street moving straight toward him. He slumped more in his seat and moved his right hand to touch the keys in the ignition.

His Volkswagen didn't look obvious, though it was parked illegally on the corner blocking the walkway. He prayed he'd blend in with the twenty legal cars parked behind him. *Hopefully the officers will let it slide that some poor shmuck just couldn't find a space in this busy city.*

The police car moved ten yards toward him, slowing to a crawl. "Shit!" Ezequiel whispered, but his expression showed that he could have shouted it. With his left hand he went into his pocket to fetch his phone.

The police car's blue lights flashed as it closed the gap between him. Pulling out his phone, he was about to punch the redial button to page Harris when the police car's tires started to screech.

The car launched ahead, blowing past him flying down the next avenue. He heard the sirens now, loud at first, then steadily growing distant.

Ezequiel found himself sweating as he eased his finger away from the send key and hand from the ignition. That was close, he thought. He looked at his watch. It was 4:10. *Come on, Matt, hurry up.*

AFTER putting clear polymer resin glue from a cement gun in his pouch around the circumference of the circle he had cut out of the cube, he slid the glass back into its place for a perfect fit. The resin mended the glass to where he was going to need a magnifying glass to see if it had been tampered with.

Releasing the suction cup from the glass, he folded the diamond-cutter and placed it in his belt. Pressing the apparatus on his hip, Harris made his upward departure from the display toward the vent. On his ascent he took some pictures of the ceiling.

His mission here was over with no harm done. The scroll map was tucked back into its place as if it never left and technically he hadn't set a foot on the lobby floor. He, Taffy, and now Chelsea had something to work with, something to dissect. This assignment was getting weirder and weirder by the minute, moving them closer to something unknown, Harris thought.

Climbing back into the vent, he disassembled the poles around the frame of the duct. With one last peep down at the lobby he watched a watchman in black suit and tie walk back to the reception desk holding a white bag.

Harris screwed the grate back into its place as quiet as he could. Crawling in the tight shaft with this clumsy harness equipment was going to be a slow feat, he thought. He was confident the guard likely couldn't hear him moving in the wall thirty feet above. Just for a precaution he moved slower, making sure his equipment didn't scrape the sides of his tight quarters.

Hang tight, Ezequiel. I'm coming.

CHAPTER 13

ABUJA, NIGERIA, A PLANNED CITY, one of the wealthiest metropolitans of Africa, glistened in all its glory. The capital city in Federal Capital Territory housed the Presidential Complex with other government buildings and residents. The complexes shared the skyline with the Millennium Tower, Abuja National Mosque, City Gates, Eagle Square, and Zuma Rock.

What he liked about *this other place*, not too far away, was that it wasn't part of the splendor of the city; it wasn't part of the skyline. It seldom showed on maps, and searching for it online to find information about the place, he couldn't find it anywhere; it was for the most part anonymous.

To Xavier, the hydropower Pedam Dam was the perfect place to hold the many meetings they conducted. As far south as he could go beyond the Three Arms Zone, Murtala Mohammed Express Way, and the reservoir sat a huge white round windowless cement building.

The HPB Building, Hydroelectricity Power Line Building, stationed about sixty workers who moved in and out of the edifice. Every day they maintained maintenance on the performance of the electric flow, pumps, and turbines. Situated eighty feet under the building was the E level basement, the third and last basement of the structure.

No one had admittance to level E except high level employees. Most employees knew, including management, that no one except the owner of the dam, Xavier Kcired, and friends had admission.

Of the many rooms within the maze of corridors on the E level, Xavier loved this conference room. The circular room walls were decorated in white marble pillars with a portion of the wall made of antique mahogany paneling that sometimes opened to video conferencing. A large rectangular African Blackwood table and eighteen black cushioned rolling chairs fit in the center where they sat.

He enjoyed the white marble bust of Marcus Garvey, Nat Turner, first president of the country's independence, Nnamdi Azikiwe, with other political leaders of nationalism that sat on mantels evenly spaced on the wall around the room. He liked to call it his association's brag or pride wall.

The most important thing he liked about the room was that it was not only sound proof, it scrambled inside and outside electronic signals. A built-in humming sound could be heard throughout many of his conferences. This congregation was for their ears only.

They were Morris Energ, Scott Xur, and himself, the so-called Three Gods of Nigeria—well, the newspapers say that, Xavier thought. Also attending the meeting was Bolaji Shagari of the SMB, Nigerian Secret Military Brigade, and Simon Biya, the Prime Minister of Cameroon.

They had all arrived each a half hour apart, escorted by chauffeurs in their Rolls-Royce and Bentley into an underground parking lot. They did this not to arouse suspicion of being together or a meeting ever took place—they'll leave in the same manner.

Of course, Scott was late, his usual ten minutes past his scheduled half hour. He blamed it on he had to drive an alternate route because he felt he was being followed. Some things never change, Xavier felt, as he opened a manila folder in front of him on the table.

Everyone wore different shades of blue Brooks Brothers, Ralph Lauren, or Nordstrom three piece suits and opened their briefcases to find their own documents. As always, when Xavier opened his folder, the meeting began.

"I briefed you already on why we're having this meeting. The question is, what to do next?" Xavier spoke. He brought a thermos of Veen water in his suitcase. He unscrewed the cap and poured a glass of the clear liquid.

"How do you know for sure the display was tampered with?" Biya asked in his French accent.

"We've created a silent alarm system if the Atlas was ever open without our authority. For the first time ever, yesterday that alarm went off. Surveillance equipment cameras were tampered with over the display and memory card missing viewing the entrance to the security room.

"This man a few days prior, posing as an IT installation vendor looking for work, was shown around the building pertaining to the computer room in the basement. That basement happens to be in the area of the security room." Xavier took a photo from his folder and slid it in front of himself on the table.

Scott picked it up across from Xavier and examined the picture of a Latino-looking man with mustache. "Dennis," Scott said, reading the name on the bottom. "Mustache looks fake."

"Probably along with his phony name and reason for looking throughout the building," Xavier explained. "Systems Networks, from which Dennis said he came, said they never sent out anybody to look for a job to work on our electrical wiring." Xavier scanned the room at the sixty-eight and above years young gentlemen wondering if they understood the seriousness of the situation.

"I'll keep an eye out, look into this," Shagari said, peering at the snapshot as it was passed around.

"If this was the CIA, does anybody believe they have the ability to know about Pandora?" Morris asked. "Or in the least conjure up the ability to pursue its mystery?"

"Should we jump to conclusions," Scott asked looking around at everyone, "that it's The Agency and not the SIS, SVR, some independent wealthy faction or corporation snooping around?"

"It's safe to assume The Agency has always been in our affairs and frankly is this time," Morris spoke out, not looking at anyone particular.

"If we're to agree on anything," Biya proposed, "it's that no one can know about this project. It must remain in the past."

Everyone nodded in agreement.

"In investigating this nuisance," Xavier said, continuing to glance at his colleagues, "I say we take our time to see what we're dealing with before we pursue and eradicate it."

"Just curious," Morris requested. "What if this is the CIA or SIS? Do we just remove the annoyance?"

Everyone looked at one another for a few seconds before Scott spoke. "I say if it comes to that, we do it real quiet like. The person or persons just disappear, no media."

"If it's a foreign government," Xavier said, "the SMB will deny everything if we proceed in assassinating these secret agents, but openly we'll give our full cooperation in getting to the bottom of the situation." He glanced at Shagari, who bowed in agreement.

"I doubt they'll find anything," Biya said. "Besides, if anyone gets too close, the evidence can easily be destroyed."

"True," Xavier responded. "But before that, we shall see who these intruders are."

From the many lights above the table, Xavier could see the conformity on everyone's faces. He cherished the meaning of out of many ideas there was one melting pot of minds in pursuit of a single objective. He thought of the motto of the United States Seal, E pluribus unum.

SOMEWHERE in Surulere, the Lagos Mainland, the slums of the state, sat a temple. The sanctuary resembled the many ramshackle houses around the area. The smells of the streets were of sewage and rot, but today the rain seemed to keep the stench at bay. The only differences were the bowels of the residences. Most homes housed lower middle class to poverty-stricken tenants.

The unnamed temple basement rooms were lavishly decorated in a rich Japanese style. The underground dojo was massive.

With the many miles of maze-like corridors and access tunnels, some false leading to dead ends and decoy training facilities, the main dojo was elusive. The dojo was actually under three houses to the left and not situated at the main entrance. The designers had their reasons.

She sat in the dark in a lotus pose wearing her black gi uniform. She felt her mind was at peace for now. Zen music of violins and flutes played and incense burned. That tranquility was soon shattered as a young boy of eight years old called her name.

"Mistress Kokawa, I'm sorry to disturb you, ma'am, but your phone kept ringing and I finally picked it up." The boy spoke nervously. "Someone called 3G."

Suraksha knew The Three Gods had summoned her again. The last time was back to back missions which took about six years. The assignments entailed a couple of assassinations for five years in the Americas and one more year assassinating Gamba and his cohorts, a major drug cartel here at home. All the missions were successful.

She'd been inactive for a year now in solitude. Though she was born and raised here at the temple, her elder Dambe and Kenjutsu masters knew not what she did when she ventured off on her incognito operations. Her only excuse for her long disappearances was that she found work that brought her back millions of American dollars.

Her Senpai, or most people would recognize her teachers as Sensei, questioned all the money she poured into the temple. She would show them her legitimate working papers and permits, and they would be quiet at least until her next adventure.

Suraksha knew all her missions were life-threatening. She lived for the thrill, but dare not tell her masters. They would say she was demented, and she was. Besides, she had an advantage. The Three Gods of Nigeria were no trivial organization. They were highly technically advanced for Africa, had global networks, and most of all, worked in secret.

AT the Dorint Sofitel Uberfahrt Hotel in Rottach-Egern, Germany, five men rented surreptitiously the entire hotel restaurant. They were seated outside at a white decorated table under a huge rust-colored canopy that blocked the bright morning sun. The backdrop illustrated the blues of Lake Tegernsee and lush green mountains of all sizes, some with snow peaks. An artist would have a ball, Lord Astor Cyril thought.

A breakfast buffet was set up on a table next to them so they hadn't been disturbed by a waiter for at least forty five minutes. They had already served themselves croissants, cold cuts, cheese, tea, and coffee.

Four of them had many things in common. Like their royal blue and black Brooks Brothers and Ralph Lauren three-piece suits, they were a part of powerful European global companies and institutions. Some were politicians in America to petroleum tycoons of Great Britain to members of the Tavistock Institute and Bilderberger Group. Director Lawerence Zamir was the only one who had retired from his organization, the Mossad.

"You're going to miss Independence Day tomorrow," Sir William Turner said in his British accent, glancing at Astor and Isaac Van Thurn, the only Americans at the table.

"For more pressing matters," Astor spoke, grinned at the gray-haired seventy-year-old man, then sipped his tea.

"Chelsea Enterprises has proven time and again that the technology works," Sir Elliott Nicholas, also British, spoke out, wiping crumbs from his white napkin on his lap. "Our Chelsea emissaries have already revealed that the molecular nanotechnology is operational, but nothing yet on Pandora. I'm beginning to wonder if we should worry about it. The company doesn't have the slightest blueprint of it. Before, we knew they had been working on MNT and Vc projects for years."

"I think this is the case of the left hand not knowing what the right hand is doing," Astor said. "Compartmentalization; so not only their associates don't know what they're doing, but their adversaries alike. It's not just Chelsea we have to scrutinize, but Livenal the same."

"That's right," Isaac agreed. "Livenal and Chelsea do have a marriage type relationship. So what do we have on Livenal?"

"That's why I beckoned this conference," Astor answered in a serious tone. "I want everyone to listen closely." Astor turned to look at Zamir and the men followed. "Zamir," Astor introduced the blond, gray hair, and sky-blue eyed man at the end of the table.

Zamir wiped his hands of croissant crumbs onto his lap napkin, sipped his coffee, then opened a black folder, revealing documents. Some things he read in his strong Israeli accent, some things he just knew.

"Xavier Kcired, founder and Chairman of Livenal," Zamir began and handed out a small picture of Xavier that went around the table. "He was the CEO of Livenal until 1989 when he became Chairman, then many CEO's took over the company until today. Benson Iroegbu has been the CEO for four years now. Xavier, of course, overall, runs everything from behind the scenes switching CEO's as he sees fit from time to time.

"Xavier started his Company at twenty-three in 1968 in America. In five years he grew globally into a billionaire, unknown for a African American at the time; hell, unknown to the world.

"How he stayed undetected was by moving most of his currency through the different Nigerian governments.

"Europeans know African leaders have billions, but we ignore their wealth because we know West and Central African nations will only slaughter each other for it. There's a cesspool of corruption in Africa without end that'll go on for generations. So we ignore the region's individual wealthy people." Zamir chuckled. "They won't live long enough to enjoy it, definitely not their kids. Why write them into the *Fortune 500* richest people in the world column?

"Xavier, fortunate for him, has survived through many of the 1979 to '85 coups in the Nigerian government by being a genius in human stem cell research, oil, and agricultural business dealings and trade. He's a bit of an aristocrat of sorts and the wealthiest black man in the world today. You might find him playing golf with us tomorrow. Individual net worth at fifteen billon."

"I've heard of this guy before," Elliott spoke. "His name was Marcus Garvey."

The fellows laughed except Astor.

Zamir continued with a tone of seriousness. "It took two years to come up with this story following only a money trail. I investigated backwards from today to the beginnings of Livenal. Two things puzzled me about my findings.

"Project Pandora was first mentioned by Livenal in 1971 and lasted three years before it was scraped. The company claimed they had found and opened Pandora's *true* Box in the South Atlantic Ocean and released a power never before seen on earth.

"Specially picked scientists from the Middle East, Asia, and Central America were chosen to undergo tests to see if this story had any substance. Over the course of three years, Pandora was active; all those scientists have mysteriously disappeared.

"Pandora was mentioned one more time in 1989 under the name Onslaught. I couldn't find any record about this project except that Livenal had spent millions of dollars hiring mercenaries that year, as if they were hunting something.

"Anyway, it had been rumored by the Nigerian press at the time that something extraterrestrial had escaped and the mercenaries were tracking it down."

Everyone stayed quiet for a few seconds as smiles gave way to Zamir and Astor's serious mugs.

Isaac gulped down the rest of his coffee before he asked, "You're saying, this possible solar weapon that may exist at Chelsea might be an alien found by Livenal, some, what, forty years ago?"

"Think about it, Isaac, all of you," Astor said persuasively, looking at each of the men. "This technology that has just sprung up out of the blue in the last four years is inexpressible. We can now build colonies not only on the moon, but the solar system, creating power grids that could last for centuries. Now we can grow our limbs back with the possibility of living forever.

"Funny Chelsea isn't giving up who their scientists are. All this technology from one company in four years. Y'all don't find this to be a little strange? Maybe they *had* opened Pandora's Box. They released something."

"Zamir," William asked with wonder. "You said two things puzzled you. What was the other?"

"Oh, yes, the other thing was what Xavier did in June of 1975," Zamir spoke. "He and his lady-friend at the time secretly, by not telling many relatives and friends, adopted a seven-month-old infant from an orphanage in America."

"Besides the strangeness of keeping that a secret," William requested, "and only God knows how they did that, what's questionable about it?"

Zamir looked around the table at each of the waiting faces for his answer.

"The infant was Nzingha," Zamir replied. "Today, the richest woman in the world, and head of Chelsea Enterprises. Her net worth at thirty point five billion."

Astor stared at Xavier's photo, collecting his thoughts as his colleagues tried bum-rushing Zamir with more questions to answers he didn't have.

Xavier's picture had a striking resemblance to an 1856 African American abolitionist, *The North Star*, Frederick Douglass.

Who was the genius? Nzingha or her estranged stepfather? Astor thought. Maybe both. Many more questions needed to be answered about this Livenal and Chelsea. He presumed if anybody in the world could find them, Zamir would. When the questions were answered, they'll be given to the council in the Trilateral Commission to discuss the next necessary actions to take.

If this seriously had something to do with an extraterrestrial presence, God help us all.

CHAPTER 14

THE OASIS CLUB RESTAURANT didn't have a sign on its entrance to welcome customers because they weren't welcome. The members-only guests with invitation-only eatery resembled a typical eight-story stone-colored building on High Street. Columbus, OH's many usual businesses on that block seldom noticed it was there.

Chelsea used the place to conduct many of her business meetings among her top employees and foreign partnerships.

Matt seemed impressed with the way the place operated, she thought, *or was he just overcome with the fact that I knew of the place at all?*

To get past the front door she used a unique card, then stood in a hall on a wall to wall red carpet furnished with purple plush couches waiting for the concierge to seat her. The building inside was disemboweled, six stories, exposing one of the most expensive restaurants in Ohio. Exclusive and elite, the chandeliers, tables, bars, and food were fashioned mostly for politicians, lawyers, and businessmen.

Let me emphasize business-*men*, Chelsea weighed, for not many women set their sights in this holy male-dominated dwelling. She sensed Harris grasped the picture and why he looked at her strangely on how she knew of the place, yet be a member.

They sat on the crown of the building, the outdoor lounging dining area, at a round table for two. Across the street and over some rooftops was a perfect view of Goodale Park and the last reminiscence of fireworks.

The fireworks started at nine over the park and had lasted for forty-five minutes ending with occasional bangs and sprinkles of white sparkles. They had just missed the grand finale of fireworks that flare-up into American flags along with eruptions of multi-colored rainbows.

Chelsea had never felt anything for the national day except she warranted the rest, so her associates had been off this Friday from work. Absent from labor all day and considering the long weekend; she felt she could solve this mystery Harris presented before her.

They were surrounded by mostly white men in costly shirts, shoes, and cologne. The only odd ones were a few tables away, her three bodyguards in black suit jackets and shades inspecting the chatting crowd.

The eighty degree weather kept her inside all day in the coziness of an air conditioner. She thought it wiser to meet Harris in the night when it was five degrees cooler. She wore black chiffon-fabric slacks and short sleeve blouse anticipating the light-silky material would help. It didn't; she was still lightly perspiring everywhere. She hated the summer.

"I assume your trip was productive," Chelsea said and sipped her Veen glass of ice water. "You're here safely talking to me."

Harris responded with a grin, sipped his Malbec wine in a Bordeaux glass, pulled out his iPad, and slid it across the table to her.

Though the iPad had its own light, the red lava lamp in front of her and the illuminated floor panels made her see Apple had created a smaller hand-held system.

Scrolling through the pictures on the seven inch screen, she examined thirty photos of the map. The first photograph showed a display case with gold plaque that read The *Atlas, Chart To The Heavens*. The multiple snapshots following were the map, all sides of the chest, inside the box, and four pictures of the Obelisk Building lobby ceiling.

"You CIA guys really do your homework," Chelsea said in a patronizing way.

She sensed him disregard her. Harris spoke quickly and to the point. "I showed my father some of the photos. He's good in ancient Greek linguistics; he says the words kept repeating warnings not to open Pandora's Box. He also says it talks about a power that can only be found by the triangular trading system. To begin the quest, you first have to pass through twin houses, a mausoleum, then ending the expedition passing through the eye of a needle."

"I know a little ancient Greek myself," Chelsea said, looking at a snapshot. "Something here speaks about something hidden in the twin houses next to the Hephaestus god. His name is Vulcan." Chelsea looked at Harris. "You know what I think? I think the twin houses are Impending Towers and the god Hephaestus is the folder we found on the basement computer. The god Vulcan is a folder also on the computer, maybe something we missed."

"I was going to say that," Harris said. "So maybe tomorrow we go back and look some things over, you know ..."

"I don't know, Matt. Where do you think all this is leading us?"

"Where do you want it to lead?" Harris asked, smiling at her. She noticed a glimmer in his eye. She knew that look all too well, too many times—a look of passion.

"Focus on the task at hand, Mr. Matt," Chelsea answered, giving Harris an angry crumpled face.

Harris's grin never wavered. "It can't hurt to try, plus now I can tell when you're mad at me you call me, Mr. Matt."

Chelsea took a gulp of her water before responding. "I'm always going to be mad at you, so don't get it twisted."

"Well then, I'll be back. Had one too many," Harris said, raising his empty wine glass.

HE had his fingers crossed the entire time until he felt it was time to make his move. He'd been watching Chelsea for days and knew by new phone conversations that she would be meeting the retired agent here, with some valuable Pandora information.

Lord Astor had told him when this mission is over man will have the gifts of the gods. It was why Astor named this project GFG, Gifts From Gods.

"We have conquered the speed of light and overcome every living disease on the face of the earth, unlocking the key to immortality," Astor told him. "Soon the power of suns will be in our hands. Man was destined to do this, can't you see? How else can man survive the harshness of the universe where all things are born to die.

"To rely on the false hopes of religion, an invisible God, is foolish. God is physical, God is us. With this new technology we can last forever, create our own big bang, remain forever young—can you not see?"

Those phrases stuck in his mind. Astor was trying to show him the high importance of this mission—pay close attention to detail. Failure is not an option.

Mission priority; obtain information about Pandora at all cost. Details; Nzingha Chelsea, indispensable, her security, expendable, Matthew R. Harris, superfluous.

What translated to him was, Chelsea could be injured, but not exterminated, even tortured if he had to. Matthew R. Harris had turn out to be a predator hunt though it still depended on which way the mission flowed. The security, well, it didn't matter either way.

He already knew Harris's profile and knew he was a dangerous formidable opponent; not only his equal, but the man had many years experience over him. In hostile situations Harris's rap sheet of reconnaissance was long and why he waited for him to go to the bathroom before he made his move.

With the many artificial trees and plants scattered about the place he felt it would be the perfect cover for blindsiding Chelsea's guards.

Surveying the place for an hour, he knew besides Chelsea's three henchmen, one being a large bald guy, there were four other men in navy blue suit jackets. These four guards, a part of the building facilities, mingled with the crowd. They all didn't look tough except the big hairless man, and he sat at a table adjacent to Chelsea and his prize, the iPad, the map.

A pity on a nice night like this all these capitalist class men pooled together without their loving spouses.

Wonderful, he thought, because what was about to go down, these customers weren't going to do anything but watch in horror. They weren't going to get their hands dirty. Chelsea's only hope of someone getting their hands dirty was in the bathroom right now washing them.

The two guards in black suit jackets who stood together at the bar in the middle of the lounge never saw him coming. One was looking Chelsea's way and the other gazing at the female bartender.

It all happened fast, even for the tough bald guy. Moving from behind a large plastic leaf, he hand-chopped the guard watching his target. After the guy grabbed his throat and hunched over, he punched him in the temple. The man didn't have the strength to yell in his pain.

The next guard, focused on the bartender, yelped as he felt his left kneecap snap from a kick. Another hand chop to the gullet stopped the cry short. A half second had gone by and he was upon his bald foe.

The big fellow was going to need more than a couple of hand-chops. He took out a ten inch glass envelope cutter from his pocket.

Using his gun would have been more efficient, but he didn't want this fight to be too noticed. *By the time everyone realizes what's going on, the only story left would be a brawl and robbery. Besides,* he thought, *I had my fingers crossed that the outcome will end in another second.*

WITHIN seconds she only saw the fight with Daniel as she looked from the iPad screen in disarray. In a split-second glance she saw her other two security guards already on the floor gasping for air. She gave another momentary look back at Daniel, who was now on the floor, his left elbow was in the wrong position and his arm was dangling. He bellowed in agony.

A white young-looking clean-cut well-groomed brown-haired man in black-suit-jacket pulled a glass envelope cutter from Daniel's shoulder.

Maybe I could slip out of here while Mr. Clean was tussling with my security, Chelsea considered, as she stood to leave. Obviously he must be after her, or the iPad, the map.

She was a half second too late. She and the assailant had already caught eye contact as he advanced toward her. Damn, Chelsea thought; did I just swear? No time to think about profanity. Her first reaction was to run, but where?

With a wall behind her, table between her and the aggressor, her fallen guards with exit behind the clean-cut lunatic, she dropped the option to run.

He didn't give her time to think as he lunged his bloody glass ripper straight for her right shoulder. At this most peculiar time, and it was only a microsecond, she noticed he was aiming for her shoulder pressure point.

She moved left sideways to the man's surprise, missing his thrust entirely. Virtually, simultaneously, she grabbed the lava lamp on the table with her left hand and bashed it across the right side of his cheek.

She was then backhand slapped across her face, knocking her back against the wall. She didn't see that coming. He recovered quickly from her blow.

When the lamp dropped from her hand, it had exploded onto the floor in a shower of hot steamy water and glass. Some people in the crowd had reacted, looking in her direction. Everything happened that fast, Chelsea grasped; only now some people caught wind of her struggle.

Dazed, but still standing holding onto the tablet computer, she watched through tearful eyes him pounce again with that icicle-looking weapon aiming for her shoulder. Her split-second reactions were to give up the item before more bodily harm.

She stood wide-eyed, jaw-dropped, and hands tightly across her chest with her back against the wall. The blade came inches from her shoulder as her attacker lunged again, but suddenly it stopped and recoiled. Someone had grabbed the man by his jacket collar and snatched him back. That somebody put their leg out so the clean-cut aggressor tripped backwards, crashing into a stool at the bar.

Harris emerged in front of her and without a word gave her a quick look up and down.

"Are you alright?" he asked.

"I think so," she responded as she watched her mugger become tackled by four bodyguards of the restaurant at the bar. Somehow they managed to wrestle that envelope cutter from his grip, but it didn't stop his onslaught.

Everyone was standing at their tables silently watching this one man fight off the security. Good, Chelsea thought, the attention was away from her now.

There were shouts and cries as each of the security guards fell one by one. She could hear snaps and cracks. *Was that bone breaking?* Some people in the crowd had their phones out nervously hitting buttons calling 911, she assumed.

"Do you have the iPad?" Harris asked.

She held it up and he grabbed her arm and tugged at it for her to follow him.

"Come on!" Harris shouted, and he moved to the exit. By sheer instinct she followed.

The tidy invader was fracturing the bones of the last two guards and working his way toward me, Chelsea witnessed as the exit door closed behind her. Harris and Chelsea dashed down eight flights of stairs in two minutes. Adrenalin was her friend today, she contemplated.

Not saying anything to the host at the entrance hall, Harris and Chelsea, speed-walking, blew past him as if he wasn't there. Rapidly they walked down the block and climbed into Harris's black Jaguar XJ Super V8.

As Harris peeled out onto the street, she could have sworn in the left side rear view mirror she saw the clean-cut man run out the front of the restaurant. She could hear sirens in the distance.

It was the first time in two years true fear had crept into her. *The very first time was with the man controlling the car, Matt. A matter of fact, all the time my life was in danger was around this guy, Matt.* She looked at him with a scowl, but suddenly realized pain throbbing in her right cheek and forehead.

"Are you sure you're alright?" he asked and involuntarily wiped the bottom of her nose with the back of his white Brioni shirt sleeve.

Even though he was in his black suit jacket, she saw blood on his white cuff. Pulling down the sun visor in front of her, she turned on its light and stared at her reflection in the mirror.

Her philtrum had lines of electric crimson blood where trickles of it had flowed. Rubbing it away with the back of her hand, she examined the right side of her face. It wasn't swollen, just a little peach. Her eight freckles were still there around the bridge of her nose, so she guessed she'd be alright because she sure felt her mugger slapped them off.

"I suppose I'll live," she answered and closed the visor.

A police car, sirens blaring and lights flashing, flew past them in the opposite direction.

"What just happened back there?" Chelsea asked, wiping sweat from her brow. She closed her eyes trying to calm down by breathing deeply.

"I was going to ask you the same question," Harris stated more than asked. "Definitely a professional assassin."

"It seems *definitely* because of your endeavors I'm in a bit of a fix again."

"My endeavors? It's your map." Harris glanced over at her. "What's your father hiding anyway?"

Chelsea huffed and folded her arms, looking straight out the windshield at fast passing street lights.

Harris sighed. "Look, I'm sorry, I didn't mean to say it that way …"

"Where are we going, Mr. Matt?" Chelsea asked as he turned left at a corner. "Don't you think we should report this to the police?"

"It's already reported to the police and the press. You don't think that was enough back there?"

"Well maybe *we* should go to the police?"

"I think going to the police could expose you to a sniper. You won't be safe."

"What makes you think after this, the guy would try again in front of the cops?"

"I would," Harris said and glimpsed at her again. "You'll be in perfect line for a sniper's riffle, especially if I missed you tonight."

She saw that seriousness in his eyes. He was a killer himself; point taken.

"I'd be incognito for a while if I were you," he continued and turned another corner. "You can stay at my hotel for the night. Don't worry, I'll sleep on the couch. Seeing that your security is immobilized, I think it would be wise that no one know your moves. At least for the weekend until we find something on what this all means, or who was that attacker."

Chelsea gave him a nod without a hitch.

She didn't like being with Harris, especially for a whole weekend, but he made a couple of logical sensible points. Her main protection was eradicated. She was a sitting duck for whoever's will.

Harris, an adversary of hers at one time, she didn't know what to think of him now. The enemy of my enemy is my friend.

CHAPTER 15

FROM THE OUTSIDE of the two-story white house, silence stood in the evening breeze. McLean, VA, on Kurtz Road, an eerie peace encircled the luxurious home. At this late hour everyone in the neighborhood usually kept things quiet. Tonight was the Fourth of July and, coming to an end in a half hour, the hoopla had died down.

Deceived by the tranquility of the night as well as he misled the public of his true identity, he was in pain. Under many aliases like Tom Davis and James Blaser, the wrong person today found his true self, Joseph Healey.

Suraksha found him through the information given to her from the SMB. On her flight into the United States using a fake ID herself, she studied Joseph Healey's file of deception.

The SMB exposed Joseph Healey, a CIA member out of four, who had visited Nigeria some years ago. The other three were too well hidden for now. That could all change today, she conceived.

Following his individuality, narrowing her research and surveillance to this house which was yet under another name—some dead police officer named Bill Short—she met Joseph when he had returned home from a party. His friends dropped him off at his house laughing and intoxicated. Perfect, Suraksha thought.

Joseph, tied to a chair in his basement, wanted to scream in pain, but the rag bound around his mouth and head muffled his cries.

He bled from his right shoulder onto his light-blue dress-shirt. She inspected the womb where she stabbed him. It wasn't that deep, she rationalized; he was only acting this way because he wanted her to stop.

"Okay," she said, throwing papers she had in her hand onto the floor. "Again, I need information about the whereabouts of your three operative playmates or Pandora."

Dressed in black jogging suit, gloves, and sneakers, she waved the nine inch Bowie knife in front of him again. Sometimes she wore a disguise, but generally she didn't need to because her victims usually never saw the light of day. That being said, she felt she had until dawn to find some answers.

They had already gone over the preliminaries of what was true and false. He had lied to her in the beginning by telling her what she wanted to hear. She knew he knew she knew a lot of information already about how the CIA worked.

"No wife, no children, your girl away for the weekend," Suraksha spoke. "My guess, it's going to be one hell of a night. You could shorten this. Tell me what I want to know. I need places, names." She pulled the white cloth from around his mouth to let it sit tightly on his chin.

She watched his arms behind his back, coupled to the chair, flinch; she knew it was fear more than pain that motivated him; fear of what she might do next.

"Look … I told you, we don't …" He coughed. "Sharing information about what we do personally is confidential, even among ourselves." He hacked violently. "… those papers are the only place … find operatives."

"What about Pandora?"

"I told you, I don't …"

"… know what you're talking about," Suraksha said, finishing his sentence. She stabbed him in the left shoulder, making sure the blade went in five inches.

He screamed like a woman, but was cut short when she put the rag back over his mouth. Pulling the knife out, he howled. Profusely sweating all over, he shook and his eyes began to roll to the back of his head.

"Oh, no you don't," she said and grabbed the green garden hose. She anticipated this and had the hose already connected to the basement faucet. She blasted him at full spray in his face flinging blood and water everywhere.

He bobbed and weaved his head trying to escape the pain, or was he trying to breathe? She didn't know which, maybe both. She turned the water off, dropped the hose, and waved the hunting knife in his mug again.

He was an ugly man, in her opinion, and he looked more repulsive the way his features twisted as so from the agony. Nice lean thirty-year-old body, though. She felt he could take the whipping.

"You ever heard of Lingchi?" Suraksha asked, not expecting him to answer. "It's an ancient method of slowly slicing the body." She looked at her two wrist watches. "We got roughly five hours before sunrise." She glanced at the hose on the floor. "I guess *we're* going to be up for a long time."

"Please ..." Joseph pleaded as she put the rag on his chin. "You have to believe me ... know anything about Pandora... way of knowing ... where my associates are ... break up after every mission." He spat and coughed.

Suraksha shook her head and stabbed him in his left thigh and he screamed once more until it was stifled by a rag over his mouth.

He started convoluting, shaking the chair, tap, tap, and rap on the gray wet bloody cement floor. His legs, fastened with rope to the chair columns, couldn't move. Just before he and the chair were about to tip over, he fainted, leaving him in a slumped sitting position, wet and bloody.

She was about to blast him with more water, but noticed something on one of the papers she threw onto the floor. Through the riddled blood and water blots, the words *asylum* and *sanctuary* caught her attention.

Showing her where to find the documents from her first assault, she had believed he'd given her the information too quickly. He's the CIA, she alleged; it's not going to be that easy, but maybe it was that easy, to throw her off, because he knew she was going to torture him anyway. He probably knew she was going to ransack the house, missing the important papers scattered about safely in this basement obscured in front of her because of her doubt. Clever guy, she thought.

She was considered deceased by the FBI and CIA, from an incident she had here in the United States two years ago. No one would be looking for her as she scoured America for the individuals who had most likely tampered with the Atlas. She'd be able to move and work without interruption. The thought exhilarated her. She smiled. She was going to be like a ghost to everyone.

Picking up the papers, then hose, she blasted the water into Ugly Joe's face.

CHAPTER 16

SHE RECOGNIZED THE DIFFERENT SHADES of blues and greens the ice and water had made in the snow. Elongated icicles of these colors went on for miles across hills and snowdrifts. The common color here, though, was white; so white that if she looked too long, she went snow blind. So white, like paper, the only way she could differentiate up from down was gravity and a gray sky separated by the horizon.

She felt the effects of the hundred below zero dry air as she ran. In her thick black and brown fur coat she scampered clumsily across an ice sheet without end. Prevailing winds bawled and disrupted the surface in a way as if it was snowing.

She couldn't see the thing chasing her, but knew it had teeth; she could hear its fangs chomping. She couldn't distinguish if it had claws, but felt the ground shake every gallop it made to close the gap between her and it. Its growl between a wolf and tiger and apparent talons scraping the ice motivated her to move faster.

Moving as nimble as she could, she still couldn't believe the air was this cold. Though her tears froze and feet frostbitten to the bone, she managed to outwit the beast, for now. She didn't know what was going to kill her first, the monster or the cold.

She thought about the dream all morning before Harris awoke. She never understood her dreams and figured most people hadn't grasped theirs either, or shouldn't. Her involuntary visions were at most times about winter storm weather—always freezing or in some situation of death by hypothermia. The creatures, she didn't want to think about at all.

Across the street from the Supreme Court of Ohio on the eighth floor of the Doubletree Suites Hotel, Chelsea bit into a green apple, examining photos of the map. Harris said he reserved the room for a month, giving himself that long to convince her that this quest was for his personal search and not some CIA sham.

She had taken a bath last night and washed her shirt, panties, and bra in the sink. After she finished taken a shower this morning, her clothes were dry to wear again. Harris, after taking his shower, had gone out to buy her an antiperspirant deodorant, some apples, and himself breakfast.

After an exhilarating, adrenalin-pumping, sweaty night, Chelsea felt liberated in freshness. Sitting at the kitchen table taking another nibble at her apple, she knew her stomach felt the same.

Harris, across from her, spoke on his cell phone as he ate his pancakes and eggs. Halfheartedly she listened to his phone conversation, something about acquiring a safe house.

He looked gorgeous in his new tight blue shirt, chest, and biceps bulging. He smelled good, too, that nice citrus aroma. She had to stop gloating over him before he noticed. Keep your focus on the map, she thought, as she inspected the pictures on the iPad. She flipped through each one, enhancing the images with the touch of her fingers.

On the four corners of the chart was the Lady of Justice and under her figure in Greek: *Do not open, you will release the evils of the world.*

What jumped at her first was the large red snake-like dragon on the top center. The other two images on the bottom left and right were interesting, too. The figure on the right was of a beautiful female dressed in a see-through gown kneeling over a gold chest, opening it only a crack. The symbol on the left was a embossed black image of a tree and waterfall.

Greek inscriptions were under the dragon titled *The Twin Houses* and beneath the image of the nearly nude woman opening the box read *The Mausoleum.* The last illustration of the tree with waterfall also scripted in Greek said *The Eye of the Needle.*

In the center of the map was a paragraph: *Within the Twin Houses dwell Hephaestus and a like god, his name is Vulcan.*

To begin quest, you first must pass through The Twin Houses, The

Mausoleum, ending passing through the eye of a needle. The power could only be found by the triangular trading system.

Last, scattered across the map were nine gold triangles that didn't seem to have a pattern. Two were near the bottom and two near the top, the others to the far left and right of each other.

Not meaning to, Chelsea exhaled loud enough for Harris to hear. What does all this mean? she pondered, shaking her head.

"… thanks, I'll call you when I get close," Harris said into his phone. He placed the phone on the table next to his plate and concentrated on consuming his food.

She glanced at Harris, surveying him devour some of his eggs, then she looked back at the screen. She did this three times, wondering if he was going to say something.

After a minute of watching him ignore her and finish his eggs, she asked, "*Hello*, so what are we doing next, Mr. Matt?"

He answered without looking up and started working on his pancakes. "Well, being that I'm your new muscle, I suggest you come to Cincinnati with—"

"What are you talking about? I'm not going to Cincinnati or anywhere with you, and you're not my bodyguard."

"Yeah," Harris said and looked at her. "I just got off the phone with a CIA friend of mine. Our tirade yesterday is already on the news. They're saying it was an assassination attempt against you and the assailant is still at large. They also said you narrowly escaped death with one of your *bodyguards*. Now I wonder who that might be."

"I didn't see you do anything but run," Chelsea said without much thought or emotion. "What kind of bodyguard are you?"

"I had to assess the situation," Harris retorted. "With my first priority, protecting you. You're welcome. There could have been more than one assassin. Besides, don't you believe in the phrase, he who fights and runs away may live to fight another day? But he who is in battle slain will never rise to fight again."

Chelsea let out another long sigh. The people at the club restaurant were nothing more than capitalistic, over-exaggerating, babbling fools, she thought. She took a couple of bites of her dissolving apple.

"What are you going to do with me, Matt?" she asked with worry in her voice.

"Look, just come with me to Cincinnati. The safe house could answer a lot of questions about professional assassins, trust me. I'm also a client."

"Are you asking or telling me?"

"I believe Daniel, your number one protection, is down. We obviously know what this single assassin can do to the rest of your security. I'll make you decide on this one yourself."

"I can't run from this guy forever. Sooner or later I'm going to have to confront this."

"I've told some trustworthy friends of mine at The Agency not to tell their superiors about us at the safe house. It'll be a safe place to find out if this hired gun is one of ours or what else might be in the cards."

"However this goes down and we discover this is your people, I'm going to negotiate a term of surrender to whatever they want."

"You submit?" Harris asked in awe. "I would have taken you to be stronger than that."

"I am being strong," Chelsea answered. "It doesn't take strength to do things; true strength is deciding what to do."

"So you already decided to surrender?" Harris asked and finished his last pancake.

"Someone wants me to fight for my life for a device I don't possess. I'll bargain for what they want so they'll leave me alone. Everyone has a price. My father may not approve, but if they want the Atlas they can have it."

"If it comes to that, I could make a sure bet diplomacy may not work."

"The art of restraining power, diplomacy," Chelsea said as she looked at the core of the apple in her hand.

For some strange reason she felt cold, like her dreams.

CHAPTER 17

FOR TWO HOURS Chelsea didn't speak as they drove into Cincinnati. She probably felt she was being kidnapped, Harris deemed. Near the end of the trip, though, she did talk about her father. She talked about the many secretive people who surrounded him; maybe they knew something more about the Atlas.

"They might be the ones hiding this special weapon," she said in a wondering way. Harris noticed she said it in a way as if maybe she didn't believe it.

Five miles from Paul Brown Stadium on the edge of the North Ohio River two huge warehouses shared ten acres of land. On the front of both windowless buildings orange words hung, *Jetro's Inc.* It stored and repaired elevator parts for most of the city. One of the warehouses, nine years young, was busy shipping parts out and transporting them in by semi-trailer trucks constantly kicking up dust and spitting exhaust everywhere.

The second warehouse hoarded decrepit elevator machinery and the Other Government Agency sanctuary.

Jetro's had abandoned the building eight years earlier, leasing it to the government. The government paid the owners to keep their name on the structure and keep quiet on why for all those years they hadn't condemned the building for demolition.

Inside the so-called abandoned warehouse, surrounded by a maze of dusty aisles where pallet racks reached five stories high the OGA, Other Government Agency data center asylum thrived. Also obscuring the OGA center in the heart of the warehouse were corroded forklifts, cranes, and rusted elevator equipment filled with cobwebs. Encompassing the actual OGA work station a twenty foot fence wall was added with wooden pallets. Floodlights illuminating the headquarters also lit spotty around the warehouse giving the illusion that some worked and some didn't.

To enter you had to remove a six foot section of the pallets and unlock the chained fence door that was camouflaged into the structure.

He got used to the constant oily grit smell of the place as he sat next to Brian at a computer. Chelsea and Sara, after introducing themselves, had gone downstairs in the basement to freshen up, Harris supposed.

The basement made directly under the center had a kitchen, five bedrooms with bathrooms, and access tunnels leading to a manhole in Jetro's adjacent storehouse parking lot and one leading to the city sewers. The place was a tad short from a fallout shelter, he contemplated.

"Thanks, I appreciate you doing this on such short notice," Harris said as he set up the webcam on one of the many computers.

"Anything for an old desperate friend," Brian said. "Maybe I could learn a thing or two. Then get the Director to listen to me when I'm speaking to him."

"Whatever, man," Harris responded, shaking his head. *The boy is still jealous after all these years. I need him, though, today. Brian was going to have to get over it.*

Harris had called Taffy from a secure phone asking him to connect to the Internet for a live video chat.

When Taffy appeared on the screen Harris briefed them on how he acquired the Atlas from Nigeria in the Obelisk Building and details of the disturbance at the Oasis.

"I'm sending you the pictures now," Harris said, handing Brian the iPad. Brian, using a FireWire cable, connected it to the computer. "Let me type in his e-mail so he could get the rest of the photos." Brian scooted over and Harris typed in the address.

Taffy hacked so hard tears rolled down his cheeks. "That's what I'm talking about, my boy," he said. He coughed more, trying to clear his throat. "You got me so excited you found this map I can't even talk. I see you've taken me serious now."

"I can't deny that something is definitely going on investigating Pandora. It's starting to get dangerous."

"Burrows always knew his life was in danger and nobody listened to him," Taffy spoke. "Not even me.

"You just remember, my dear boy, our middle name is danger. We don't take threats; we give 'em."

Harris watched for the first time Taffy chuckle a little from his own saying, but it was cut short by a cough. *Well, he almost got the laugh out; it was good enough for me.*

Harris gazed at Taffy's patchy beard and pale-thinning face as he coughed more into a rag. *I didn't want to see this—him deteriorating.*

"Get some rest, sir," Harris said. "I'll have this solved soon in no time."

"You better," Taffy responded, and his face faded from the screen.

"The old man doesn't look too well," Brian spoke. "You may think nothing of this coming from me, but I'm sorry about him. He was a great man."

"He still is," Harris replied as the ladies came from downstairs.

"I know you guys have obviously met already," Harris said, looking at Sara and Chelsea. "Brian, this is Nzingha Chelsea, and Nzingha, this is Brian."

Brian extended his hand, and Chelsea shook it.

"I've heard so much about you," Brian said, smiling. "Matt has already briefed us on your situation. It's a pleasure to meet you."

"I bet," Chelsea responded, "but this is Matt's charade, I seem to be just here for the ride."

Harris noticed Brian couldn't stop smiling at Chelsea, who was now dressed in a plan white shirt. She could have been one of the agents. Sara had seemingly given her one of her shirts; they were about the same size.

Brian was hit like most males who witness Chelsea for the first time. He was hit with her unquestionable exotic beauty. Harris laughed internally; *simple boy.*

Chelsea scanned fifteen monitors behind them built over a table by some racks and stands.

"Nice video surveillance," she complemented. "It seems like you have every place in here covered. Doesn't always work, though. Somehow some creep seems to always slip through." She glanced at Harris.

"Anyway," Harris said, "I know everyone's time here is precious. I'm going to put the map on the big screen."

He sent the last attachments of the Atlas photos to Taffy, then downloaded the snapshots from the iPad into the main hard drive. Chelsea and Sara found some black rolling chairs and sat behind the fellas at the main computers.

Harris set each of the thirty pictures to show for fifteen seconds, like looping wallpaper, on a forty inch screen stationed on a stand above them. For almost eight minutes it showed all the photos before repeating.

"Nice treasure map," Brian said. "Too bad I can't read Greek."

"Interesting," Sara said. "I like the dragon."

"Again, you guys," Harris spoke, "I appreciate you traveling for hours here this weekend."

Harris felt this all could be a dead end. They may never solve this mysterious map's cryptography. "So, do you guys know if you have any agents out there looking for super devices in the Chelsea Company?"

Brian peeked at Chelsea before responding. "Matt, I remember a time the mentioning of our names, I'd have to kill your friend there. The Director has already changed the SOF team." He shook his head. "There's so many compartmentalized organizations these days in the name of national security I couldn't have told you what was going on if you tortured me."

Harris folded his arms and sat back in his chair with a grim face. "Nothing, huh? I mean, could you throw me a rumor?"

"Sorry, guy," Brian said. "I could throw you something else, though." He glanced at Sara, who was still busy scrutinizing the photos. "In 2016, the next presidential election, there'll be a shift in Asia."

"Watch your mouth, Mr.," Sara said, glancing at Brian, then back at the monitor.

"I didn't tell it," Brian pleaded.

"I think I see something, guys," Sara said. Everyone looked at the monitor. "Brian, go back to the lobby ceiling photos."

Brian, using the keyboard, moved to one of the photos of the lobby ceiling and paused it.

"What do you see?" she asked.

"Some kind of constellation, of course," Harris responded for everybody.

"Now flip back to the full view of the map."

Brian guided the wallpaper pictures to the map.

"Now, what do you see?" Sara asked again.

Chelsea opened her eyes wide and so did Harris.

"Yeah, I see it," Chelsea replied for the both of them, "the same constellation."

There it was, Harris professed; nine gold triangles that at first seemed scattered across the map showed the same formation as the lobby ceiling. If he drew a line connecting all the triangles, it would have represented a stick man with his right arm longer than the other or just simply a cross. It was the same, though repeated, for the stars on the gold lobby ceiling.

"What constellation is this?" Chelsea asked no one in particular.

"About to find out right now," Brian answered. Moving to another computer, he searched the Internet. "Okay, nine star constellations. Coming up we have the Taurus constellation, which has nineteen stars."

Everyone gathered around Brian as he continued verbalizing what the Internet revealed. "Within Taurus, Pleiades has nine bright stars, but they don't quite look like our cross or stick man here. Ah, yes, here we go; the constellation Cygnus, nine major stars known as the Northern Cross in contrast to the Southern Cross, the Crux constellation which only has four major stars."

"Bingo," Harris whispered. "Cygnus it is."

"Could mean nothing or it could mean everything," Sara said.

"Does this mean anything to you?" Harris asked Chelsea.

Chelsea shrugged, staring at the monitor.

"Well, guys," Harris spoke, "I'm going to drive my friend here back to her towers to find a bit more information about all this. I'll probably drop her home and be back here sometime tonight. Maybe you'll have more for me about this map. Then I'll tamper with your computers a little more, you know, just to make sure you have nothing new on the Chelsea Company." Harris winked at Chelsea and she rolled her eyes.

"Under our extreme supervision, of course," Sara spoke with a counterfeit smile.

CHAPTER 18

THE TWO HOUR RIDE back to Columbus was more pleasant, Harris thought, or in the least, more interesting. He presumed, maybe she figured she was going home for good this time. For starters, and most important, they found a pit stop, a diner cafe, and ordered food to go. Harris ordered a turkey burger and fries and Chelsea managed to find three apples and two bananas.

The highway was somewhat as clear as the afternoon sky. It was all smooth sailing into Columbus, Harris assumed, behind the wheel of his Jaguar and Chelsea as his co-pilot.

Chelsea, checking her phone messages, shook her head before speaking. "I have a lot of missed calls, thirty to be exact, and ten text messages." After five minutes of reading her posts, she sighed. "A lot of people want to know where I am and if I'm still alive." She smiled. "I'll call them in a few, for now I kind of like the affection, the camaraderie."

"I would figure so, Ms. Chelsea, owner of a conglomerate," Harris said, driving with one hand and stuffed some fries into his mouth with the other.

"Most of the calls were two to three hours ago," Chelsea said, scrunching her brow. "Funny my phone didn't ring at all."

"Our safe houses have electronic scramblers; makes it harder for others to track calls to our location."

"I'd figure so, Mr. Matt, retired CIA specialist." She then bit into her apple, forcefully mocking the way he ate his fries.

Harris smiled; that was cute, he thought. "You ever stop to wonder if the Livenal Company has anything to do with this?"

"What are you insinuating, if my father has something to do with this?"

"Not necessarily your father, but maybe someone else in his company, associates."

"I don't know," Chelsea said, mixing eating her banana and apple. "He's never, if hardly ever, talked to me about the Atlas. When I was a teenager maybe, and he vaguely talked about it then. It's a surprise I even remember."

"How's your relationship with your father? Does he—"

"Like any father. Let's play a little quid pro quo since we're getting personal. What was your mission really about when you were investigating me?"

Like me, Harris thought, *Nzingha knew it was going to be a long trip and this time didn't want to remain silent.*

"Alright, but I don't want to know about your father. If you want to play, I need to know if you yourself are the actual scientist behind these inventions from your company."

"You first, Matt," she said and gulped down some Gerber Pure bottled water.

"Okay, well … for starters … well, I'll start backwards and if you have any questions we'll go from there." He cleared his throat. "Infiltrating the Chelsea Company was my last mission before my retirement. The Agency claimed they had the Vc technology and that they didn't need another entity controlling that power. So they simply gave me the go-ahead to end the mission. Ending the mission means to cut the head of the snake."

"Imbeciles." Chelsea chuckled. "Just to let you in on something; at that time they never had the Vc technology. It was still in its early stages. It was only fully formulated about a year and a half ago. If they would have killed me, they would have got nothing; imbeciles." She shook her head.

"Your turn. What's your true function in this technology?"

"If the world knew who the scientists were, they would be sought after by every nation on the earth," Chelsea said and sighed. "I trust what I'm about to tell you will stay with you to your grave. Anyway, they'll just deny it. I would deny it, if I were them.

"I *paid* five scientists, who'll remain nameless, to *say* for the rest of their lives that they've created all the technology for Chelsea. Many years from now when this knowledge becomes more conventional they'll divulge themselves."

"So I see you're still not going to tell me your involvement?"

"Actually I have."

Harris did a double take, looking at Chelsea.

"I said I *paid* five scientists to *say* they created the technology."

"Oh, I see," Harris said. Carefully lifting his coffee from the cup holder, he took a sip. "You don't want to come out and just say you're the one behind the technology."

Chelsea grinned, finishing her apple, then started working on completing her banana.

"Let me ask you this," Harris inquired. "And you could shake no or nod, yes. Did you … I mean, did *they* create all of it, CAI, MEG, Vc, and now PE?"

She nodded, glanced at him, and neatly folded her banana peel and apple core in a napkin. "Okay, I'll admit to you this one time," Chelsea said and took a deep breath. "I'd say science is my raison d'etre."

"I think I had it figured all along," Harris said, his mouth wide open. "Wow, you're like a genius."

"Am I? I hadn't figured you out."

"Yeah, but you have to admit, you had a good time."

"Don't flatter yourself."

"So, do you believe in miracles now?"

"No, but I do believe you wanted to be done with the mission you had against me. Maybe had sympathy that I could change the world, and how could that be accomplished if the scientist is dead."

Not a bad assumption—maybe a bit of a mind reader, too, Harris conjectured, but he wasn't going to reveal his thoughts on that.

As Chelsea answered her many text messages, he contemplated deeply on their conversation. Wow, he pondered. Glancing at Chelsea every once in a while, he concluded that she's truly a whiz kid, and that within itself was a miracle. From that moment on it was hard to look at her in a sensual way. She didn't gain his respect; she demanded it, by default.

SHE felt she was in a secure place, *her* safe house; not quite her home, but second to, The Impending Towers.

Arriving 5:30 in the afternoon on a Saturday, when most people were off or the few who worked were gone, she still managed to talk to a hand full of executives about her adventure at the Oasis. She found out her bodyguards were alive in the hospital on her expense and reassured the attacker was still at large.

She also talked to her father on her company phone for fifteen minutes, assuring him everything was alright and it was back to work as usual, though that was a understatement. She left out the fact that her bodyguards failed at their job and Harris picked up the slack.

After a half hour, detecting Harris's impatience, she cut some of the conversations short to find herself back in the data room basement in front of computer 560.

"It seems we're in a bit of a jam again," Chelsea said, looking at Harris who sat beside her.

"It's amazing this folder was right next to Hephaestus and I didn't see it," Harris said, rubbing his chin. "Taffy would have detected it the first time."

"You weren't looking for it at the time," Chelsea said and typed in 612560 to open the Vulcan folder, numbers they had programmed before to open Hephaestus, leading them to the Atlas.

RESTRICTED, the computer seemed to holler again. The Vulcan folder was as stubborn as ever, Chelsea thought. She had tried everything.

She had tried the numerical numbers backwards, scrambled, and all the phrases Harris gave her before from Pandora, Prometheus, to Hesiod.

RESTRICTED, RESTRICTED, the computer flaunted in red.

"You wouldn't happen to have anymore clues written on paper somewhere?" she asked.

"Afraid I'm all out," he responded. "You know what I know about this. Your guess is as good as mine."

"Hiding things in plain sight," Chelsea said to herself more than Harris. "Isn't Spock a Vulcan on *Star Trek*?" she asked herself again. "Let's try Spock." She typed in the name which gave her the same results as before. "No, not that, uh, *Star Trek*. Nope not that either."

"Look up the god Vulcan online," Harris suggested, "and see what we come up with."

Chelsea connected to the Internet and found the Greek god Vulcan. "The god of fire," she read the screen. "Also known as Mulciber or Sethlans. He's depicted here holding a thunderbolt; he also has a few sons."

She typed in as many names as she could find trying to unlock the folder with all of the god's aliases to the sons and uncles.

It frustrated her that she had such things on her server and couldn't access them, but possibly some stranger out there could; a stranger like Harris's deceased government scientist pal.

She felt she was always great at solving conundrums, especially her own. This was all within her realm, the Atlas, her computer ciphers. Why was she coming up blank? She studied quantum physics, Maxwell's equations, and solved the Fundamental model of Particles and Interactions. Her company was even asked by world scientists to help work on the Hadron Collider. She was among other things an entrepreneur, a physicist, a naturalist—mathematician, polyglot for crying out loud—though she just couldn't decipher this map and Greek gods.

Then, just like that, an idea formulated. She had thought about it before, but Harris had interrupted her. Harris wasn't going to like this and neither was the other individual she thought about, but it was worth a try. She talked to just about everyone in the building today but him, so she needed to give him a call anyway on general principle.

"Remember I said I had an operator who managed things here at one time?" Chelsea questioned.

Harris answered, "Yeah," without much confidence.

"Well, I'm going to call the manager who used to work in this room when it was under the east tower. He practically built this place piece by piece."

"Yes, now I remember. I also remember saying not to talk—"

Chelsea picked up her cell phone and hit the automatic dial button next to Aaron's name.

Harris shook his head, showing her his disapproval in her defiance.

Aaron picked up on the second ring. "Nzingha," he addressed, "it's great to hear from you. I heard you were in the building, but didn't believe it. Are you alright?"

"Fine. It's the weekend; I didn't want to hassle too many people about too many things," Chelsea responded.

"Oh, of course not. You rattled the media instead. Did you not see the news about you and some—"

"Look, I'd rather not talk about the media; I have something important to talk to you about," Chelsea said, glanced at Harris, then back at the computer screen that aggravated her so.

"Go ahead, shoot. What's up?"

"I'm in the old server room. Remember when you first started and was head of the IT department?"

"Yeah."

"When this data center was under the east tower?"

"Yeah."

"You knew about most programs and files back then. I was wondering, did you ever come across a folder called Hephaestus or Vulcan? These folders are on computer 560 and I can't imagine why I can't access them."

"Hephaestus, Vulcan," Aaron whispered into the phone as if thinking aloud.

"Preferably Vulcan, if you remember anything."

Aaron stayed quiet for a few seconds before responding as if trying to get his story straight. "Yeah, actually I do. You should, too, though it was a long time ago. I remember a business meeting we had with your father. He asked me to store some folders on our computers for backup precautions. Most of it was business related, then there were those folders you mentioned.

"At the time I didn't see much to the folders, just a bunch of symbols and meaningless Greek gods. It looked like one of those role playing games. Ten years is a long time for all this to mean something now."

"Do you have a password to access the Vulcan folder?" Chelsea asked with new anticipation.

"I think so, but I'm not too sure," Aaron spoke. "Try tomb, or grave, something like that. It should open either folder."

She tried, tomb, grave, mausoleum, and crypt, with restricted behind every word adding to her growing dissatisfaction.

"You know what? I'm in the building," Aaron stated. "Let me come down there and take a crack at it."

"No! That's all right, I ..." Chelsea noticed it was too late; silence followed with a dial tone. She gave Harris a grim expression. "Sorry, he's coming down."

"Great," Harris conveyed. "So much for keeping secrets."

In five minutes Aaron had made it into the small black and white server room.

"Hi, my name's Matt," Harris said, standing with his hand out. "I don't believe we've properly met."

"No, we haven't," Aaron said, shaking Harris's hand reluctantly.

Chelsea could see the tension in Aaron; he didn't like this one bit. She noticed Harris didn't care for the exchange either, but he seemed the more gentleman today. *Of course, Matt had to be; he wasn't on his own turf, he was on mine.*

"What's he doing here?" Aaron asked, grabbing a chair to sit on the left of Chelsea while Harris sat at her right.

"Just doing a little investigating is all." She smiled. "Now, about that password?"

"Try vault," Aaron spoke, looking around as if trying to pull the password out of the air.

Restricted.

"Um … wait a minute, now I remember. Type in L dot, R dot, P dot."

"What's L.R.P. stand for?" Harris asked.

Aaron peeped at Chelsea as if trying to get her approval to tell. She ignored him, hitting keys for the new code. Giving in, he glanced at Harris kindly and said, "Last resting place."

The Vulcan folder opened.

Now who would have thought of that? Chelsea speculated. How did he know the password and she didn't? Aaron and Harris moved closer to Chelsea to get a better view of the screen. She clicked on a PDF file called Vulcan and it opened showing a single page on antique ephemera paper just like the Prometheus docs. They all read the fancy script.

In the city of Bath. In the land of the Royal crescent and circus lies St. John, the mausoleum, Lilith.

Everyone remained silent for a minute reading it over and over.

"Lilith," Chelsea spoke, "Jewish mythology developed in the ancient Babylonian Talmud. In Jewish folklore, Lilith is Adam's first wife created at the same time as Adam. She refused to be subservient to him and so left the Garden of Eden. God then made Eve from Adam's rib so she'd be submissive. Anyway, Lilith is generally thought to be related to a class of female demons."

"For a nonbeliever, you were always into related biblical things," Harris spoke to Chelsea.

"I think I can help," Aaron said. "I think I know were the City of Bath is and the Royal Crescent. It's in England. I visited there some eight years ago on a telecommunication business meeting. I have a detailed map of the Royal Crescent and the area around it at home."

"Matt has the Atlas and you have the location of the mausoleum," Chelsea said and smiled. "A little teamwork and cracking this enigma is starting to slowly work itself out."

"It seems so," Harris said tiredly.

Concurrently Aaron said, "Yeah," with the same enthusiasm.

Chelsea smiled at the two guys on her left and right. "Aaron, it would be much appreciated if you get that map of England from your house. I'm possibly thinking about taking a quick trip to Europe to see how involved my father is in all this. This time I think I'll investigate before I ask him anything."

For sure Matt has given me an inquisitive itch; a bug that doesn't seem to want to go away. What involvement, if any, does my father have? A power to generate a star, extraterrestrial presents, science at its breaking point seems to surround me and my father. It always had.

What was Matt up to? What picture was he painting here? What was Matt and his father really trying to discover?

We seem to have been pulled into this web of mystery together again, and it seemed more complex this time. This time, so he claimed, he wasn't working for the government.

Chelsea drove with Aaron and Harris trailing in his Jaguar. Using Highway 71, they made it to Clintonville in ten minutes, Aaron's home.

CHAPTER 19

THE CLINTONVILLE NEIGHORHOOD reminded her of a place out of a holiday story. The landscape always remained the same no matter what time of year.

Today it was blanketed in full green trees and grass in the same exact fashion if it had been packed with snow or orange leaves. The residence five blocks away from each other all hidden behind huge trees from the main road seemed to be one happy unit. Everyone knew everybody else and went to the same stores, kids' same little league, and exchanged gifts for Halloween, Christmas, etcetera.

Aaron's two-story red brick house resembled an oil painting of an early 1900 cottage with contemporary interior. She had visited here two times before for business, on company time. This visit ensued to be the first time it was recreational.

On this trip something kept racking her brain. For the whole ten minute drive she felt Aaron had his timeline of business endeavors wrong. Maybe it was just a glitch of memory on her part. She stored it in the back of her mind to ask him about it later.

She glimpsed at her watch; 7:30. The sun in the western sky still hung bright as she stepped into Aaron's house with Harris.

"Make yourselves at home, guys," Aaron said. "Just give me a minute to settle in, then I'll get that map." He disappeared into a back room from the living room.

"Nice home," Harris said as he sat on the huge white couch with many pillows.

Chelsea remained standing, pacing the room in front of the clean unused fireplace. Something's not right, she thought. She couldn't restrain the glitch in her brain and forced it forward, expanding her thoughts while she waited.

She remembered ten years ago her father needing help to back up a few programs on some of her computers. She seemed not to keep in mind Aaron ever going on a business meeting for telecommunications in England.

Vasquez, Harvey, and their crew of executives went on that trip. Aaron wasn't part of that team. He never was. This happened only eight years ago. Could she have forgotten that she sent Aaron, too? Three minutes had gone by and Aaron was still in the back.

"Are you alright?" Harris asked. "You're sweating. You look a little overheated. I know you and heat disagree. Why don't you sit down?"

She glanced at Harris as if she understood what he said, but ignored him. She could have sworn she heard Aaron talking to someone in the back room. She was more keen to the surroundings; Harris wasn't.

She noticed Harris never sensed Aaron come from the back room from behind him with a wooden Rawlings two-tone blue baseball bat. She stood in horror as Aaron in full swing bashed the bat into the back of Harris's head, giving off the sound of a thud. The stroke launched his whole body forward into a convulsing stupor before he collapsed onto the white rug.

"What the hell did you just do?" Chelsea asked, her face stuck in astonishment.

"I need that Atlas on the iPad. Does he still have it?" Aaron requested comely.

"Aaron, what the hell is going on, and how did you know he had it on an iPad?"

"There's too many questions and not enough answers. Tell me where the iPad is and I'll tell you what's going on. We haven't much time." Aaron spoke demandingly as Chelsea glimpsed at the bat still in his grip.

She noticed he observed her glance, and he put the bat down by the window.

"Nzingha, I'm not going to hurt you …" He said it with his hands stretched out as if he was giving himself up. "You know I could never do that."

Chelsea tightened her arms across her chest. "No, I don't know that. He doesn't have the iPad; it's at a … *safe place.*"

"Come on, Nzingha, this guy's a spy for the government, we both know that. He's dangerous. As soon as he gets all the information from you, he'll kill you as he tried before.

"We're wasting time. I need to know exactly where the Atlas photos are."

"Why do you need the Atlas, Aaron?" Chelsea asked. Her heart was racing. She backed up, she was sweating more now; events were moving too fast. "Why all of a sudden it's so important to you? How did you even know he had it on the …"

He bent over Harris's body checking his pants and suit jacket pockets.

He didn't find an iPad, but she noticed he found Harris's car keys.

"Some important people are coming to pick it up. How about the car? It has to be in the car."

"Who's coming?"

Aaron stood and walked toward Chelsea as she watched him size her up. "Come outside with me to his car," he spoke persistently.

"You're acting uncanny right now. Almost as if you're another person. Who's got you like this? Maybe we can work something out."

Aaron moved to her face. "You can't work anything out with these people. They already have things worked out. I like you; I really do, but let's go." He grabbed her by the back of her right bicep, guiding her toward the door.

"I see you're scared," Chelsea spoke, stern. "You're not thinking rationally."

As he moved her toward the door and she became reluctant to leave, his fingers bit into her arm more forcefully. "We can get the authorities," she now pleaded.

"They're the authorities."

"We can …" She knocked over a vase of flowers with her left elbow from an end table and the flowers and water fell on Harris's head. Aaron tugged on her more, leading her to the door. "Aaron, you're hurting me."

He pulled her violently toward him so they were face to face again. "How long have you known me? I don't want to hurt you. I just need this done before they get here. If you don't cooperate, they'll make you talk anyway, and I don't think they'll be as polite as I. If *we* get this Atlas they want, this will be over quickly, then you'll thank me later for saving your life."

"Or you'll be cursing me for firing you," Chelsea said as he shoved her out the door.

Outside in the driveway for four minutes cursing, he found no Atlas in the Jaguar.

For the whole four minutes she wondered did her trick work. Knocking over the vase was no accident. *Was there enough water in the two foot vessel to wake Matt up?*

She had known Aaron for over ten years, but never fancied getting close enough to date him until recently. It seemed as soon as she picked a mate, they turned on her. What luck, she thought sarcastically. This aura of science that surrounded her had made her closest friends insane. She remembered a saying she told herself at her PE, nanomedicine meeting. Humble beginnings will soon fall between the cracks from greed, and here was the first sample of greed, Aaron.

She had tried to stall him as long as she could by discussing the nature of their long-lasting relationship as colleagues. He spoke to her, but didn't deviate from checking the car, then shoved her back into the house with Harris still in the same position on the floor. *Mmm,* she pondered, *not enough water and probably not enough time for him to recuperate.*

She thought about escaping, but the car keys to the vehicles were on Aaron and there was no way around getting the keys from him. *Just running away was an option, but where am I going? Am I to leave this situation alone without closure? Am I to leave Matt's fate to whomever Aaron said was coming?*

Aaron moved into his kitchen and went through the draws in a frenzy, knocking silverware onto the floor. He finally found what he was looking for; duct tape, scissors, and rope.

"I'm calling the authorities," Chelsea said, taking out her cell phone.

"Go ahead," he said and dropped everything onto the couch and faced her. "What are you going to tell them? I'll tell you what I'm going to say when the police get here. This guy over here broke in and was trying to rob me, so I knocked his ass out. Remember, he's in my house. A matter of fact, the guys coming here will call them off anyway." He looked at his watch. "They'll be here any minute."

"I'm leaving," Chelsea said, and Aaron grabbed her upper arm again forcefully.

"Before you go, maybe I should search you for that iPad." His eyes explored her body up and down; she saw the sexuality in his look. She'd never seen Aaron look at her with such passion, and he wasn't immediately looking for an iPad.

"You don't want to do that," Chelsea said, grabbing his hand holding her arm. "What's got into you, guy?"

He seemed to come to his senses as he blinked at her a couple of times. He let her go, wiped sweat from his brow, and breathed in deeply.

"You said the map was in a safe place," he said. "You should make it easy on yourself. If you don't tell me, they're going to get it out of you one way or the other."

"It sounds to me these guys might kill us anyway," Chelsea responded.

Aaron answered her with a bleak look. When he picked up the tape and rope from the couch, again she noticed something amiss.

For one thing, Aaron was no criminal, Chelsea hypothesized, and if he was, not a good one. He seemed not to notice the small details. The scissors were missing.

She was disappointed in him. He also missed her purposely knock over the vase. Maybe it was because of his whipped up non-thought-out plan to confiscate the Atlas.

Aaron bent over Harris, uncoiling the rope to tie Harris's hands, she figured.

Aaron let out a high pitched scream, making her jump and squeal. His lack of detail had done him in, Chelsea concluded. Evidently the vase stunt worked.

Harris imbedded the scissors deep into Aaron's left shoulder. He wobbled to his knees, bringing Aaron to his. Now the two were nose to nose. After Harris pulled the scissors out, Aaron grabbed his bleeding shoulder, whimpering.

"I just evened the playing field," Harris whispered to Aaron. He then punched him in the jaw. Aaron spun onto his back, taking Harris's place on the floor. He searched Aaron's pockets and retrieved his car keys.

He then threw the scissors across the room, staggered to his feet, rubbed the back of his head, and moved toward the door. "Your friend there will be alright," Harris spoke, not really looking at Chelsea. "You can stay if you want, but if I were you, I wouldn't be here when his buddies show up."

Chelsea for the moment made a judicious assessment of the scene and followed Harris out the door.

HE parked his car where most cars were parked on the winding street road. He deliberately didn't drive into his informant's driveway. He preferred to walk a block and observe the house a few feet away for a few minutes before knocking on the front door. In the driveway he noticed his contact's Porsche and fresh tire marks of another car he couldn't figure out.

After his informant invited him in, he cautiously looked around the house, then eased his hand off his Five-seven in his shoulder holster.

He looked at his watch; 8:40. It was apparent he was too late; his targets had just fled. His contact, sitting on the couch, groaned and winced, holding his left shoulder that was bleeding, staining his brown shirt and hand. He stared at the pitiful man waiting for an explanation.

"They left about ten minutes ago," Aaron said. "He's driving a black Jaguar XJ. I checked thoroughly; I don't believe they had the Atlas with them."

"*You don't believe?*" he asked Aaron apathetically.

"I had him knocked out. I checked his pockets, his car ..."

"Did you get anything out of the woman?"

"She wouldn't tell me shit. All she said was that it was in a safe place. I mean, what's that ..."

Aaron's voice drifted from him. *The woman, Ms. Chelsea, said it was in a safe place. She was naive; I wonder what she could have meant by, it was in a safe place?*

Her running around with an ex-agent wasn't her style. She must know the significance of the Atlas. Agent, safe place, kept jingling in his brain. It was a shot in the wind, but he was going to give it a whirl.

He took out his cell phone and dialed a number with his thumb.

Aaron became silent from explaining his situation as he was being disregarded.

"Wild Mike," a male voice on the other end said. "What can I do for ya?"

"What lily pads do we have in Ohio?" Wild Mike asked, though that wasn't his official name.

"Hold on," the voice said, and it sounded as if someone started ruffling paper.

Wild Mike was the nickname of his father, a mercenary who used to be a colonel in the U.S. Army. They could have called him Wild Mike junior, but his father was inactive. His benefactors chose the name without the junior because it just fit. Like father, like son; they both were sociopathic killers—for the country, of course.

"I've only come up with one," the man on the phone said. "It's at the Ohio-Kentucky border. I'll text you the coordinates now."

"Much obliged," Wild Mike said and hung up. He looked at Aaron with cold eyes. "Is there anything else?"

"Yeah," Aaron said, grunting he rubbed his swollen jaw. "They might be headed to a chapel, St. John or the Royal Crescent in Bath, England."

"Anything else?"

"No, that's about it," Aaron said.

Mike watched Aaron look at him with uncertainty—with uneasiness he felt was more like it.

"You said a bunch of people were coming to straighten this all out," Aaron spoke with worry in his voice. "I've so far only see you. I'll soon be out of a job because of all this. You said your people would compensate me pretty—"

His hand coming down with one blow from the butt of his gun, Mike hit him in the temple. Knocked out instantly, Aaron slumped on the couch.

He couldn't just shoot the contact in this nice neighborhood; somebody will hear. Then they would have seen a strange man walking to his car. That strange man being him, he was going to have to dispose of the contact some other way.

England, safe place, retired agent, and the usual soon to be dead body all for an Atlas that supposed to lead everyone to the most powerful device on earth. This could be one big waste of time. They were paying for his services so he didn't care in the end if he came up empty. In the meanwhile he was going to have a little fun and do his job methodically by following every lead.

The cell phone beeped; he received his text message.

CHAPTER 20

HARRIS WAS UNEASY ABOUT IT, but she convinced him to make a pit stop at her towers to grab a bag of changeable clothes. They might be wrinkled, but at least they were clean, she simplified. Then it was back to the two-hour ride to Cincinnati.

The setting sun hid behind swirling red and lilac clouds while most of the sky dimmed royal blue. The humidity was still up late in the day, but Chelsea didn't care. Most of her time was spent in an air conditioned car with only one person complaining.

"I'm definitely going to get sick of this cold air, lady," Harris said, trying to unwrap clear plastic from a turkey sandwich and drive.

"Unless that knot on the back of your head makes you sick first." She rubbed the back of his skull for a few seconds with her warm fingers examining the swollen strawberry-size bump. "You think maybe you should see a doctor?"

"I think I'll be alright," Harris responded and shot her a quick smirk. "Trust me, I've been hit with much worse things." His grin grew.

"Okay." Chelsea shyly smiled, bringing her dimples out more than she felt she should. "Yes, I care, Matt, but you're not special. I care when anybody is hurt."

"So, do you know who Aaron's friends might be?"

"I was beginning to suspect someone linked with my father," Chelsea said and took in a deep breath. "If you don't know already, I believe some years ago someone in his company had sent an assassin here to the States to eliminate my competitors; the reason and result, to hasten the productivity of my science. But the thing with this Atlas, if it's someone in his company, why would they want something back they already possess?"

"Someone doesn't want us to see what's inside," Harris said. "I haven't ruled Livenal out totally but I'm starting to believe more and more that this man who attacked you is one of ours. The way he fought the security at the Oasis was one sign, then something Aaron said when I came to. He said, whoever was coming will probably dismiss the authorities if you called them. Definitely a sure sign of Langley deep undercover field agents."

"I don't know what you got me into, my staff turning on me, but I think all this should be carefully looked into before I consult my father."

"See? Now that's why you shouldn't have told Aaron what we're doing."

"You might be right, but I thought he could have helped, and we do need help." She stared out the window. "I've known him for more than ten years."

"Knowing somebody and getting to know somebody are two different things."

"And *you* would know huh? Though, maybe we were lucky. We would've never known the password or that he was a double agent unless I called for his help."

"Sort of a blessing in disguise."

She bit into one of her apples. "I could make a couple of calls, rent a private jet, and charter a flight in no time. I haven't been to England in a while."

Harris gave her a smile of approval.

After finishing her apple, the rest of the trip was fuzzy; her eyelids drooped as did the sun in the western horizon. She was more tired than she had thought, plausibly because of all the excitement. After a couple of yawns and the radio playing some smooth jazz melodies she was asleep.

She was cold, freezing, and alone. She had been walking in the snow what seemed like forever. Everywhere she looked were blankets of white dunes, a desert of snowdrifts. The wind howled and snow fell from the sky like forever dropping white confetti.

Thunder cracked over and over again. Lightning struck the ground closer and closer. Alone, she ran just to get out of the way of the strikes. She was cold and already knew her feet, hands, and the tip of her nose was frostbitten black.

The dry air made it hard to breathe. She couldn't breathe … running … freezing … bitter … frigid and blinded by white. The sky was spinning vanilla, cream, and ivory. She tried to swallow, she couldn't breathe. She fell face-down in the snow nude, alone, and knew she was going to freeze to death.

When she awoke she startled herself and Harris. She noticed she had her head on his shoulder and picked it up instantly.

"Sorry," Chelsea said and wiped small beads of perspiration from her hairline.

"It's alright," he responded. "We're almost there. Are you alright? The AC's up almost full blast. I'm freezing, but you look a little flush."

"I'm fine," she answered. "I survived worse."

"Tell me about it," Harris said and rubbed the back of his head.

It wasn't true, Chelsea rationalized. She hated her dreams. A nightmare was more like it. *Why can't I dream about anything else other than the cold?*

CHELSEA had gone downstairs to take a shower and Sara strapped a ice pack on the back of Harris's head.

"Good and bad news bud," Brian said, typing at a computer. "The bad news is, I had to tell the Director about our little maneuver out here. We're using company facilities. Good news is, he said to look into this little operation of yours and see if it has any relevance."

"If you guys haven't already," Harris said.

"I don't think so; he seemed agitated when I had to tell him where we are. He said we have a week to figure it out, then he needed us to start on a project."

"It's true, Matt," Sara cut in. "When he's usually interested, he gives us more time than a week to figure things out."

"Well, somebody's gunning hard for this map," Harris said. "The director doesn't know everything?"

Sara laughed. "No, usually he does, and if he was interested, I would have agreed with you that he might know about this Atlas and sent a rogue agent to pick it up. But since we're on it, why send another agent, then show no real interest to us other than, hurry up, you got a week?"

"How about your friend downstairs?" Brian asked. "You got wacked pretty good by one of her buds."

"I don't know," Harris answered. "I haven't ruled out that option."

"Well, Nzingha has chartered a plane for us, ten tomorrow morning," Sara spoke. "Maybe we'll find some answers in the United Kingdom."

As the conversation shifted to the Atlas, Harris left the two agents at the computers to argue over the symbols and went downstairs. He took the iPad with him, stating he needed to ask Chelsea something about it. Probably to add on to their squabbles, Harris figured they thought.

After walking through a long hall and through a door that was usually locked he found the room Chelsea occupied. The door was open a crack; he knocked.

"Come in," Chelsea voiced from behind.

He unstrapped the ice pack attached to his head before he entered.

The room tried to simulate an average bedroom, but the common person knew better. Besides a bed, desk, dresser drawer, and closet, there were no windows. No smell of outside garbage or flowers—no stench of the city or country; no sounds of the outside, only the hum of the central air system. One would no doubt soon sense you were simply in a basement.

Chelsea sat at the dresser drawer fixing her short brown-black hair in the mirror. The wrinkles were hidden well in her black shirt and slacks, the clothes she had brought from her towers. The faint scent of apricot filled his nose.

"How was the shower?" Harris asked, standing by the door.

"The cold water was fine," she replied.

"Oh, you have to let it run—"

"It was fine," she said and smiled.

"Oh, yeah, I forgot you like … here, I wanted to give you this," Harris said, handing her the iPad. "It's yours anyway."

She took it and placed it on the dresser. "I'll look at it again, but please, no, I don't want it. I think it would be much safer in your hands."

Harris folded his arms, hiding the freezing ice pack between his bosom and hands.

For a second he glanced at Chelsea's visage with sexual hunting eyes. He didn't mean to, but he was attracted to the luster of her ochre skin tone, smooth like a teen. He wondered was it natural or did she do something to get it that way.

Snap out of it, he thought. "So, you ready for your trip to London tomorrow?" he asked.

"Sure," she answered. He watched her peek at the half hidden pack in his hands. "How's your head?"

"I think I'll live," he said, then looked away from her at the floor. "I haven't said thank you since the many incidences, but ..." He looked at her. "Thank you, for listening to me and the water on the head."

Chelsea shook her head sorrowfully, then managed a grin from the side of her mouth. "You're welcome, but I have a feeling I'm going to soon regret this."

He left her room with that last statement stamped in his mind. They might all regret this mission, his friends and foes alike. We all might be trying to kill each other in search of nothing but someone's sick game.

CHAPTER 21

SHE NARROWLY ESCAPED the safe house in Buffalo, NY. She wasn't great in performing stealth operations. She enjoyed being the element of surprise by sending a message. On this mission she felt she was somewhere in the middle. She wasn't quite sending a message, but more like collecting information, investigating, then maybe becoming the element of surprise, maybe.

Usually 3G did the investigating and she did the dirty work. Not being used to this part of the field apparently led to almost getting captured and could have led to her death. She had to bump her skills up to the next level.

At the Buffalo sanctuary on the waterfront in an 1800 abandoned fish storage warehouse some agents had tried stopping her to ask questions on why she was snooping around.

The only good thing about her first encounter was that they exposed themselves, as she uncovered herself. Knowing they weren't the agents she was looking for, she made a run for it. Hopefully they considered she just drifted to the wrong area and didn't expose her to the entire network of CIA safe havens.

Hidden cameras had detected her; she felt she wasn't going to make the same mistake at this new safe house. Scarcely escaping on her rented Aprilia motorcycle had brought her here to Cincinnati.

Suraksha last time pried around the safe house about eleven o'clock in the morning. This time she was going to do it three hours earlier part of bringing her talent to the next level.

She smiled. They sure don't change much, she whispered. The other place was near an abandoned storehouse near a lake. This one was an abandoned depot near a river. *Jetro's Inc.*, the front read like the identical warehouse adjacent to it that already had workers moving about starting their day.

She entered the building from the rear avoiding the bottle-cap size camera over a locked door and crawled through a half broken window. Using her gloved hands, it was easy breaking the rest of the dusty glass so that it didn't fall and shatter; waking up any alarms or light sleeping agents.

Inside was a labyrinth of aisles of corroded mechanical gears and machine parts of all sizes. It resembled a vast gray and black graveyard where elevator equipment came to die. Morning sunlight shot through low windows with dust swirling in its rays like millions of gnats. If it weren't for some lights in the ceiling, the place would have been pitch black.

Suraksha moved through the slate, ash, and charcoal gray world, cautiously keeping in mind every part of the place was booby trapped. So far she spotted six cameras and avoided them. Her black jogging outfit made it easy for her to move through the shadows.

Lost in the maze of passageways full of pallet racks jam-packed with pallets, she felt she was walking in circles. Growing frustrated, she murmured, "Think, Suraksha, think."

She realized her misstep. It wasn't around to enter this hidden fortress of solitude; it was up. She looked up at a section of five-story pallet racks and spotted another tiny camera. She started her climb, avoiding the surveillance.

HE knew exactly where to go. He parked his black Cadillac Escalade across the street from the functioning warehouse of *Jetro's Inc..*

He watched two trucks leave the premises this early morning before he got out his car to leisurely head to his target. He wanted to survey the place before knocking on the front door, or maybe this time he might use the back.

Some pigeons flew directly over him. He slowed his pace, hoping at least one of them would let loose on his head. None did. Damn, he thought, not a good sign. He checked the cartridge in his gun; he couldn't have it jamming, not on a delicate mission like a predator hunt.

For some reason today he wasn't feeling lucky so he hoped hope was on his side. *Sometimes I just have to go in there and do what I'm supposed to do. Simply do what I was hired to do. Yeah, that simple—damn, I wish one of those damn birds shitted on my head. I would feel so much better.*

ELEVEN forty-five, the digital clock read. He had to get up in ten minutes. Harris lay in his bed facing the clock with one eye open. Five minutes seemed to pass by in seconds, then the first alarm on the clock went off beeping like a heartbeat. He hit the button on top of the clock turning the alarm off.

Uh, just five more minutes until the second and final alarm, he figured. He had set his clock to go off twice before the ten minutes was up, giving him time to be lazy if he wanted to. He was figuring on how he felt when he got up the first time, sluggish or energetic. He was feeling sluggish—he'll just go back to sleep and wait on the final alarm.

Eleven fifty-five seemed to come faster than the first five minutes and the alarm beeped again like a steady heartbeat. He still felt too sluggish to get up and hit the alarm button again. To his surprise the alarm kept beeping. "Damn buzzer," he mumbled. He hit the button again and again and it kept beeping and beeping.

He now truly awoke and was slapped with a harsh reality. He lay on top of the sheets on his bed dressed in white shirt and tan slacks in his own simulated room of the OGA center. The digital clock by his bed read 8:05 AM and the clock alarm hadn't gone off at all; it was the OGA's distress signal.

The intercom above his head, also designed in every room, flashed red with a steady heartbeat like beep. *The place has been breached and nobody seemed to notice.*

Harris leaped out of bed, grabbed his .45 handgun on the small table next to him, slipped on his shoes, and ran out the room without tying them.

Fumbling into the hall, he couldn't decide on what to do first, tie his shoes or knock on doors to warn his associates. He hammered on Chelsea's door first, then moved to Brian's and did the same. Sara happened to open her door before he reached there and he bent down to tie his shoes.

"I think we've been compromised," Sara said, fully dressed, standing in the hall holding a Walther P22.

"You think?" Harris asked sarcastically.

"Hey, what's going on?" Chelsea inquired groggily as she came out of her room.

She only wore her black shirt which merely covered her upper thighs. Wow, her legs, knees, feet sure looked—he had to pass on the look right now. He was in a moment that could be a life or death situation.

"Sara," Harris said and finished tying his shoes. "Get Brian up and have him meet me upstairs. Get Nzingha and our gear ready to leave out the back, tunnel 2, double time."

Sara nodded as Harris unlocked the door to the tunnel leading upstairs to the computers.

The intruder, probably the agent at the Oasis, will never know he was detected, Harris knew. The alarm only went off in the lower facilities. He might be able to surprise him, capture maybe, and get some answers.

Pointed in front of him, his gun was secure in both hands. He cautiously moved through the tunnel toward the stairs. Gradually he walked up the fifteen steps to reach the main computer level. He heard the closing of a door behind him. He glanced back to see Brian in the hall with his gun drawn at his side. Harris put his index finger to his lips, pointed upstairs, and waved Brian to him.

In half-a-second Brian made it to the bottom step. "What do we have?" he asked, whispering.

"Could be our friend from the Oasis," Harris whispered over his shoulder. "Who else would know about this place?"

Brian bowed in agreement and clicked his pistol off the safety.

"I'm going to confront the intruder. Keep an eye on the situation for a minute, then back me up."

"Always," Brian said. "I got your back, hero."

Whatever, just back me up and try not to get us both killed, was what Harris really wanted to say, but now wasn't the time. He smirked at Brian and continued his climb up the steps.

Ever so meticulously Harris moved into the center of the computer area, the hub of OGA.

"You!" Harris said with his gun aimed at the prowler.

There she was in black jogging suit steadfast from his approach, the agent from Livenal. She stood bent over one of the computers, typing.

What kind of deception was this? Harris reflected. Wasn't she supposed to have perished in a building explosion two years ago?

"Was wondering if you guys have more of these photos," she said without looking at Harris, who moved closer with his gun on her. "I seem to have found a screensaver of the Atlas on one of your computers. I can't seem to retrieve the rest of the photos though. Do you have the password?"

"Suraksha Using, so the papers called you," Harris said. "The Chelsea Company assassin is alive. I'd say you're a modern Houdini, Ken Kesey at best. I'm here to inform you I'm making an arrest."

He seemed to get her attention for a second, and as she swung her head staring at him with those lifeless blue-gray eyes, a grin formed. He couldn't tell if she was African American or Asian, but he did notice she had a pretty smile. In reality it was the eyes and grin of a wolf.

"Are you going to arrest a ghost, Mr. Agent?" she asked callously. "It's conclusive you're the guys I'm looking for."

"I'll ask the questions," Harris said. "For starters, how the hell did you find this place?"

"Wouldn't you like to know?"

"The time for playing games is over," Harris said, waving his gun. "Place your hands on your head."

"Of course, Mr. Agent," Suraksha said and motioned to raise her hands. "But who says I'm playing games?"

As she was about to put her hands on her head, a two foot bamboo pole shot out from her right sleeve.

The pole slammed into Harris's right firing hand and he dropped his gun. Another pole ejected from her left sleeve, which she grabbed and continued to swing.

He knew this dance, Kenjutsu. He avoided most of her strikes, which came lightning fast. Her stick just missed his throat and chest, but wacked his wrist. He yelped from the sting and launched a counter assault.

Fluently he grabbed her by the left wrist and flung her over his back, using the momentum of her lashes. She slammed into the table of keyboards behind him. He attacked again, trying to use elbow and wrist joint locks, but she wiggled her way out.

She answered by kicking him in the chest, knocking him back into a bunch of computer monitors.

Harris saw a glimpse of a frown as if she just realized the method of his style of fighting. She'd also been in this waltz before when he was disguised some years earlier. Yes, Suraksha, we have fought before, remember? Harris wanted to say.

"Hey!" Brian yelled at Suraksha, pointing his gun at her.

The tables seemed to have turned. Harris recalled being in a similar predicament in the Impending Towers some years ago.

Suraksha didn't give Brian time to think, and roundhouse kicked one of her sneakers off her foot so that it soared across the room into his face. In repeating the same move with her other leg, her second sneaker hurled into his mug with a direct hit a microsecond behind the other.

Obscuring his view and giving him a bloody nose, Suraksha dove on Brian, toppling him onto his back. Losing his gun, she punched him with all her might in the solar plexus. Grasping his chest, he gasped for air and she aimed her bamboo stick to thrust into his throat.

Harris interrupted her with a full kick to her abdomen, spinning her on her back, causing her to lose her pole.

Harris, seeking the upward advantage, helped by gravity, punched downward upon her with the fullness of his strength. His knuckles connected with her chin, but her head automatically rolled with the punch, attempting to lessen the blow, Harris knew. She front kicked him in the stomach, evidently to knock him back, he assumed.

She was good, Harris distinguished; very professional, but so was he. He always kept his body fit and took her blow while also rolling with the kick. He punched downward again, linking with her chin and this time causing her to go limp. He shook his hand. *Damn, that hurt;* he hit her as if she was a man.

He was about to tend to the coughing Brian laid out on the floor rubbing his chest when he noticed another familiar face on one of the security cameras.

The clean cut well dressed man from the Oasis moved vigilantly through the back door of the warehouse. The man took out a gun, placing it at his side, and continued traveling as if he knew where to go.

Harris glanced at Suraksha on the floor, figuring they didn't come together, then decided it would be best working out the scenario later on their flight. For starters, maybe they could kill two birds with one stone. Protocol was, if a lily pad was compromised, it had to be destroyed.

"Are you alright?" Harris asked Brian, helping him to his feet. "We have to go."

"I'm fine," Brian said, coughing. "Why, we got the …" He coughed again and wiped blood from his nose with the back of his hand. "We got a grip on things here."

"Apparently not," Harris said, retrieving their guns. "We have this agent here, most likely from Nigeria and another coming, I just caught on the camera. It's the one I told you about at the Oasis."

"Are you sure?" Brian asked, holding his stomach and walking to the security monitors. "The boss is not going to like this."

Harris moved to the stairs leading to the bowels of the center. "We have to go. This place is done."

Harris left with Brian on his heels. Brian locked the door after coming in from the tunnel leading to the computers upstairs.

"I have all our stuff we're—" Sara said, pointing to two black duffle bags on the floor at her feet. She stopped in midsentence when she saw Brian's face. "What happened up there?"

"I'll explain later," Harris answered and picked up one of the bags. "This Atlas is hotter than I thought. We have two different agents who compromised our position."

Brian nodded assuring Sara, and Harris spoke on, "One's immobilized, the other on his way. Do you have the destruction codes?"

Sara dipped her head at Harris and glanced nervously at Brian.

Harris acknowledged Chelsea with a, everything is going to be alright stare. She affirmed with an edgy look holding on tight to her bag on her shoulder.

The girls obviously weren't used to this sort of skirmish, Harris thought, so it was his job to map out a plan for everyone to get out safely. As much as he wanted to confront the man from the Oasis, he went on a gut feeling to let it pass for now. Besides, he might not have to do anything if the man was caught in the wind of this soon to be destroyed building—mind over muscle, in this case pressing one button over face to face confrontation.

Brian picked up the remaining bag and they were off jogging down the three hundred foot long, dull lit passageway, tunnel 2, which Harris knew led to the occupied Jetro's parking lot and their cars.

At the end of the tunnel was a huge silver airlock door. Sara punched in a code to open the door from a computer panel built into the wall. The door unbolted and everyone made it out the tunnel and into the sewer below Jetro's parking lot. Sara punched in another code and scanned her thumb on a scanner next to the computer.

Shutting down, the CPU's unemotional voice said. *You have two minutes and counting for departure. Goodbye.*

"You never thought you were going on an adventure today, did you?" Harris asked Chelsea and went into his pocket for his mini flashlight.

"No, I suppose not," she responded. "But co-existing with you these last couple of days I'm beginning not to be astonished."

Harris smiled at Chelsea as Brian helped Sara close the heavy door. Instantly everything turned pitch black. Sara wiped her hands together, took out her flashlight, turned it on, and said, "It's done."

Jetro's abandoned building was going to get that demolition a lot of people anticipated after all, Harris thought.

CHAPTER 22

COULD THEY HAVE DECIDED THAT FAST to annihilate the place? he wondered. They didn't give him the audacity to negotiate terms of exchange or surrender. They didn't invite him to a friendly mano a mano. He laughed, thinking sarcastically, *cowards*.

He knew this was the right place as he witnessed white pulsating lights flashing in the ceiling like pulsar stars.

He knew that meant the place was compromised and might self destruct in four, sometimes two minutes. *Cowards,* he assumed again.

In one of the aisles he stopped in his tracks and started back pedaling. Too late, he calculated, and watched what he knew as the center of OGA light up in an array of sparks and lightning. He turned around and ran as fast as he could to where he came in.

Hopefully it won't be too late. He knew it was bad luck entering the building without getting shitted on by the birds. The failure of the act led him to believe he was jinxed.

He knew the building wasn't going to explode in a fire ball, but more in a demolition fashion. He could survive this if a beam didn't fall on his head as the building collapsed onto itself.

He saw everything in slow motion as he ran. The building implosion commenced as he was five feet from a nearby window. No time to open the window, he thought, and jumped.

The shockwave from the first blast helped propel him through the glass window. Most of the heavier particles and steel joists fell away from him while hot dust and soot shot out around him like cannon fire.

Hitting the grassy ground outside, he rolled twice from the building as clouds of dirt engulfed the area.

Huge charcoal and earth yellow churning clouds bubbled and expanded in every direction around the elapsed perimeter of the elder Jetro's warehouse.

After the pop of charges went off, the demolition drowned out its sound. The collapsed construction roared like the fictional creature Godzilla mixed with a thousand huge trees splintering. The ground shook as metal fell on top of metal, causing echoes of moans and shrieks, then silence followed by an increasing choking haze of gray and brown.

He got up slowly coughing, covered head to toe in gray ash as the grass and sidewalks about. Gray snow fell everywhere as he squinted trying to assess the damage. As far as he could see in the center of the smog was a smoldering graveyard of debris of brick and twisted metal.

He knew the documents and computers were specifically set ablaze, so there was no retrieving data in the rubble. Recovering the Atlas was going to have to come from the individuals who did this.

"Speak of the devil," he said to himself.

Though a gray cloud still blotted out the sun in the vicinity, he spotted taupe-colored silhouettes of apparently stunned bystanders from the adjacent *Jetro's* building. What peeked his interest were the human images behind those spectators evacuating the scene in a car.

"Shit!" he said out loud and took off running.

A sting in his ankle, back burning, and eyes tearing from the accumulating dust, he still pushed on. Scampering with a limp past about six flabbergasted observing Jetro's workers, who might not have seen him in the mist, he moved to his car across the street. A black Jaguar drove past him as he climbed into his Escalade.

He started the engine and thought about his injuries that he knew he was going to have to tend to later. He fought through the agony of a sprained ankle from his first fall and bleeding gashes on his back from thrown metal shrapnel.

The thrill in pursuing his targets was too great, intoxicating. Taking out his Five-seven, he laid it on the passenger's seat and pulled out onto the street. He had to stop that car.

THEY had decided to take his car for many reasons. The first and main reason was not to look too suspicious driving out of the parking lot. It was better for one car to leave the scene of destruction than two, Harris guessed.

Second, simply why drive two cars to an airport that was around the corner—okay, maybe he just was comfortable driving, reason three.

"Great, that'll be fine," Chelsea said into her cell phone in the passenger seat. "We'll see, Paul in hangar fifty-five."

"Hold your head back and let me see," Sara said in the back seat with Brian.

"I'm okay, I'm okay," Brian said, snatching the tissue from Sara's hand and wiping his still bleeding nose.

"Men," Sara said, shaking her head.

"There should be some ice on the plane for that," Chelsea said, glancing back at Brian. Brian held his head back, cleaning his nose.

"What's our flight situation?" Harris asked Chelsea.

"The same as before, Lunken Field. I had them bump up our flight a half hour." Chelsea looked at her watch. "So that should be—"

The car abruptly jolted and swayed, making the passengers grab the hand straps above the windows. Sara gave a yipe.

Harris mumbled under his breath, "What the hell?"

Looking in his rear-view mirror, he noticed the big black car that had hit them from behind. The dusty Cadillac Escalade in no time drove toward his side of the vehicle. The Escalade alongside his car had its passenger window down, and the owner pointed a gun in his face.

For a split second Harris saw the man behind the wheel. The man resembled one of those African tribesmen covered in white paint from head to toe. The paint here was made of gray ash. The man from the Oasis had survived!

"Everyone keep your heads down!" Harris screamed and slammed his foot on the brake.

His car, going seventy miles per hour on Columbia Pkwy, tires squealed and lurched everyone forward. Harris and Chelsea's seatbelts almost squeezed the life out of them, but saved them from flying into the windshield. Sara and Brian crashed into the seats in front of them.

The Escalade shot ahead of Harris's car.

Three automobiles on the highway, their tires screeching, barely made it out of the way of the Jaguar as it almost came to a stop. Harris then hit the gas, launching the car forward again, slowly catching up behind the Escalade.

Harris took his .45 from his shoulder holster while driving with one hand. "Brian, are you with me?" he yelled.

"I think my nose is broken now," Brian responded, sounding like someone with stuffy sinuses.

"Sara!" Harris bellowed.

"I'm on it," she said, taking out her gun.

Harris glanced at Chelsea, who was squinting holding onto the dashboard with her left hand and clutching the center of her shirt with her right.

She wasn't enjoying herself, he thought. He smirked; he lived for this. *Sorry, Nzingha, but we're going for a ride.*

He drove his car into the back of the Escalade, making it swerve and everyone in his car jerk their heads.

Vehicles on the freeway bobbed and weaved, honking their horns in near collisions to get out of the way of the highway chaos of two cars. With both vehicles reaching speeds of seventy, Harris moved into position for the PiT maneuver.

Harris smashed his car's left front bumper into his assailant car's right backside. The Escalade started to fishtail. The cars sounded like many soda cans being crunched as metal and plastic bent out of shape. Blue and white smoke engulfed them as the tires of both cars spun and skidded against the friction of the asphalt.

He was good, Harris analyzed. As the Escalade veered to one side he could see the driver turning the steering wheel in the same direction with one hand. Harris noticed the Escalade's anti-lock brakes moved the car sideways in front of his Jaguar. This position gave the man a clear shot into Harris's windshield. With the man's free hand, Harris watched him fire his gun out the passenger window.

The blast from the gun was loud, like a cherry bomb, and blew a half-dollar hole in the windshield above Harris's head and out the back side window.

Let's see how good he is, Harris thought. He hit his brakes again just enough so he could swing his car around to the Escalade's left backside and fishtailed him there.

Got him! he yelled the thought as his car shot ahead through white clouds of burning rubber. The Escalade did a full spin and slammed into the guardrail.

Multiple sirens could be heard in the distance. *That'll keep him occupied for a while.*

"Is anybody hit?" Harris asked, glancing around at everyone.

"No," everyone said almost together.

"Shook up is all," Chelsea said, holding her chest slumped down in her seat. "Whiplashed, but that might be an understatement. Next time I ride in the back."

Harris glimpsed in the rear-view mirror witnessing two police vehicles surround the Escalade that still hugged the railing that separated the opposite traffic.

We'll meet again, Harris mused, but not today. He put away his gun and peeked at Chelsea, who seemed relieved that he did.

"You were saying our flight goes out, in what?" Harris asked Chelsea. "An hour?"

He observed Chelsea, still feeling her chest, responded nervously, "Yes, an hour."

Harris cruised his front-end dented car and bullet hole windshield to the speed of sixty. They made it to municipal airport, Lunken Field, in ten minutes.

CHAPTER 23

CHELSEA'S STYLISH QUALITIES were great considering the fast turnaround time for the plane, Harris observed. They only paid the price for an absent flight attendant, leaving them the two pilots. They all hid out inside the plane in hangar 55 for about thirty-five minutes until the captain, Paul, and his co-pilot showed up.

Harris enlightened Sara and Chelsea about the encounter with Suraksha. Chelsea was shocked as he was that Suraksha was alive and hadn't died in a warehouse explosion as the media had it some years ago.

"Things are never what they seem lately," Chelsea declared.

"Just know there are two people gunning for this map," Harris reminded everyone. *Considering Suraksha survived this recent warehouse destruction.*

As he described the scrap, Sara checked Brian's nose, determined it wasn't broken, placed an icepack on it, and stopped the bleeding.

Harris also talked about his theory on the Agency sending a splinter cell or plausible deniability assassin to retrieve the Atlas. Harris noticed Sara and Chelsea were concerned with his story while Brian more for his nose. Brian then took a nap on one of the couches.

Finally airborne in a Gulfstream jet, Harris took a good look at the lavish cabin. Two gray couches, six seated dinner table, numerous window chairs facing each other, and carpet was stretched out extravagantly in the thirty-five foot long area of the passenger accommodation.

Paul clarified to Chelsea that they'll arrive at Filton Airfield in

England in eight hours and Chelsea relayed it to the rest. She also explained the airport was the closest to the City of Bath.

Sara waking Brian, helped themselves in the galley as Harris sat facing Chelsea, who stared out the window at fast passing clouds.

"Sorry," Harris apologized, "because of our hasty departure the only food aboard is French-style grilled salmon."

Chelsea glimpsed at him, crossed her legs, and continued her stare out the window into the sky blue.

"I did manage to find this." He smiled and held in front of him a green pear half wrapped in a napkin. He handed it to her, which drew her attention. Accepting the pear, she didn't return the favor of a smile. "So what do you think about the involvement of Livenal?" Harris asked. "Clearly this is their agent."

"I know where this is going," Chelsea responded. "I've had a long debating conversation with my father and he knew nothing about that assassin. He contacted the Nigerian authorities on the matter and they've been investigating since."

"I want you to truly know," Harris said, "I'm uninterested if it was your father's doing or not. Frankly I believe you and your father. It's the great interest someone else obviously has for this Atlas that concerns me.

"I laughed at my stepfather for taking this whole thing seriously. I should have never doubted him. I'm finding out that not only someone in Nigeria has and had great interest in your company, but someone in the shadows of our government.

"This being evident from what we experienced, then someone in this government feels that the secret of the Atlas is a real threat. With the perpetrators being dangerous to the point of committing murder and threatening our lives, I know you'd agree that this should be your last trip.

"You should speak to your father, up your security, and let me cue you in from webcam on details of what I find. The agent from this invisible government isn't going to stop. He'll soon find us in England from his mole, your executive, Aaron."

"Late executive," Chelsea spoke. "I can't deny the fact that my company has some shadowy characters who could be linked to Livenal and maybe always had.

"On another note, you did drag me out here in seeking help about the Atlas. I'm as curious as you are about its secrets. I want you to know that I want to know what my father is up to, too, if anything, without informing him right away. It'll be interesting to know who else in my company or his knows about this."

"This'll be a dangerous path if you take it. Protecting you isn't guaranteed. Everyone has a job to do. Yours is commerce."

Chelsea bit into her pear and he watched some of the juice form on the corner of her mouth. She removed it by dapping at her mouth with her napkin, sensually in his opinion.

"I don't know whether to be flattered or embarrassed about your statement," Chelsea responded. "I'm a big girl, but I do see your point in this quest becoming life-threatening—correction; it already is."

Sara approached them with two cups in her hands. "Sorry to interrupt," Sara said. "Just bringing you guys some coffee." She handed a cup to Harris and he took it with a nod. She handed the other to Chelsea. "It's a regular, two sugars—"

"Thank you, but no thanks. I don't drink coffee," Chelsea said, smiled, then took another bite out of her pear.

"Well then, non-coffee drinker, more for me," Sara said, smiled, sipped the hot drink, then walked back to her seat.

"I was thinking about your father," Chelsea spoke. "What is he dying from? We can quid pro quo; you keep me alive on this quest, maybe I can help your father. You may need me more ways than one."

"Lung cancer," Harris replied with a dismal look. "He has lung cancer. I'm afraid he's terminally ill. He doesn't have much time."

Chelsea looked into his eyes as he looked into hers, and he sensed she became sad for a moment. She looked away and out the window again.

"I could cure him, you know," she whispered.

"I've heard rumors of your nanomachines entering damaged human cells and repairing them. The news has it that it's at its early stages. Sounds like the beginnings of M.E.G. all over again. It took the U.S.

in red tape of regulations two years to accept that. I don't want to get into things you discovered which our government as in the FDA hasn't released yet."

Chelsea stared at him with the most unblinking somber look. "The nanomachines work," she spoke softly. "I can cure your father, and that's what I'll do when we get back. It's our government's legislators and bureaucrats who have everything in a deadlock."

"I would appreciate that, I really would," Harris said, smiling again. "I'd like to think the stubborn old man would, too, but he's a prideful dude."

"I'm sure he's kind," Chelsea said. "I'm sure you get your kind heart from him, but I don't see it much in you, because of all that pride."

Harris understood what she meant and looked at her curiously as she stared out the window. He simplified her saying that his father taught him kindness and arrogance well. Good guess again, Chelsea, he thought. He and Taffy are one and the same.

A few hours later they gossiped around the table about the latest clues from the Atlas. They spoke about the City of Bath, St. John's Hospital, a burial chamber, and if Lilith could exist there. They also dialogued about the likelihood of human destiny to live forever if they could recreate another sun.

There were dangers to a great invention like this, Harris pondered. If it's not made perfect, another sun could disrupt magnetic fields throughout our solar system and wreak havoc upon the earth. He wondered if such a power could be controlled or should be found.

Maybe these perpetrators are right, this power should remain hidden. The killing didn't start until curious minds wanted to know. To keep things concealed; was that the rogue agent's purpose in pursuing us? Are they out of the loop and trying to recover the data? Are they doing this for honor or greed? Most times it was for selfish gain. He wondered if he should chase these queries to find out. Then he thought, *what I'm I doing chasing powers beyond my comprehension? I'm retired for crying out loud, but I've come so far.*

Chelsea sat by herself and didn't gather around them when they had their conversation. She soon fell asleep in her chair and Harris placed a blanket over her. He speculated about her place in all this. As she always evaluated him, he now appraised her.

She was a loner, as some scientists are. The question is, despite the many people who surrounded her, was she a lonesome person or wanted to be a loner by choice? He came to the conclusion she wanted nothing more but to be alone for awhile away from the usual horde of constant business to embark on a quest of possible death. Maybe it was exhilarating to her, for now.

CHAPTER 24

AFTER SHOWING THEIR PASSPORTS TO CUSTOMS, they were okay to enter the country with firearms because of their government security clearance status. At Filton Airfield they exchanged their money to pounds at a post office, rented a four door blue Rover, and drove to the City of Bath, Somerset.

Harris reminded everyone to adjust their watches to United Kingdom time, which was five hours ahead of the US. He knew they weren't going to do much tonight now, 10:30, but they could get things started.

Harris had visited England more times than he could remember so the group selected him to drive since he was used to left side vehicles. That eliminated one problem, he thought, because everyone knew who the chauffeur was. Next, after forty minutes of riding around in circles, they found St. John's Hospital. Their last quandary was finding out about the hospital and the existence of Lilith.

Sara volunteered, and walked into the hospital administrative office alone. She had found out for the team it was a almshouse, a retirement home for the poor, and was closed for the night to guest.

Sara, the great communicator Harris knew she was, asked the overnight administrator for a list of residents long departed. She told a story of her great grandmother who stayed at this hospital in 1901. She was trying to retrieve her grandmother's records that had been lost in a fire many years ago. Sara said she conveyed to the young male administrator in a sexual English tone that she wanted confirmation of Lilith's residency, her grandmother.

He showed her to the computer and told her to help herself, but she only had a few minutes before he was going to ask her to leave and come back in the morning. Though he sat right next to her, helping her start her search on the computer, his attention was more on a program on the telly called *Peep Show*.

Sara explained when she typed in Lilith and the information appeared on the screen he never saw her take a snapshot from her phone. She also took a picture of a directional map incased in glass on the counter and grabbed a brochure.

Small-time detective work, Harris presumed, but effective. When Sara finally made it back to the car to tell her story, she boasted that she had something interesting to show. She wasn't revealing the piece of the tale until they found a hotel.

Three Abbey Green, eight blocks behind St. John, Harris reserved rooms on the first floor for the evening and tomorrow. Known as a hotel, it resembled a townhouse that blended with the rest of the buildings in the area.

They coped with the family-size suite arranging that Sara was going to sleep in the king size brown canopy bed in the main room and Chelsea on a twin bed. The men settled in another room on different single beds.

In the white living room they gathered next to the immobile fireplace to discover what Sara had on her phone. Harris noticed the portrait of the Royal Crescent over the fireplace, in the window's plush tan curtains, and huge couch made him feel he didn't do too bad picking the lodge.

"I found our Lilith," Sara said and handed her phone to Chelsea, who sat with her on the sofa. "Enlarge the screen with your fingers and look at the full name and year."

Harris watched Chelsea frown as if mystified, or was she enlightened? Sara looked at Chelsea as if to say, *well, don't you know*, and Chelsea shrugged. Chelsea handed the phone to Harris, who sat across from her in a chair next to Brian. As Brian looked over Harris's shoulder at the tiny screen, they now knew why Chelsea looked the way she did.

Disregarding other names on the deceased list, Harris focused on Lilith. It was the full name that baffled him as everyone else.

Lilith Chelsea 1974 to 1992 cremation, chapel vault.

"Could this be a coincidence?" Harris asked Chelsea.

"Or you never told anyone you had a sister," Brian suggested to Chelsea. "Or you never knew you had one."

"It's like I never knew I had one," Chelsea answered everyone's inquisitive curiosities. She folded her legs and sat back. "Interesting, but not crazy to think I could have a sister or cousin. She was born in the same year I was. I never knew my parents. I wound up in an orphanage as an infant."

"You ever ask your stepfather about your real family?" Harris asked.

"Of course," Chelsea replied. "He always told me he never knew and never wanted to know, but I could always go to the orphanage to find out myself. I never did, never considered it to be important. Always felt if my real parents thought I was insignificant, then trying to find them would be pointless. Of course, I still thought about it through periods of my life and looked up the orphanage some ten years ago. I found it was abandoned five years prior to that with the history of the archives lost."

"So this could be a coincidence," Sara said. "Or a twist of fate that you actually found a lost deceased relative while intertwined in this mystery we're trying to solve."

"What makes you think this could be her sister?" Harris asked Brian curiously. "Could be an aunt or cousin, like Nzingha said."

Brian shrugged before answering. "I looked at the dates; she died young, so I just assumed …"

Brian's voice faded from him for a second. *Brian was right, Lilith died at eighteen in a old age home. Could this be another riddle?* Handing the phone back to Sara, that's what he suggested to the group. "The Atlas is affiliated with Nzingha's father, so this could be another clue. Who dies in an old age home at eighteen?"

"This is definitely another piece of the puzzle," Sara said. "We need to get into that hospital. Though keep in mind the evening hours. I got a glimpse of the place inside; it didn't seem heavily guarded."

"We should start this as soon as the place opens, first thing in the morning," Harris said. "We haven't much time; our black op friend will soon discover where we are."

"When you find Lilith," Chelsea said staring at Harris, "I want to be there."

"I suggest you stay here," Harris recommended. "This could get a bit hairy if—"

"I have to do this."

"Nzingha, seriously, stay here, I'll collect the information you need. You don't want to risk your life over something that might not have any relationship to you. Besides, if anything was to happen, I think I'll never forgive myself for dragging you into this."

"It's too late for self-responsibility now," Chelsea responded, and Harris sensed she was growing agitated. "I didn't chart a plane all the way over here to sit in a hotel—"

"Let her come," Brian cut in. "Maybe we can use her. The more people on this operation, the faster it'll go. Besides, showing my black and blue face may not go so well if I have to be persuasive with the staff."

Harris shook his head in disagreement and caught a smile on Chelsea's face. He didn't like it, but Brian had a point.

They came up with a simple plan where Sara and Brian were going to be the distraction while Harris and Chelsea snuck into the temple vault.

Sara and Brian separately were going to ask for a tour of the place for their imaginary elderly relatives before registering. After a few minutes casing the place checking the staff and security positions, they were going to call Harris.

Chelsea was going to shadow Harris and become his eyes behind his head. Brian also suggested to bring the iPad along in case they needed to compare clues at the site. They all agreed.

Reading the brochure and finding the almshouse on the Internet, Sara and Brian came up with plenty of questions to ask the administrators, figuring to at least get an hour out of their visit. They all studied the hospital directional map on Sara's phone to get an idea of the place.

Having Bluetooths in their ears should make it easy for them to contact each other for a fast executed plan, Harris thought. This wasn't his best operation, but it was going to have to do.

Everyone took turns in the shower, then drifted off to their own space in the living room. Being that it was 8:30 at night in the Americas, Chelsea was on her cell phone announcing she won't be at the office for a couple of days and discussed future business transactions. Harris also overheard her say if anybody saw Aaron, not to permit him in the building.

From the hospitality of the hotel, Harris ordered a late night dinner for his crew. They discussed their positions of the mission again as they ate, then finally went to their assigned beds. Harris had a feeling; when the sun came up over England, it was going to be a big day.

ST. JOHN'S Hospital opened 8:00 Monday morning. Sara went in first, Brian twenty minutes after, then Harris and Chelsea twenty minutes after that.

Harris left the car in the back of the hospital after Brian and Sara told him about the rear exits. If things went well, he'd pick up Sara and Brian in front after checking the catacombs. If things went wrong, everyone was to leave out the back doors.

Sara advised Harris in his Bluetooth that the hospital was short staffed in the morning hours until noon. From fourteen personnel who were supposed to be on the site, there were only nine.

"Though some budget cuts were made," one red shirt staffer commented, "it's still the best run retirement home in Bath."

Harris knew Sara had her way with certain individuals by engaging in a common conversation to then deceptively attain information.

Brian, the observant person he was, told Harris about the hospital security cameras. On Brian's tour he learned most of the cameras were in the living quarters and not around the chapel.

"Perhaps they think God doesn't need cameras to watch over his dead," Brian said in the three-way calling conversation. Harris neither Sara responded to Brian's typical humor.

Ignoring Sara and Brian's constant chatter with the staff in his

Bluetooth, Harris with Chelsea circumvented through a maze of buildings.

St. John's Hospital, retirement home, was an eight block mishmash of two to three story grade one buildings. The Georgian city reminded Harris of many places in England with its sash windows and Bath Stone structures.

"Walk where I walk," Harris told Chelsea as he guided her past some cameras protruding from the roofs of some houses. They cautiously but ever so casually moved through a courtyard of pillars, arches, and huge pots of colorful flowers making their way toward the chapel.

Taking out the pamphlet, Harris glanced at it, then looked up at the top of a vine-covered archway placed on brown antique pillars. Stained of ancient corrosion and nearly covered in trailing plants, a slab in the arch read *Founded 1174*.

"I believe this is the back of the chapel," Harris said. "Past this gate and down the corridor should lead to the columbarium." Wrapping his hand around one of the bars on the rusted iron black gate, he shook it. "Locked, like I figured, but that shouldn't be a problem."

Tapping Harris on the shoulder, Chelsea said, "This might be a problem."

Harris let go of the bars just in time to see an elderly lady slowly walk from the corner of a building behind them. Clothed in a white dress and bonnet with black bag on her right shoulder and cane in her left hand, she hobbled straight toward them.

The lady had her head down most of the way and when she finally looked up she stood in front of them with a smile.

"Morning, luv," she said to Harris, and he nodded. "Going for my morning stroll to the chapel. I always used the back way before I go to the front because I love the flowers in the yard. They always look nice on such a lovely day." She then noticed Chelsea. "You kids looking for your folks?"

"Me and the missus seemed to have taken a wrong turn," Harris said, turning his voice into a British accent. "Do you know where to the main office?"

"That load of bollocks is back that way." The lady's smiling face turned uptight and pointed behind herself. "You tiddlers have a good one."

"Ta, cheerio," Harris responded and watched her hobble along and disappear around the corner of the chapel.

Chelsea rolled her eyes at Harris. "Do people use *cheerio* anymore?"

"She's old," Harris spoke. "Now look out while I work on this fence." As Chelsea turned watching the yard, Harris took out his master key. The old fence lock easily clicked open. He touched Chelsea lightly on the shoulder and she followed him into the darkness of a passageway. She left the gate open a notch, making it look as if it was closed without locking it.

The tight hallway led to narrow spiral stairs that went two stories down. Chelsea bumped into his back as they descended single file in the shadowy slightly sunlit staircase. "Sorry," she blurted out.

Harris could tell the water-stained, moss-patched and green-streaked stone walls and stairs where indeed old. He could smell the dampness of mold as the sunlight on their backs dwindled from the curving passage. A new light shown at the end of the coiled stairway.

The stones here were newer, but of the same color, raw umber. The columbarium opened wide enough for a group of people to stand, and lights in the ceiling lit the place enough to show four bedecked walls.

The PO box incorporated bronze walls structure had sculpted leaves made by each niche with a vine attached to all of them which led to the ceiling. The artificial vines connected at a center point in the ceiling as if a huge tree was above, that colossal tree being the church, of course, Harris assumed.

Harris and Chelsea spread out searching the numerous wall faceplates for Lilith.

"They're situated alphabetically," Chelsea said, her voice echoing.

From two different directions, following the names, they met in the middle of the back wall. They had to squat as *Chelsea Lilith 1974-1992* plaque was closer to the floor.

"Here goes nothing," Harris said, taking out his master key. He jiggled with the lock on the bottom of the box-shaped alcove. "Damn, my key's too big." He scratched his head. "You wouldn't happen to have a bobby pin, would you?"

"Wait a second, look at this," Chelsea said, pointing to an etch on the metallic wall leaf.

Looking closely, Harris saw a thumbprint on the middle of the leaf with a pinhole for a light. He glanced at the other box nooks around the room that also had thumbprint leaves.

He placed his thumb on the leaf above Lilith, a nameplate that read *Chase Eli 1922-2005*. The small aperture lit red, then faded. He did the same to the Lilith leaf. The tiny light glowed red, then diminished.

"Here goes nothing," Chelsea said and placed her thumb on the leaf of Lilith. The tiny light flushed green.

Simultaneously Harris and Chelsea looked at each other, then stared back at the wall as the alcove advanced from its cavity. "Told you, you might need me," Chelsea continued. "Only relatives can open these chambers."

"Meaning you might have had a sister," Harris said, glimpsing at the astounded look on her face.

"I usually don't go around sneaking and stealing in church mausoleums," Chelsea said as if she was talking to herself. "To improve in life is to change, and to be perfect is to change often. I needed to know."

Pulling the box fully from the wall, she placed it on the floor in front of her and glanced at Harris as if asking his permission to open it.

Harris nodded at her, then looked about the chamber, spotting two other passageways besides the one they came in. He hadn't checked them, but had a strong feeling they led up to the chapel main floor. Optimistically he thought so far nobody had come and disturbed the few minutes needed to discover their treasure.

He could hear in his Bluetooth Sara and Brian's conversations coming to a conclusion. "If you can, guys, see if you could make it downstairs to the chapel," Harris said, pressing the Bluetooth more to his ear. "We should be tidying up by then."

"Confirmed," they both responded.

Chelsea opened the top of the box and carefully removed the white hand-size Greek style urn. Harris watched her turn the porcelain jar reading the Phoenician inscription.

"Place below the monolith," Chelsea whispered. She stood and so did Harris. She glanced at him again before she opened the top of the urn.

Harris felt like a kid in a candy store. *What's inside? What surprises are in the jar today, Ms. Storekeeper?*

Chelsea tipped the urn over on its side so whatever was inside fell onto her hand. Expecting to see white powdery sand remains, instead a glass key fell in her palm.

"I know what this is," Chelsea said, rattling the key in her hand. She stared at Harris in what he saw as her thinking for a few seconds, watching him take the Bluetooth out of his ear. "The Obelisk Building was originally called The Monolith during its construction. The last few days, before its grand opening, it was changed."

"Is that so? That means—"

"Yes, Matt, back to Nigeria," Chelsea said and closed the urn and put it back into its box. She put the box into its cavity in the wall and watched the green light fade.

"Look at this," she said, taking the iPad from her pocket. She turned it on and found one of the pictures of the Atlas. "The power could only be found by the triangular trading system."

"That's right," Harris said. "The manufacture of slaves and raw materials between Africa, the Americas, and Europe. Just as your towers in the Americas, this crypt here in Eng—"

Harris saw the Glock G22 with some kind of attachments to it creep from behind Chelsea's head. He first thought it was Brian, but since when did he have attachments to his gun? Then he saw the clean cut man step into view. The man maybe came from one of the passages leading to the chapel main floor. Maybe he'd been hiding in the shadows of the room all along. How the man managed to skip the police back in the States and make it here so quickly told Harris he was definitely a Company agent.

He was far from covered in gray ash since the last time they met. He saw his expressionless face clearly for the first time. In a pristine auburn shirt with black tie and suit jacket, the man was well groomed. His straight russet hair was as spruced as could be, and black leather gloves held the Glock firm.

The man must have followed us. How did he know where to find us? Harris wondered. I have the upper hand for now he thought, he'll soon be outnumbered. Come on, Brian, Sara, hurry up.

CHAPTER 25

WHEN CHELSEA TURNED AND SAW THE GUN, she quivered in what Harris saw as panic. Hyperventilating, she eased back, retreating toward Harris holding the iPad nervously to her chest like a child not wanting to give up her candy. He glimpsed at her casually without thinking slip the key into her pocket. He hoped, and yes he had to use the word hope this time, that the well-mannered man didn't see.

"Normally," the man spoke, "we wouldn't say our names out loud, *Matthew Roger Harris,* but this isn't a normal situation, is it?" He spoke properly, sounding every syllable Harris discerned.

Many things flashed in his brain. *The guy knew my true full name. It was tangible he was a Langley assassin, on a mission, a killer like me.* Harris put his hands into the air and Chelsea followed.

"I never wanted it this way." The man continued gazing at Harris, holding his gun in his face. "Agent versus agent. Ms. Chelsea, hand me the iPad and this will be over. Matthew, I need you to hand over your weapons. Slowly."

"We all know this isn't going to end well," Harris said, leisurely going for his shoulder holster. "Field assassins never leave a stone unturned."

"It won't end well for you," the man responded.

"Neither you," a familiar voice said, echoing in the chamber.

Sara came from one of the passageways aiming her P22 at the man's head.

"We have new orders," the man said, keeping his gun and eye on Harris. "We can call Director Grass and straighten this out."

"Yes," Sara said, moving closer toward the man. "We'll straighten this all out, by first you dropping that gun."

Sara, you're moving in to close, Harris shouted in his conscience and wanted to scream it out loud. Her lack of skill as a field agent was showing, and in this profession it could get her—

It was too late to warn Sara, Harris knew, and too late to take out his gun and shoot the man; the man was too quick. Harris saw his young self in the man and knew he had to make a move swiftly and control the situation.

The man grabbed Sara's arm and firing hand, bringing her toward him and at the same time he knocked her gun away for it to slide across the floor far behind them.

It was his opportunity to make his move, Harris perceived, his only opportunity.

No! Harris's mind howled emphatically, and he dove onto the man, but again it was too late. Everything moved in slow motion, including his lunge.

He imagined being submerged in a pool and trying to jump on his enemy. The bullet, leaving the gun, as if under water, seemed to travel in the same fashion.

The man shot Sara.

Before Harris leaped onto his assailant, the attacker twisted Sara's arm in his arm, making her cry out in pain. The man had put his gun to her temple and without hesitation fired, silencing her yell and splattering trickles of blood on his face and jacket. The echo of the gun blast seemed to continually ring in Harris's ears.

Before Sara's body dropped, Harris tackled the man, slamming him into the back plaque wall.

Chelsea screamed as Sara lay still on the floor, blood pooling around her head.

The man's gun was also knocked away over Harris's shoulder to glide near Chelsea's feet. Harris glimpsed Chelsea back away to the opposite wall using her left hand to half cover her eyes with the iPad. She used her other hand to cover her mouth, composing gagging sounds.

Harris knew Chelsea couldn't bear to see Sara's skull fragments with gray matter smeared on the walls and floor. He concluded she wasn't going to be much help in this fight if she hadn't run away already. He felt she would be in her right mind to do so.

For five seconds Harris and the man were in accord, blocking each others strikes. Punches, kicks, ducking, bobbing, and weaving were equally executed until the man caught Harris more than once. He punched Harris in the stomach, then started to break his arm, but Harris managed to wiggle free. He kicked Harris in the leg, just missing his kneecap. He then bear-hug-lifted Harris and slammed him onto the floor.

The man punched down on Harris repeatedly, bloodying his nose, lips, and the side of his right eye. As the man held onto Harris's shirt with his left hand and balled up his right hand in a fist to punch Harris again, he heard the click from the hammer of a gun—his gun.

"Please, stop," Chelsea said, holding the Glock with both hands shaking in the man's face. She followed the man's head as he rose erect, his hands in the air.

"Ms. Chelsea," the man said, breathing heavily. "However do you know about guns?"

"Enough to stop you from doing this."

"Think again," the man said, showing an emotionless face once more. "Think again."

There was another click of a hammer from a gun. Chelsea showed an expression of perplexity as she saw one more Glock pointed at her.

Harris wobbled to his feet, gauging the situation.

The man put his hands down and smiled.

"Brian, what the hell are you doing?" Harris asked.

"Country first, my friend," Brian said to Harris, then looked at Chelsea. "Hand it over real easy like."

Chelsea handed Brian the gun as if she was relieved to do so, and he slipped it into his shoulder holster.

Still pointing his gun at her, he demanded, "now give me the iPad."

Chelsea went into her pocket and handed him the iPad, and he put it into his pocket.

"You had plenty of time to give The Agency that map," Harris said, then asked, "why now?"

"I was going to do it at the safe house," Brian answered. "But we all know how that ended. Didn't know its importance then. Could have been a bunch of smoke and mirrors, until your discovery today." Brian looked at Chelsea again. "You're going to have to hand over that key, too, honey."

"Was Sara's life worth this, Brian?" Harris asked. "One of our own? Did Grass put you up to this and didn't tell Sara?" Harris watched the smirking man he fought move toward Brian, to retrieve his gun and prize. "A house divided can't stand."

"You know the code, ol'boy; the sacrifice of one to save many," Brian retorted. "Or maybe two."

Harris knew his life was over if that assassin agent got to Brian and retrieved his weapon. Harris recognized he had a better chance at living by beating Brian and taking those guns. Harris grasped the assassin knew it, too, and he made his move. As he pounced onto Brian, in his peripheral vision he saw the assassin double back to look for Sara's gun.

Brian fired his gun and Harris felt a sharp sting in his left shoulder. He was used to the burning sensation of a bullet; he'd felt it many times before in his arm, leg, and lower back. He'd been waiting a long time to beat the crap out of Brian so it was easy to ignore the pain.

Harris slammed into Brian, crashing him into the wall. As Brian lost his gun and became dazed, Harris spoke softly in his ear, "Punk." He elbowed him in the chin, knocking him unconscious. Harris then grabbed Chelsea's arm. "Let go!"

A bullet smashed next to them into the floor, throwing stone fragments everywhere. They raced into one of the hallways and up some stairs leading to the main chapel.

"What about the iPad?" Chelsea blurted out in a full dash skipping up two steps at a time.

Two more projectiles shattered the ancient walls behind them. Harris could hear the firing of two different guns. The man was quick, Harris identified, a lot faster than he ever was. This assassin had already made it to Brian and was firing Sara's gun and his own Glock 22.

"Keep moving," Harris responded to Chelsea as they made it to the top of the staircase and into an assembly hall.

Wincing, he took out his gun and placed it by his side as he and Chelsea ran past aisles of pews.

Taking his gun from his left shoulder holster released pins of pain in his shoulder. He could feel the wet warmness of his blood dripping down the side of his blue shirt. He was glad he switched his shirt in the hotel from white.

The church looked interesting; he recognized the Medieval and Roman mixed architecture. He wished he'd have time to really observe.

The twenty elderly people who occupied the pews never paid attention to Chelsea and himself as they ran by. It was amazing the senior citizens never heard the commotion of gunshots and screams downstairs.

Coming out in front of the church brought them to the front of the hospital. Harris couldn't tell if it was the pain in his shoulder making the sun brighter in his imagination to the point of giving him a headache or the sun was actually that bright. He knew he had to find somewhere to recuperate and think up his next move and fast.

"We're in front," Chelsea said timidly and out of breath. "The car is in the back."

"We're not going to the car," Harris said. Hunched over and holding his shoulder with his right hand, they jogged down the next block. "That'll be the first place that guy will attempt a shoot-out with me and I'm in no condition."

"Me neither," Chelsea said, "and I sustained no injuries."

Harris would have laughed if he wasn't in so much pain. "We're getting a hackney," he said. "We need to find a hotel outside this city and reevaluate our situation."

"That's an understatement," Chelsea said, looking at him up and down. "I think you should go to the hospital; the authorities need to be involved. Bobbies will soon be all over that chapel."

"You don't get it, do you? These people don't play by the rules. They *are* the rule. You're familiar on how governments work."

He knew Chelsea understood by her impassive reaction. He put away his gun and wiped blood from his face the best way he could with his shirt sleeves.

Chelsea shook her head sorrowfully, so he figured he didn't do a good job cleaning himself. Yeah, he weighed, he looked a mess.

He looked back a few times to see if they were followed. It appeared clear. Chelsea then hailed a black cab.

HE paced the room looking through his victims belongings. He checked Harris's laptop to find it was locked. He asked Brian for the laptop password but he didn't know. Wild Mike considered taking the laptop to his organization's hackers but knew Harris would have remotely wiped it clean by the time it reached them.

Matthew was astute, as I figured he would be. The agent also didn't take the rented car that he put a tracking device on before he stepped into the chapel.

He didn't put up much of a fight either, Wild Mike measured, *he wasn't that long into retirement.* Mike wondered why his benefactors had put Harris on such a high pedestal. Though his number one rule was, to never underestimate your opponent, he felt his first real contact with Harris was no sweat.

Mike knew when he retired agents it was always a sneak attack. This agent, Harris, knew it was coming and he barely escaped with his life, his iPad and belonging confiscated. Mike felt in his favor it wasn't a bad first round. It also helped to cross his fingers and knock on wood before going to battle.

"What about the authorities finding Sara's body?" Brian asked Mike in the living room of the Three Abbey Green Hotel. "They'll eventually track her whereabouts here."

"It'll be cleaned up before then," Mike responded. "I need your version story of the map. What's your friend's next move?"

He needed to be five steps ahead of Harris, or six steps would be better. He needed to keep the surprise element alive to make his profession effective.

"First of all, he's not my friend," Brian said, sitting on the couch.

Mike sat in a chair across from him, sat back, and crossed his legs.

"I don't know for sure the whole story," Brian continued. "I don't know if this is going to make sense, but some young dead relative left a key for Nzingha to open, something below a monolith. Matt turned his phone off when I heard Nzingha say she knew what the key was for. How I knew they were talking about a key was right before I tried to control the situation I saw Nzingha slip it into her pocket so that you wouldn't see."

"Where do you think," Mike asked, "or if you had to guess, where would you say this monolith is?"

"Truthfully I have no freaking idea, but if I had to guess, I'd say somewhere in Nigeria."

"Why there?"

"Like I said, it's just a feeling I have. I mean everything seems to point there. The Atlas is from there. Nzingha's father is there. Nzingha had no clue of a blood relative until now. Though Nzingha claims her stepfather knows nothing, like Britons would say, that's a bunch of bollocks. He knows something. *His* map led Nzingha to *her* relative. If she or I wanted to find out about this relative you'd have to ask her stepfather, who's in Nigeria.

"So, what do you plan on telling the director about this mess we've created—"

"Very good," Mike said and took out his Glock 22 with silencer. The gun gave the sound between a cough and sneeze as Mike shot Brian point blank in the forehead.

Some of the back of Brian's head and brains was splattered across the floor behind the couch and on the wall. A perfect quarter size hole smoked in the center of his forehead. His eyes were still open, but rolled back looking up at the ceiling. His head, chin up, was laid back on the couch as if he was praying.

Funny the way some people perish, Mike thought. He uncrossed his legs, sat up, and dropped his gun on the couch next to the body.

He took out his cell phone and dialed a number.

"Wild Mike," a voice said out the phone. "What can I do for ya?"

"Going to need a cleanup asap at the Three Abbey Green hotel, City of Bath," Mike responded into the phone. "Time sensitive because of possible police investigation of fallen agents. Two stars lost, one unreachable, the other here at the hotel."

"I confirm," the voice responded. "Sounds like operation Let God Sort Them Out, dispatching a team now. ETA thirty minutes. Is there anything else?"

"Yes, one more thing. I need an STP on agent Matthew Roger Harris and aliases and Nzingha Chelsea."

"Not a problem, sir," the voice on the phone answered. "That might take some time, though. We're talking forty-five minutes."

It was time he couldn't spare, Mike evaluated, but it was going to have to do. The STP, Satellite Tracking Position or some people in his organization called it Satellite Tracking People, had millions of cell phones to go through to finally pinpoint a single individual's phone. Forty-five minutes he guessed was a pretty good turnaround time. Tracking a rogue agent's many names wasn't easy.

He knew one thing was inevitable at this point. His next stop was somewhere in Nigeria.

CHAPTER 26

CHELSEA ADMITTED TO HERSELF that Harris was the most durable man she'd known personally. She didn't mean in physical strength, but in wits and will. She cherished that in a man; it reminded her of her stepfather.

Harris was beaten, shot, betrayed, and a friend died before his eyes, but he still maintained his composure on what had to be done next. *Let's not forget his stepfather was dying. Now that was a man*, Chelsea ruminated. She knew if this had happened to her she would have vomited and fainted. She expected he was trained in this method of toughness from the Agency. She wondered if he had any true feelings.

And to talk about fainting, she felt like it now. She didn't know if it was because of the traumatic events that had taken place an hour ago or running in the heat. She knew if she didn't find an air-conditioned room soon, the great man she knew Harris was was going to also have to carry her. They both were perspiring to the point of dehydration when they made it to the Holiday Inn in Bristol.

Harris had thrown their cell phones out the black cab window, claiming the assassin agent would track them.

As he gauged his wounds in the hotel, she bought bathroom essentials, bandages, Peroxide, aspirin, and groceries—lots of Gatorade.

Next order of business, using the hotel phone, Chelsea booked a night flight out to Lagos, Nigeria. The Bristol Airport, three miles away, will be crowded, Harris conveyed to her. They'll blend in. Chelsea liked a man who could think under pressure, particularly with a bullet in his shoulder.

She then watched him take bandages, Peroxide, and his Bowie knife, and close the door behind himself in the bathroom. She knew what he was about to do. From the grunting and sometimes occasional shouts it was obvious he was digging in his wound to retrieve the bullet.

After Chelsea turned the air conditioner on full, she grabbed two bottles of Gatorade, opened one, and gulped down the red liquid inside. In a couple of swallows a quarter of the drink was left. She was dying of thirst, she discerned; dehydrated was more like it. Almost all the moisture in her body was gone.

Standing by the bathroom door, she asked, "Do you need any help?"

"Yes …" he said, moaning. "Talk to me … anything." He groaned again behind the door.

"Oh," Chelsea said, not knowing where to start. She knew she had to come up with something to keep his mind from the pain as she heard him grumble. "Um, I'm sorry for the loss of your friend, Sara."

He let out a long whimper.

"Oh, I mean … uh, I'm sorry, I shouldn't have started—"

"No, it's alright," Harris responded. "Losing an operative comes with the territory. She'll be missed and deeply remembered."

"I didn't know her long but, she seemed genuine."

"Who taught you how to hold a gun?" Harris asked.

"My father, a long time ago."

Harris whimpered for a few seconds before replying, "Your father's a good man … he …" He groaned again.

"You sure you don't need help?" she asked, putting her ear to the door, and heard running water.

"Most good fathers teach their daughters defense techniques," Harris said, ignoring her assistance. "Today you were a lifesaver."

"I guess. If you want to call it that."

"So what do you think the key might open?"

"Don't know," Chelsea answered, now leaning on the wall and finishing her first drink. "It's exciting to know I have a relative. I wonder what my father is going to say about this." She heard the running water grow stronger and him mutter in agony.

"I'm done," Harris said. "I got that sucker. It was in there pretty deep. I'm going to take one of your cold showers and try and numb the pain, or at least try and take my mind off it.

"Hey, Nzingha."

"Yeah?"

"Thanks for talking."

"Yeah," Chelsea responded, moved away from the door and sat on the couch. She opened her second Gatorade and drank.

She tried to calm herself, but her mind was racing making the headache she had grow more potent. Despite a condition her doctor called controlled hyperpyrexia, where her temperature stayed at a hundred and nine degrees, she had worries about her recent events.

Who was Lilith Chelsea? Why were agents double-crossing agents? Who would make one of my closest executives backstab me? What was the connection of the Livenal assassin's involvement again? Who helped her fake her death? Did my father know about Lilith?

An obvious picture was beginning to develop. If the United States government was after this Atlas, there must be some kind of truth to the weapon. Lilith possibly could hold the answers to this new solar-powered device.

The clues and Atlas led her to believe, if you find Lilith, she'd find the weapon, perhaps hidden in Pandora's Box. One thing was for sure; everything was pointing to her father—Nigeria.

Chelsea got up, sat at a desk, and turned on the computer. They requested the Internet as part of room service and she checked her stocks, offshore, and FINMA accounts trying to keep her mind at ease. If everything in her life went wrong, she knew finances and physics were always something she could rely on. Those things were second nature, just so simply logical.

When Harris came out the bathroom with just his pants on, she hoped he didn't see her eyes for a split second bulge. Besides his bandaged left shoulder, all she saw was muscles. Tan well-shaped chest, biceps, and six pack abdomen; from years of working out, she figured. She stood to take her shower.

"You look terrible," she said, lying to herself.

He smiled, showing a face of cuts and bruises. "You don't look so hot yourself," he retorted. "Looks like you're about to pass out."

"Yeah, well, that's because I am." She passed him to go into the bathroom.

She lost herself in the cold spray of water. Since she was a little girl her father taught her how to remain calm when she felt disoriented from her high temperature. Her father would put on jazz music and teach her methods of meditation in tai chi, and her headache and nauseating feelings would go away. Many times he had also swayed her to sleep with ancient Zen melodies.

She remembered him once singing a song to her by Billie Holiday, "In my solitude, you haunt me, with dreadful ease, of days gone by."

Smelling the rose-scented Yardley soap, she subconsciously smoothed the suds on her body and meditated in sentiments of energy in life, human values, and self-cultivation. *Female couldn't live without male as light couldn't be without dark. How would I know how great the light was if I weren't in the dark?*

Snagged into this undertaking with Harris, she conjectured she might be in a quandary where she may have to fight for her life. Was she ready for a quest like this?

She at first felt devastated and wanted to vomit when she witnessed Sara's death, but at the same time she felt compelled to become strong. *Only the strong survive, but strength wasn't in muscle nor the most intelligent, but the one who could most adapt to change.* This was all new to her—heart wrenching, but thrilling.

If she had to fight on this mission to stay alive, she felt she had to be sensitive to her opponent and become the center of gravity. The soft and flexible will defeat the hard and strong all the time.

She reflected upon her tai chi ch'uan defense fighting of joint locks, palm strikes, and pushing her enemy away. She would do this fighting in close range, long, and everywhere in between.

Control my breathing, she kept brooding, *and I'll be able to fight for a long time. Control my breathing and I'll be able to, surprising as it may sound, help Matt.* She had come so far and knew she was already in too deep.

Letting the bitter water dance rhythms on her face and body was ever more relaxing as it washed away the soap. Her headache and feeling of nausea slowly crept away.

Stepping out of the tub, she noticed dried bloody tissues in the silver garbage pail and tiny sprinkles of blood around the sink and floor. It almost brought her headache back that this was all real and someone was just murdered in front of her for the first time in her life.

Matt and I were in a real fight for our lives and this was really his blood. Alright, lady, Chelsea whispered. *Don't throw up and piss on yourself just yet. Deal with it. This won't be forever.*

Chelsea came out the bathroom wrapped in two white towels to find Harris at the computer typing. He had his chest covered in a towel, shivering as if *he* just came out of a cold shower.

"I'll lower the AC," Chelsea said, moving to the radiator under the window.

"You can leave it, I know you—"

"It's alright, I'm fine now," she said. She moved the radiator dial from high to low. "You could have cleaned the sink and floor of blood better."

"Sorry about that," Harris said, not looking up from typing. "On the next operation I do on myself I'll try not to make such a mess."

Standing behind Harris at the computer, she saw on the right side of the screen a frail old man coughing in a bed.

"Is that your stepfather?" Chelsea asked.

Harris nodded, then typed more. "I usually talk to him online face to face, but since our supplies have been lost I'm talking to him through a chatroom. I can see him, but he can't see me. This computer doesn't have a webcam."

"Do you think he might be in danger?" Chelsea asked.

"He would know; he was head of the CIA once. Considering his condition, I don't think so; he might not live until tomorrow.

"He told me he went over some old documents he overlooked and wrote down from the late Anthony Burrows website. That site is now down. He said Burrows spoke about the government already working on and storing a solar powered technology at Area 51. To complete this technology, they knew they had to go into Nigeria and spy on Livenal, rumored to have the completion of the technology in a hidden lab.

"I know first-hand, if Livenal had any such weapon, it was long abandoned or moved to different locations."

"I'm afraid to ask how long you've personally been snooping around Livenal," Chelsea said, "or know what else is at Area 51."

Harris smiled at her, then stared at the screen as his stepfather, Taffy, wrote *hurry up, son, time is wasting and time lingers for no one.*

Chelsea stared at the coughing man on the screen and wanted to cry. She hated when people suffered.

Harris typed *I'll have final answers for you in a couple of days. I'll see you soon.*

"I'm finished here if you want to use the computer," Harris said. "I already by remote access crashed my laptop knowing it's in enemy hands now." He grabbed his bottle of water that had been sitting on the desk.

"No, you can turn it off," Chelsea answered and moved toward the kitchen. "Maybe later."

Harris sat on the couch and she washed some green grapes in a bowl in the sink.

"I used my credit card for the flight," she continued. "If they can track our phones, couldn't they track our cards?"

"Yes, but it won't tell our location every single minute of the day like our phones. The time they track our whereabouts by credit card we should be long gone from the area."

Chelsea sat next to Harris on the couch and ate some grapes from her bowl. "Very good, Mr. Matthew Roger Harris."

"You said Mr. Matthew with my full name. What's your beef now, besides our near death experience?"

"Like if that isn't—"

"I told you not to come. I did protect you. You came out alive."

"Scarcely."

"You're welcome."

"So I assume," she changed the subject purposely to tease him, "what we're looking for will be in the basement of the Obelisk Building. Place below the monolith, so the urn said."

"This has to be the final clue," Harris said. "The map said the power could only be found by the triangular trading system.

"Taking slaves to work in the Americas, *you first must pass through the Twin Houses*, like your Impending Towers in Ohio. After slaves labored American products, it was shipped to Europe, *passing through The Mausoleum*, like the key you found here in England in the tomb of a church. Last, after the product of goods was given to Europe, it made trade easy going back into Africa to get more slaves to go back to the Americas. *Ending passing through the eye of a needle*, your stepfather's Obelisk Building in Nigeria. Everything is interconnected, like the Atlas says."

"It's not going to be easy getting into the basement of the Obelisk Building," Chelsea said with worry.

"You let me worry about that," Harris said and smirked. "I have some connections in Nigeria and I got you. Your father owns the building. We're going to walk right through the front door."

"What are you going to do when you find your answers, Matt Roger Harris?" Chelsea asked.

"Take a picture for my father is all, just like I did with the Atlas," Harris said and rumpled his face from the pain in his shoulder from shifting on the couch. "I remember a time when nobody knew my name. The very utterance of it was death. You now knowing my Christian name has definitely sealed my fate of ever being an agent again."

Chelsea smiled and looked down at what his towel didn't obscure, a five-inch scar on the left side of his ripped stomach.

"What happened there?" she asked, lightly touching the scar before he responded. "It looks like it must have been pretty serious some time ago."

"If I tell you that story I'd definitely have to kill you. I could tell you, though, it was a pretty electrifying knife fight."

"Do all your scars have stories?" Chelsea asked, looking into his desert sand eyes that seemed to sparkle; she didn't know why, maybe she was hypnotized for the moment. She saw that he noticed her stare and they simultaneously made themselves more comfortable on the couch.

"Only the scars that hurt," he responded.

She felt her temperature rise again, but this time it didn't come with queasiness or a headache. She would call it a natural high.

"When we get back from this, your father will be my first priority. He'll be cured ... Matt." She moved her head closer to his head, her breathing a little heavier now.

"You're a good person, Nzingha," Harris said. He lightly grabbed her chin, and caressed it. With his thumb he touched her full lips, circling to etch out the shape or feel how soft they were.

They stared into each others eyes for two seconds. In those two seconds she didn't know what she was looking for or waiting for. She just knew excitement rose from the bottom of her abdomen to her head like little sparks of electric currents.

Harris cupped the side of her cheeks and they kissed.

Cold, but his lips were soft. With her eyes nearly closed, she softly bit and pulled his lips and watched his face flinch in pain. She laughed inside. *Oops, sorry; forgot you were just in a ferocious fight.*

She closed her eyes and felt his tongue on her tongue as he moved one of his hands to the back of her head. He moved his hand back and forth through her hair as he pushed her head toward him, his tongue twisting deeper into her mouth. Chewing on each others mouth and tongue, like sucking the pulp out a kiwano melon, Chelsea put her hand on the back of his head, stroking the waves in his short hair.

Chelsea pondered on what was happening, thinking of her desires, putting her passionate needs first. Come back to reality, she thought. This man will never love her the way love should be. *Look at his life and look at mine. He was retired, yes, but do you ever really retire from this? Look at their situation now.*

With the separation of saliva and smacking sound of their mouths, she abruptly stopped the kiss. Opening her eyes, she watched him sit back on the couch painfully and puzzled; the pain from his physical agony, but the puzzlement must have been from her unexpected halt in smooching.

She looked at him not with irritation nor happiness, but with significance. "You can't promise me this isn't going to end."

He sighed and looked away, his eyes darting around everywhere but at her. He took a gulp of his water before responding, "No, I can't."

"You're an honest man, Matt," Chelsea said and looked down at the seams of the couch. "Not many men would have said that at this particular moment."

She was never a spontaneous person, especially when it came to relationships. She knew he must have had all kinds of women on his many missions. He sought after her on one of them and they could have ... *He would consider me an amateur where I literally had three relationships in my lifetime. He could get any woman he wanted; why would he settle for old lame me anyway?*

Harris let her sleep in the bedroom while he took the sofa, claiming the soft bed would only make his agonizing body hurt more. They decided together it would be best to get a little rest before the long flight to Nigeria.

WRAPPED in metal, she handled the cold and hundred mile per hour winds that whipped around her. They had walked many meters over snowdrifts and hills looking for a city. She couldn't tell what type of conurbation, but maybe they were simply looking for civilization.

The clique of travelers were growing inpatient, but she had faith they'd arrive at their destination. Over the next hill she saw the top of a steel tower, maybe twenty, thirty miles in the distance. They were almost home.

Snow fell and lightning flashed, but the cold didn't bother them as they moved in armor shaped like their bodies which made them six feet taller. Their robot-like casings helped them move at a unbelievable pace for the average running human.

Something dinged against her metal body as if she was hit by a wrench. Just her luck, she thought, as she saw the softball size chunk of ice in the snow.

"Run!" Chelsea screamed into the intercom in her suit.

Blessed with the great speed of their machine bodies, they still couldn't escape the hailstorm. The hailstones at first came down like pebbles pelting their metal and the snow packed ground like the rhythm of hard rain. Then came the baseball followed by softball size hailstones that ripped them apart one by one.

They were slaughtered—tortured, for they didn't die right away. After the ice projectiles ripped through the metal cans, the humans were trapped inside with nowhere to go.

A piece of ice slammed into Chelsea's right leg as if she was shot by a rifle buckshot. She screamed as she lay in the snow and ice entangled in metal and wires. Another piece hit her in the arm, then stomach and left leg. The ice then hit her in the same spots again and again.

It felt agonizing as she was being fired upon and her body hadn't gone numb. She screamed and squealed as well as squirmed about, urinating on herself simultaneously. The pain wouldn't subside, bringing her to whimper and cry hysterically. She regurgitated blood ferociously from her mouth and nose unremittingly. The cold seeped in, the awful cold.

Sweating, Chelsea jumped when Harris touched her on the shoulder in her bed.

"Come on, we have to go or we'll miss our flight," Harris said over her in a new clean blue shirt.

"Sure, sure," she said and wiped sweat from her brow. "Just give me a minute to wash my face."

"Okay, but hurry up, we got to go. Are you okay? You were in some deep sleep. I tried to wake you five minutes ago, but you wouldn't budge."

"I'm fine, just need to freshen up is all."

She detested her dreams. She desired to never sleep again.

CHAPTER 27

ARRIVING IN LAGOS NIGERIA two in the morning on Tuesday Harris felt they were making great time, especially for being shot in the shoulder seventeen hours earlier.

He couldn't bring his gun with him on this trip, fearing authorities would ask too many questions. He left his gun in a safe deposit box at the hotel and pulled out a fake ID. He was sure Ezequiel would provide him with the rest of the necessities.

He wasted no time on the commercial airliner explaining his plan to Chelsea. The problem wasn't getting into the building, but more working past a door that was presumably going to be restricted to Chelsea herself. He told her he had ways of manipulating locked doors, just direct him to the one.

Harris loathed disturbing Ezequiel so early in the morning, but he knew Ezequiel would understand he wasn't the type of guy who'd show up during peak hours.

Ezequiel really woke up when he introduced Chelsea to him and she entered his house.

"Wow," Ezequiel said, "thee Ms. Chelsea, the richest woman in the world." He couldn't stop shaking her hand. After a few minutes of being starstruck, Harris brought Ezequiel back to the mission at hand.

Bringing him up to date on their current events, Ezequiel provided him with a black suit jacket, skeleton keys, digital camera, cell phone, and .45. Ezequiel's last task was escorting them to the Obelisk Building in his silver Nissan.

Most of the rainy and gray early morning they waited two blocks from the Obelisk Building rehearsing their A, B, and C plans. Overall the plan was; Harris, escorted by Chelsea, was going to enter the building and head to the basement. As fast as they could, before someone in the security camera room became suspicious, Chelsea was to find the door that the glass key fit.

They were going to have to play it by ear, make it up as they went along. This was his first half-ass, unorthodox mission and he laughed wondering if they'd ever get through the day.

Worst case scenario, we'll get caught by building security and Nzingha would just straighten it out with her father; case closed. He laughed again at their haphazard intentions as 6:00 rolled around. Harris and Chelsea departed the car to begin, in his eyes, this foolish operation.

Ezequiel never stopped smiling at Chelsea, following her with his eyes as she left the car. *Doesn't he know she was far beyond his pay grade?* Harris believed. *But I guess it's okay to dream. Don't worry, buddy, I'm in the same dream,* Harris rationalized, pertaining to getting this job done and courting her.

Harris and Chelsea huddled under the one umbrella Ezequiel provided as rain slammed above them and the pavement.

Trickles of employees started six in the morning entering the Obelisk Building. It was the time Harris decided best to go in instead of eight when the place was bustling with people kicking each other to be first in the elevators. Harris wanted to blend in, but not be in full swing of the morning crowd, just enough to be unsuspicious.

He spotted the Yeside store familiar to him now. After they watched two men in business suits enter the building in the south lobby, Chelsea glanced at Harris and they walked in.

The image Harris figured they portrayed was that he was the bodyguard and she was here on business. There shouldn't be too many questions asked. Keeping a stern and serious demeanor and hiding a black eye with shades should be convincing enough.

There was the Atlas display, *Chart To The Heavens,* glistening in all its glory in the middle of the lobby, Harris noticed. It seemed to radiate in a dreamy sort of way, he surveyed, or did he have a new-found respect for its worth?

Harris observed the two men, using their thumb, touch the turnstile and the waist-high gate let them in.

Chelsea moved with enthusiasm toward the large brown reception desk. The man behind the desk had his head down looking for something as Chelsea and Harris approached. He found what he was looking for and slapped a clipboard on top of the shiny granite counter.

"*Ekaaro, Bawo ni,*" Chelsea said in a Yoruba twang. "I've come to monitor progress with the interns in the basement training rooms—"

"Hello to you, too, madam," the security interrupted her. Not looking up, he searched for something else. "You're going to have to sign in."

"Just have it noted that my escort has a firearm," Chelsea spoke sternly. "And if he still has to sign in, you need to let him through the gate."

When the guard found a pen, he almost dropped it. "Ms. Chelsea … I'm sure … I don't think your security needs to … sorry, Ms. Chelsea."

"It's okay," Chelsea responded, keeping a serious face. "Just need you to open up for him is all." She thumbed at Harris.

"Not a problem, Ms. Chelsea," the guard said, looking for the button. "Again, sorry for your inconvenience." He was all smiles, and Chelsea nodded at him.

The gate automatically opened for Harris, and Chelsea put her thumb on an indicator on the right side of the turnstile, letting herself through.

He glanced up at a memorable vent in the gold celestial designed ceiling above the Atlas. Interesting, he thought; from down here the vent was practically invisible blending in with the architecture of the ceiling.

"What's the need for saying I have a weapon?" Harris whispered as they moved toward the elevators.

"You said we shouldn't appear dubious," Chelsea answered, whispering back. "That's what I would normally say to the front desk. Sometimes my security is checked in, sometimes not."

The elevator came and they entered. Chelsea pressed B3 and as the doors closed they saw a few more people come through the gates. Whatever they were going to do, they were going to have to make it quick. If a building crowded with people wasn't going to be a problem, that assassin agent might be.

"Why the third basement down?" Harris asked.

"Because it's the most restricted area," Chelsea responded, not looking at him, showing her confidence. "I know the other basements too well. The least place I visit is B3. What we're looking for will feasibly be there."

Harris smiled; *you're the lady who knows.*

When the doors opened, they stepped out into a lime-green hallway that seemed to go on forever in both directions. The first thing he noticed was the yellow restricted sign on the wall as he turned right following Chelsea. Next, he noticed dome cameras in the ceiling every twenty feet.

"I'm not saying you don't know where you're going," Harris asked, "but why right?" She seemed to smile at his ignorance without actually smiling, Harris noticed.

"The other way is a long path to the janitor's supply room and an exit stairway. This way is to an out of date data center and two other doors I don't know about."

"Got you," Harris said, following her close.

They passed four overhead cameras. The hallway then curved just enough so if he looked down the hall from the elevator he wouldn't had seen the three doors. Chelsea walked past the first door, then stopped and stared at the other two. All three doors had signs on them, *Restricted Area C-level Authorized Personal Only.*

"I suppose the door we passed must be the server room, eeny?" Harris asked and Chelsea gave a nod. "Leaving us with meeny and miny." Harris moved to the door at the very end of the hall. "I have a feeling about this one."

Chelsea stood over Harris, attempting to block the ceiling camera with her body. He handed her the umbrella, then bent down fiddling with the door using his skeleton keys.

"How long before you open it?" Chelsea asked and folded her arms bear-hugging the umbrella while tapping its long slender end on her leg.

"Give me a second," Harris said and jiggled his key in the lock. In fifteen seconds Harris heard a click and a green light on an indicator box on the wall next to the handle flashed green. He glanced at Chelsea and opened the door.

Lights automatically came on, showing a large conference room. Harris and Chelsea stood in the threshold observing the brown carpet floor, shiny black marble table, leather chairs, and many video conferencing screens built in kingwood paneled walls.

"I've never been here before, but this isn't it," Chelsea said, and they both looked at each other puzzled and turned their heads simultaneously toward the middle door Harris called miny.

Working his master key on the middle door, Chelsea stood the same way, blocking the camera's sight with her body. Harris worked on the door, opening it in the same manner as the other. In fifteen seconds a green light near the knob flashed, unlocking the door.

Instantly lights from above brightened a twenty foot long hallway. As they stepped past the entrance, Chelsea let the door behind them shut. Harris looked at her and she nodded for him to continue. He took the gesture as to say this had to be the place they were looking for.

Walking down the hall, he felt a surge of eagerness for somehow he knew this was the place, too, without saying it was.

At the end of the hall it opened into a huge chamber. Harris looked at Chelsea, not sure if he himself was amazed or not. His face must have looked wedged between puzzlement and astonishment. She nodded at him again as to say it was alright to feel confused for she was, too.

"Surely never been in this part of the building," Chelsea said, her voice echoed.

The hall had put them in the middle of a chamber that went left and right for about eighty feet. Every square patterned panel in the forty foot high ceiling lit up, making the place as bright as a clear summer day. The sand and lion-colored granite walls and floors would have shined like a mirror if it weren't for a light film of dust. The grime exposed their footprints as they walked about.

The things that did twinkle bright and warrant most of their attention were six round chrome safe doors as large as the Big Ben clock face in London. Three vault doors were to the left of them and three on their right.

He felt like Alice in *Alice in Wonderland* when she drank the contents of a bottle labeled *Drink Me.*

They both walked up to one of the behemoth glittering metallic doors of a safe. With their heads cocked back, they not only marveled at its size, but the size of the chamber around them.

Okay, Harris visualized, and took off his shades, let's get down to business before someone realizes they shouldn't be here and crashes the party.

"Your father sure knows how to store his loot," Harris said, and Chelsea gave him a sinister look. "Just kidding, just kidding."

On the left bottom side of each safe was a keypad, inscription, and keyhole. He saw that Chelsea noticed it, too, and took out the glass key they found a day ago from her back pocket.

"It looks like it fits," Chelsea spoke. "You think it works for all the safes?"

"Who knows," Harris said scrutinizing words and numbers etched in the wall. "Let's start with this." He read out loud. "Genesis, one, twenty-eight. I know a little scripture, but I'm not that good in reciting chapters and verses."

"I'm no priest," Chelsea avowed, "but Genesis one, twenty-eight is basically about God's creation of the world and man." She moved to the next safe to their left. "This one says Ezekiel, one, four. About the vision of a wheel in the sky Ezekiel saw."

"For someone who doesn't believe you sure know—"

"You have to study a conviction, before condemning."

"I say put the key into all of them and see which one opens," Harris spoke, backing up to get a better picture of the vaults.

"We might not have to," Chelsea said and waved him over to the last safe on the left.

As he approached the safe and read the inscription, he shrugged. "What does any of this mean?"

Chelsea gave him a serious peculiar look, the look his stepfather would give, like *you're stupid*. She then, without saying a word, effortlessly jabbed the glass key into the hole and turned.

The sound of turning mechanisms could be heard. Adding to the noise was the squeal of gears unlocking, with the harmonious click of latches opening like many briefcases but only amplified ten times louder.

Harris opened his mouth in amazement. *What did the wall say again? Isaiah 34:14.* "What does that mean?" he asked himself aloud, barely realizing Chelsea heard.

"I realized Isaiah thirty-four, fourteen from watching the *History Channel*," Chelsea replied. "I learned Lilith in the book of Isaiah is depicted by some scholars as a night creature or owl."

They backed up as the vault began to open. The safe door unbolted, swung far and wide with the hiss of air escaping.

Peculiar, he acknowledged. When the door opened a fracture, he saw dust in swarms puff out, then, as if rewinding a DVD on playback, some of it was sucked back into the room. Some kind of HVAC, air purifier, he presumed.

The considerable heavy hatch silently opened for a minute, then stopped, showing a full round hole of gloom the same size as its door. They walked up to the gap and peered inside.

Chelsea nudged her head toward the glass key as it dissolved into the keyhole. The bow of it quivered, then shattered into pieces, raining crystal tears onto the floor.

"Only to be used once," Harris said, standing at the entrance. "The keyhole ate the key. Do you want to go in first?"

Chelsea stuck her head inside the dark, then pulled back and shook her head no.

"Ah, scaredy-cat," Harris said and motioned that he was going to climb in. He looked at Chelsea with an anxious grin and retracted, thinking better of his actions.

"Let me see the umbrella," Harris demanded with his hand out. She handed it to him and he raised the umbrella to his face—his smirk widened.

Chelsea met his smile. "I like a man who can think," she said.

Harris figured the double canopy *GustBuster*; open, a diameter of 68 inches, closed, the five foot long umbrella should set off any trap inside. He *hoped,* and he used that word sparingly, but this time actually meant it, that the umbrella might save him. *That extra four-inch aluminum spike at the end should account for something.*

He pushed the full umbrella into the night of the maw before them. Waving the umbrella around, it touched nothing but air. Reaching in more, making the umbrella an extension of his arm, he waited for a motion detector to trigger a trap and slice the umbrella in half—or something. Something did happen, making him immediately contract his arm as if he touched a hot stove.

The lights flickered on.

"Scaredy-cat," Chelsea said, and they both gazed into the chamber.

Light stretched along the ridges of the ceiling and seams of the floor. It brightened a cube-shaped room embellished in square bronze tiled walls, floor, and ceiling.

In the center sat a four meter high brass structure he couldn't quite describe right away. At first gaze it looked like a brass replica of the crystal ship the infant Kal-El traveled in to get to earth from Krypton in the 1978 *Superman* movie.

To study the object with more observing eyes, it was a three dimensional hexagon with a bunch of triangles of all sizes interconnected perfectly attached within.

He remembered in college it was called a birectified 5-simplex. This whole sculpture was tilted sideways, balanced from growing out of the floor by one of its points. In the center, protected by the triangle shapes, was a four-foot Greek style ancient clay jar incased in glass.

This could only be one thing, Harris considered. He saw it on Chelsea's face, too, her admiration. The clay jar had to be Pandora's Box. In the story of the eighth century Greek poet Hesiod's, *Theogony* and *Works and Days,* a woman who was hypothetical to be Pandora, opens a jar. Centuries later, the word *jar* was translated into box.

Tapping the umbrella across the floor like a blind man, he was looking for more traps. He then walked in. Chelsea followed and they examined the room. Staring at the walls, Harris noticed they were littered vertically with embossed hieroglyphs and Phoenician writings.

Chelsea read some of them out loud. "To create an evil that cannot be undone. A beautiful evil, God's gift to man. Only hope was left within her unbreakable house, she remained under the lip of the jar and did not fly away. It is not possible to escape the mind of God.

"The walls seem to be full of the poet Hesiod's poems, written in Greek and Egyptian hieroglyphics."

"What does this say?" Harris asked, standing in front of the odd shaped structure in the middle of the room.

Chelsea moved from the wall to stand next to Harris. Following his stare, she saw the small metallic seal on the floor in front of the configuration.

"It says, pithos; Greek, for jar." Chelsea looked at the abstract object before her. "The object the jar is in is called an octacube, also called a twenty-four cell. It's a puzzle like construction. I've seen drawings and small mock-ups of cubes like this, but I've never seen one built before with such detail."

"I, too, have seen simple drawings of this, but it's the first time I ever saw such a thing built," Harris spoke. "Remarkable. Your father has some fancy secrets."

"Indeed he does," Chelsea said as they both circled the octacube. "I'm almost afraid to dig in his back yard for what I might find."

He perceived the octacube differently from the side. Replicating optical art, the structure seemed to change into a different shape from its sides. The side of the octacube resembled magnetic field lines of the sun. *Most people would recognize it as the sun's corona. What the hell is this?* Harris pondered. Something was hidden here, something … He touched one of the crossbars of the cube. It had the feel of smooth cold metal.

His mind was racing now. Cryptographies of this quest formed in his thoughts, crashing at him all at once; stories of an alien presence—clues leading them to Europe and Africa, the triangular trading system, The Atlas, Lilith Chelsea, Pandora—all this to discover a hidden solar weapon. Harris marveled at this, figuring something big was about to happen or had happened.

To observe all this, from a man on vacation's perspective, was a bit much to take in, but extraordinary. He had no purpose, no mission, just purely observational. It was almost like meditating—sitting back in a comfortable seat with his head back in a planetarium staring into a canopy of stars and planets in total darkness.

"Come, I want you to look at something," Harris said, grabbing Chelsea's warm hand. She looked at him strangely as if he shouldn't have grasped her hand, but he overlooked it; he was too excited. He showed her the side of the octacube, then directed her back to the front. "Neat, huh?"

"I'd have to say peculiar, yes," Chelsea said, taking her hand back. "The front looks like a hexagon with triangles, but on the sides the triangles seem to turn into what the sun looks like during an eclipse. Like fire dancing on the sun's surface."

Eloquently put, Harris imagined, like fire dancing on the sun.

"What should we do?" Chelsea asked, but he knew that she knew she shouldn't have asked. "Should we ... no-way we could open that jar."

"You think we should? I think we should, but first." Harris took out his camera and started taking pictures. After he finished snapping twenty pictures at different angles of the configuration, he walked around the room. "How do you think we can get it out of there? There most be a mechanism to trigger its release."

Chelsea joined him in looking around at the walls. "I don't know about this," she said.

"You know these symbols. What do they say?"

"I don't see anything about releasing a jar," Chelsea answered, moving her head up and down trying to read the inscriptions quickly. "All gifted ... all giving," Chelsea read out loud.

Oh, hell, Harris deliberated and moved away from the wall to stand in front of the octacube. Leaving Chelsea to search the walls, he brought the umbrella up and eased it into the design. He imagined trying to guide a needle into a cluster of enormous nerve cells. He wanted to tap the glass to see how thick it was.

He heard a click and withdrew the umbrella; he was scared again, he guessed. Well, at least Chelsea didn't see his anxiety this time as she occupied herself with the hieroglyphs. He must have triggered a motion detector, though no deathtrap was released to kill him. Instead, the glass encasing the jar slowly contracted into the brass obtuse triangles.

"Psst," Harris uttered to Chelsea, like if he called her name he would ruin the dynamics of what was happening.

She heard and right away turned from the wall and moved to stand next to him. "What have you done?" she asked, whispering as if she, too, didn't want to spoil what was happening.

The glass dissipated into the frames, leaving the jar exposed on an alloy platform.

Harris took the umbrella and poked it back in past the triangles. He leaned in more, placing the pointed tip of the umbrella on the pot. Nothing happened so far. He then leaned in with his left arm, reaching for the lid of the vessel.

"Careful," Chelsea said. She grabbed one of his back pants pockets, helping to balance him as he made his slow dive into the cube. Cute, he thought; they looked like two little kids helping each other steal their father's cookies high up on a shelf in a jar.

He could see the pot's engraved depictions of a woman kneeling, holding up a jar over her head with fire shooting out of it. Another illustration was of a flying horse-like creature with a lion's head. His left hand finally touched the lid. This could be a trap, he thought, but he didn't come all this way for nothing.

Surprisingly the lid easily came off and he placed it with care on the side of the pot. He was sweating, struggling from the weight of the lid, making sure it didn't fall between the brass frames.

He glanced back at Chelsea, and she acknowledged him in a go-ahead way. *You look into the jar because I'm not.* She'll be an accessory to the crime, but not actually do it, Harris figured.

The first thing that hit him was the smell. It wasn't strong, but he'd smelled it before—the rank smell of week-old rotting steak, the smell of death.

He peeked back at Chelsea, who noticed the stench, too, and rumpled her nose. The second thing that hit him was what he saw. Half of his body inside the cube and moving his head over the crest of the jar, he saw the top of a beige and tan colored adult-size skull. Inching in more, he witnessed the entire skeletal remains.

The skeleton was in a fetal position with its hands crossed on its chest. The last thing that hit him was the brown rolled up scroll on the lap of the skeleton. Dipping his hand into the jar, he went for it, then heard another click.

"What are you …" Chelsea continued to whisper.

Harris removed his hand and in his nervousness, falling off balance, he had to grab something. He missed grabbing the scroll and ripped half the index finger from the carcass while grabbing the side of the jar. He shrugged in his moment of confusion, palmed the half digit and contracted himself from the construction as the glass casing spontaneously, like a Venus fly trap, closed around the jar.

"What did you do?" Chelsea asked, matching his tenseness.

"I tried to grab …" He was going to explain to her the whole situation about the skeleton and the finger, but thought against it when the room changed color.

The lights in the room turned blue. In the left corner a hologram flickered on, showing a cluster of stars.

Traces of Chelsea's ambient technology were all over the place, Harris realized. It *was* her father's establishment.

When Chelsea and he moved closer to the hologram, he noticed the Cygnus constellation. The floating image then showed six planets circling a star. The second planet from the star was labeled Kepler-22b.

In the next instant everything happened in accord. The deathtrap Harris had hoped not to spring was sprung. The hologram sputtered off, blue flames shot out of the jar in the center of the octacube, and the vault door began to close.

"I think this would be a great time to abandon our curiosities," Harris said, put the finger into his back pocket, and grabbed Chelsea's hand.

Chelsea held Harris's hand tightly, not flinching in objection in any way. They exited the vault just in time for it to slam shut, resonating a clanging sound throughout the hall. The sound of mechanisms locking echoed in the well-lit chamber of safes.

CHAPTER 28

"WHAT DID YOU SEE?" Chelsea asked. "There was a foul smell when you opened the jar."

"Skeletal remains of someone," Harris responded. "Most likely—"

"Lilith; Lilith Chelsea," Chelsea interrupted and stared at the floor as if pondering.

"We won't know for sure, but that scroll on the skeleton's lap might have told us something."

"Scroll? There was a scroll?"

Harris nodded. It was burnt now, Harris knew, and locked behind that door. *Her father was hiding something.* He was about to tell her about the finger he accidently confiscated when he heard the voices.

It was too late to hide out of view from the new visitors. Harris was too amazed about their situation, too lax, and too engaged in trying to explain to Chelsea what he saw in the jar.

Five building security guards and one female guard with sunglasses and black cap finally crashed his party. The guards raised their weapons, what Harris saw as police issued X26 Tasers.

"Sir, step away from her," one guard said, pointing his Taser toward Harris.

"Madame Chelsea, please step away from him," another guard said, also pointing a Taser gun at Harris.

"Guys, it's alright, I ..." Chelsea tried to explain.

Two of the guards right away grabbed Chelsea by the shoulders and pulled her toward their circle.

"Easy, guys," Harris said with his hands in the air. "I'm with her. Listen to what Ms. Chelsea has to say for a minute."

"Place that umbrella on the floor," one of the guards said, approaching him.

"No, they don't have to listen to what Ms. Chelsea has to say," the female guard spoke and took off her shades.

You, again, Harris exclaimed in thought. He right away knew who the Asian, African, but most likely Filipino woman was—Suraksha. Things just went from bad to worse real quickly, Harris presumed. That would be two burning buildings she escaped from.

"Guys, I said it's okay," Chelsea shouted in a stern voice. "He's with me."

"No, he's not," Suraksha said, also in a firm tone. "He still works for the CIA. Once an agent, always an agent. He's come to steal something from these safes."

"You can't be serious —" Chelsea responded.

"Oh, but I am," Suraksha said. "He can't take the thing with him, so he's just taken pictures of it like he did with the Atlas, to give to his agency."

"For his sick …" Chelsea retorted. "Who the hell are you to talk … murderer. Who do you work for? Do you work for my father?"

"Guys." Suraksha snapped her fingers for one of the guards to restrain Harris. "Who I work for doesn't matter. You believe this agent whose life is dedicated to the C—I—A?" She pronounced CIA aggravatingly slow.

"Wait a minute," Harris said and went into his jacket pocket.

The one guard next to him tense, moved the Taser closer to Harris, but stopped when he saw the digital camera in his hand. "Here, I don't need the pictures." Harris bent down and slid the camera across the floor for it to stop at the guard's feet.

Suraksha right away stomped on the camera with the heel of her boot, smashing it, the crunching sound echoing. Suraksha shook her head disappointingly. "Surely you can do better than that," she said. "The images will be on your mind for the asking of your colleagues.

"Hand over your weapon. You'll be detained by the SMB as a spy, Mr. Agent."

So you work for the Nigerian Secret Brigade. Harris figured as much. *No wonder you're so good in deception tactics.*

When I meant things went bad to worse was just an understatement, Harris measured. He saw and knew Chelsea recognized it, too. One of the guards who lifted his head wasn't who they perceived him to be.

The well groomed man from the Oasis Club and columbarium in England was dressed in black pants and suit jacket like the building security; the assassin.

"Ms. Chelsea, we'll handle this situation," Mike said with his chin tucked in and head hung low. When he went to grab Chelsea, she had thrown another guard in his path.

"You stay away from me!" Chelsea shouted and looked at the other three guards, who already surrounded her. "Guys, this man is not one of you. He's an imposter."

"Sir," one of the guards standing next to Chelsea asked Mike, "Let me see your security pass, again."

Mike answered the man by jabbing his Taser into the guard's chest.

Shit! All hell just broke loose, Harris understood. He had to make a move. His first priority was to try and get Chelsea away from the assassin agent.

Suraksha wasn't the immediate threat, for he knew she wasn't here to harm Chelsea; she was, though, here to harm him, no doubt. He'd like to call this his plan B escape route.

He slapped the guard next to him in the face with his umbrella and leg-swept him onto the floor. The guard was more stunned than hurt, Harris knew, from the way he hit him. He dropped him so it would clear a way to Chelsea.

Suraksha wasn't as slow as the guard, though. *Damn,* Harris contemplated. He knew Suraksha hadn't spotted the commotion of Chelsea's security guards getting their asses kicked, moving the agent closer and closer to his target as Chelsea retreated. *Suraksha was too focused on me and already had her bamboo blades out and swinging. She moved too swiftly for me to reach into my shoulder holster for my gun. All I have is this damn umbrella.*

He blocked her strikes, high then low, to the left then right in succession. Harris managed to knock one of her sticks onto the floor. She followed up using her right leg in a roundhouse high-kick to his face.

The fight was over that fast. It might have surprised her; the fight was that simple, Harris thought, and he fell backwards to the floor. Little did she know his shoulder was not only hurting him, but that kick in the face seemed to only make it worse. Losing his umbrella, it reeled across the floor.

The assassin agent was working on the last guard before making his way to Chelsea. Harris noticed Suraksha grasped the situation. Good, Harris thought, the enemy of my enemy is my friend for right now.

Suraksha gave Harris an ominous glimpse from cold azure eyes. It was the kind of look, *like you better not get up.*

One guard was knocked out, sprawled across the floor. Another was squirming away from Mike with one good arm, screaming. Mike had broken both the guards' legs and left arm. The last guard by Chelsea's side just lost his Taser and a couple of teeth from a few of Mike's hand strikes. With a leg sweep and help from a punch in the chest the man went down in front of Mike, too.

Suraksha kicked Mike in the back. He fell forward in a clumsy way past Chelsea, tumbled, and got back on his feet. Mike faced Suraksha, both of them in a fighting stance.

Chelsea moved toward Harris to be stopped by the now standing guard Harris had slapped onto the floor.

"Madame, I was given strict orders for you not to go near this man," the guard said, blocking her way. "The Nigerian Police Force will be here soon."

"By whom?" Chelsea asked.

"By the highest—"

"He's right, Nzingha," Harris said, wincing as he staggered to a sitting position. "You shouldn't be around me. Get outta here!"

Throwing a side fist, Suraksha connected with Mike's face, but he wasn't fazed. Her many kicks were blocked and her remaining bamboo stick was confiscated. Mike, with her baton, bashed Suraksha across the face hard enough to whack her hat off, knocking her to the floor to join the rest of the guards in agony.

It was too late for him to make a move; the assassin was too swift, Harris thought. The agent jumped on the remaining standing guard, tackling him to the floor.

"Nzingha, go!" Harris shouted. "I'll handle this!" He pulled out his .45 pistol.

When he noticed she saw the gun, Chelsea moved to the ingress in the hallway, the exit of this chamber of safes. Harris liked to call it the chamber of hell.

"Matt, I can't just …" Chelsea said, standing by the threshold holding onto the wall. For the first time it looked like she cared for him, Harris sensed.

As Mike wrestled with the guard, Harris staggered to his feet. He pointed his gun at Mike's back while he punched the guard continuously into a bloody pulp.

"Alright, Mr., put your hands–" Harris said, but was caught off guard by Mike's back-leg-sweep. He was good; he really was good, Harris distinguished. *The assassin must have seen me in his peripheral vision.*

Harris felt, in his prime, he was never that agile and strong enough to take out a room full of security and two expert martial artists. Well, he considered himself as half a martial artist considering he was shot in the shoulder and supposed to be on vacation for the last two years.

With the back-leg-sweep, Mike swung like a figure skater in a whirlwind, knocking Harris back onto the floor onto his back. *Damn, my shoulder; it has to be bleeding again.*

Mike grabbed one of Suraksha's sticks and slapped Harris's pistol out of his hand. When he attempted to strike him again, Harris used his side and armpit to blunt the blow. He then ripped the stick from Mike, gripping it with his armpit and hand, and knocked it away from them both for it to clatter along the floor. Damn, I needed that, Harris discerned.

Mike put a knee in Harris's chest. He grimaced in pain, not so much from the knee, but from his shoulder that had been throbbing since these squabbles began. Then there was the umbrella his head happened to land on when the assassin toppled him. *If my situation wasn't aggravating enough, faith had to land me here on top of this stupid umbrella.*

"It's about time you stay down," Mike the assassin said through clenched teeth. Mike took out his Glock, aiming it in Harris's face at point blank range.

With the actions of a desperate man, Harris grabbed anything. He happened to grab for the umbrella and hit Mike in the shoulder with it in an attempt not to give his opponent such precise aim. The umbrella fell back to his right side on the floor and opened up like a huge sturdy parachute with no purpose. *Freaking umbrella*, Harris screamed in thought, *it'll undeniably be the death of me, or …*

Mike, if he had any expression at all, it was a smirk. "Bad luck to open an umbrella inside," Mike said. "Doesn't look like luck is on your side today."

Harris had to think rapidly. *Brains over brawn and agility.* He chewed over what Chelsea said to him not too long ago. She said she liked a man who could think. *The assassin agent was quick, yes but it was what he did with his quickness now that was going to count.*

Harris did it in one motion. He held the assassin's right wrist firing hand with his left hand and simultaneously with his free hand pressed the button to close the umbrella and jabbed that four inch aluminum spike at the end into the right side of the assassin's neck.

He made sure he plunged the barb directly into his carotid artery, under the chin at the right side of the windpipe and out the side of his neck. Bull's-eye, Harris thought, then spoke, "What about the lucky closed umbrella?"

Mike's surprised face quivered and mouth gaped as he dropped his gun and fell to Harris's side. He grabbed his neck in a frantic attempt to stop his blood from spraying when the point came out. He tried to grasp his neck tighter as blood started to ooze and creep through his fingers from all directions. It was like trying to plug an overpowering hole in a dam.

Harris felt he had to pat himself on the back. *That assassin should be admiring me now; brains over brawn. I missed the obvious jugular vein and went straight for the carotid artery—yeah, with that stupid umbrella.*

Harris, on the floor in a sitting position, painfully crawled away from his adversary, who was making gurgling sounds with blood materializing around his head.

The assassin was experiencing hypovolemic shock and will soon fade from life, Harris thought. He was about to reach for his .45 when a shadow cast over him.

Suraksha, with her long hair up in a bun, looked young and attractive to him for a second, but the scowl on her face said this fight wasn't over.

There was no chance for me to get my hand on that gun before she was to make her move. My new lucky umbrella wasn't going to do much in this situation either. She advanced toward him with one of her batons in her hand—*shit!*

Harris heard a thud, and Suraksha froze in her tracks, then shook. It was like she got shot and didn't know it. Her brain wanted her to come forward, but her body just said no.

Harris saw Chelsea still at the hallway opening with a weird shocked look on her face.

Mike's body gave one good shake, then his hands went slack still around his own throat.

So what happened to Suraksha? Who's left? Who wants to take a shot at me next? Harris watched Suraksha drop to the floor in a heap.

Ezequiel stood where Suraksha once was with one of her bamboo rods in his hand. He was in his fake mustache disguise. *Wasn't he a sight for sore eyes? Saved by him again.*

Harris smiled as Ezequiel held his hand out. Harris picked up his gun, holstered it, and grabbed Ezequiel's hand as he lifted him to his feet. He hunched over, wincing in pain, and grabbed his shoulder.

"It feels like I've been on that floor forever getting my ass handed to me," Harris spoke.

"Yeah, well, lucky Nzingha recognized me and let me in or it would have been handed to ya," Ezequiel said with seriousness. "More trouble is coming our way. Two NPF vehicles are out front right now, no doubt waiting for backup."

Harris glanced back at Mike one last time. He was skillful, Harris recognized, but today luck wasn't on his side.

Harris put a philosophy together for himself, giving hope respect, just for today. *Hope in the face of luck is a better result from my work toward future things to come because one day or another my luck is going to run out.*

Harris walked to Chelsea, who stared at the carnage behind them.

"You know I can't stay with you when authorities arrive," Harris said. Flinching at first, he lightly touched her under her soft chin with his index finger. "I wouldn't suggest you running off with me either."

Chelsea stared at him to where he could see emerald specks in the iris of her dark green eyes. That second they stared at each other seemed like many minutes to Harris.

Her facial expression illustrated concern. He could see it in the center of her head between her thin eyebrows, the way her forehead almost creased together. She had a look, like they weren't going to see each other again or she was going to cry for all that has happened was too much for her. He couldn't yet determine which.

"I've no reason to run," Chelsea said, glancing again back at the devastation behind them. "Yes, they'll see you as a spy." She spoke as if she read his mind; for he couldn't have said it better himself.

Harris gave Chelsea a big smile figuring, she'll be alright; her father will take good care of her.

He kissed her on her warm forehead. "Thanks for a good ride, lady. I'll hopefully see you in the States," Harris said, and a smile developed on her face. Good, he considered, he would have liked to kiss her on the lips, but he knew it wasn't the right place. He was far too hurt and far too out of time. It was time for a plan C retreat strategy.

"Come on, man," Ezequiel said nervously. "We have to go. There's a back exit on the other side of the hall."

Harris could feel Chelsea's stare burning onto his back, like receiving a tattoo, as he hastily withdrew.

CHAPTER 29

THIS IS WHERE HOPE SHITS ON ME AGAIN. *Taffy had drifted off into a coma while I was off on possibly the end of this little venture.*

After picking up his car in the wee hours at the airport in Cincinnati, ten hours later he found himself standing over Taffy for twenty minutes contemplating. Over and over again he rotated the brownish-gray bone in his hand.

The man in front of Harris asleep in his hospital bed with intravenous tubes connected to vital sign monitors, respiratory ventilator, and oxygen mask didn't look like who he was supposed to be. Instead of Jeremy Taffy, former Commander of Forscom, Director of the FBI, Director of the CIA, and father figure from the age of nine, was now some shriveled up portion of an old man.

This thing that lay before him looked like a malnourished individual whose barber deliberately botched his head of hair and beard. Where once fingernails were pristine clear were now yellow with black streaks. The glasses on his face were slanted and sliding off his thin nose.

The doctors said they didn't know why now his immune system stopped working and somehow overnight he developed a form of cardiotoxicity.

He wanted to report to Taffy that he didn't find any solar weapon or alien presence, but found many other weird things. Harris wondered and wanted to converse with his father in contemplating if the octacube itself was the weapon. It did represent the sun in a square-like way. Maybe it was a replica of a bigger real weapon.

What did Lilith Chelsea have to do with it? Why was possibly her skeletal remains in the center of the cube? Was Lilith Chelsea the center of all this? Did we find Pandora's true jar? The hope that was left in the jar—was she the hope, the ancient Lilith, Adam's first wife?

What was the meaning of Kepler-22b and the other five planets with the Cygnus constellation riddled on the lobby ceiling of the Obelisk Building? Did that have something to do with extraterrestrials? Maybe the alien's location.

What would my father have to say about all this? What would he say about the evidence involving Anthony Burrows' untimely death and the Atlas leading to the chamber of safes and the octacube? He had hoped his father would touch the evidence of this piece of finger in his hand. He hoped to tell his father he loved him, whether they disentangled the quest or not. He felt hope was in the same line as a wish or a dream. He despised hope again. *Hope; the thin line of a lie.*

Harris felt like crying, but knew what Taffy would say, "Come on now, boy. Now you're going to make us both cry and how is that going to look?" Harris wanted to laugh at the statement, but knew his father wouldn't and he'd stare at him, giving him that face like, you're stupid. Who cries and laughs at the same incident but a crazy person.

Harris at that second noticed something different about the room, and anger welled inside him. Something in the room was missing. Taffy's notes, his laptop, and all his papers were missing.

His notes about Pandora were confiscated by who? Who cared for such things Taffy searched for for some years to where it was now so important? Yes, Taffy was getting close to something. No, not Taffy, but I was getting close to something, and now this Pandora was essential to somebody.

Harris was about to interrogate every doctor and nurse who came through Taffy's room in the past couple of days. He then thought better of the idea and calmed himself down to where he felt he had to think rationally about the situation. Being over emotional had only confused the circumstances.

His answers were most likely right outside the door in the waiting room. He could keep this whole thing quiet and not stir whoever took the stuff. *Pretending to be null about the thievery was dollars to doughnuts the best thing for a sneak attack later or at least find some answers.*

Harris had almost forgotten John Goldman sat in the waiting room of Pennsylvania Hospital waiting for him to come out of Taffy's room. Harris's mind when he first arrived was dead set on seeing Taffy, but now he needed answers.

John put the magazine down, but kept his legs crossed as Harris approached and sat next to him on a brown leather couch.

"Again, sorry about your old man's condition," John began. "He's a legend to me, too, you know."

Harris responded with a nod.

"Sorry, I had to see you on such sensitive uneasy circumstances," John said in a low voice, "but rumors are spreading like wildfire at Langley. The Director wants an immediate investigation on downed agents, and he wants you to come in for questioning. What happened out there?"

"Long story, and I'm afraid you and Joseph are the only friends I got right now," Harris also spoke in a whisper. "First give me the rumors."

"You might want to say only friend. Joseph has been missing for five days now. His girlfriend and family don't know where he is. Some friends had taken him home after the Fourth of July celebration and that was the last time he was ever seen."

"Shit, that agent must have got to him," Harris said. "John, this might not be over. I believe the CGFSI is at work here. My father spoke of this before he … Our lives could be still in danger."

"You might be right," John spoke, uncrossed his legs and sat up. Every time a doctor or nurse walked by they became silent. "My boss was visited the other day by some so-called bureaucrats. They claimed that they heard you went rogue and murdered Sara and Brian and possibly Joseph. They said you were on some deranged quest for some kind of imaginary solar weapon."

"That confirms that assassin I encountered was a CGFSI agent," Harris spoke. "Well, some of what they said is true. I was looking for a solar weapon that never existed, but so were they. So what does your boss think?"

"The Director didn't believe it for a minute. First of all, he knows what they're working on at Area 51. He also knows Nigeria declares to have caught a United States spy the other day.

"The Nigerian secret service has privately released his picture to us for identification. The deceased agent isn't one of ours. Well, not directly ours. The Director did a hasty research and found the man is a mercenary, *nom de plume* Wild Mike. Not ours. You're right, differently a mark of the CGFSI."

"If that's the case, then they must have been here and confiscated Taffy's belongings."

John nodded in agreement. "The nurses told me a day after Taffy went into coma a couple of men in suits came. Whatever significance Taffy's notes had, they now possess."

"Well, not everything," Harris said and patted his back pocket, not expecting John to understand the finger-bone in it.

"The director urgently wants to speak to you, Matt. It looks like the CGFSI wants to wipe out the old team."

Harris thought for a second. Who could he trust? When the CGFSI was involved, it was never good. He wondered did they have a hand in speeding up his father's condition.

The Continuity of Governments Freemasons Skull and Bones Illuminatists, in short the CGFSI, were no cryptocracy to piss on. He recognized, they drove hard on their cause, and usually never stop until it was met, even if it took hundreds of years.

He knew they had the strength of the United States, the valor of Europe behind them, and had in the least been four hundred years old in a make up of different affluent organizations around the world, all on one objective. Whatever they wanted, they got. They had centuries of practice in power and they weren't going to change now.

He understood, they had been writing a furtive history that had been said would last long after this civilization. It was their aim. For four hundred years they had been creating wars with heroes and villains. Harris thought of it like moving figures on a chest board using the world how they see fit.

In this game he wouldn't know who to trust. He saw with his

own eyes his colleague turn on him. Chelsea wasn't even safe from turncoats.

Could they have killed my father? The taste of revenge was on his tongue, but he had to remain calm. These people played the game ruthlessly, and he knew if he wanted to play, he had to play it cautiously and quietly.

"I know we worked together many times in the past," Harris said, putting a hand onto John's shoulder. "I have to know I could trust you before I talk to the Director."

They looked each other in the eyes and John nodded.

"I need you to quietly get me in to talk to General J. Powell," Harris spoke. "Next I need to get into our forensic lab and see a specialist. It has to be someone we can trust. Someone who won't go yapping their mouth all over the place. Can you do that?"

"Sure, not a problem," John said and shrugged. "I'm on it. I have one guy in mind; I just have to find out his work schedule."

"Yeah, but I mean right now, tonight," Harris said and showed a simple face with no smile.

"Tonight?" John repeated with not much confidence in his voice from just a second earlier.

Harris continued his intent look.

"Damn, what do you have, a piece of the weapon everyone's looking for?"

Harris smiled. "Don't know yet, but I'll explain on the way."

Harris clarified to John how Sara died and Brian betrayed him, along with other details of his quest with Chelsea as his witness and where his stepfather fit in. He hadn't yet told him why he needed forensics and felt he didn't need to for he'd soon find out.

Identifying who the bone belonged to could mean nothing or it could mean everything. *There was no need to cause any alarm about a finger belonging to an unidentified eighteen year old or ancient skeleton in a jar with a scroll on its lap to anyone, especially the CGFSI.*

CHAPTER 30

OH, SWEET, SO SWEET, *a familiar shower, a familiar house, and clean clothes.*

She repeatedly scrubbed her sleek legs, torso, and underarms using the velvety soap and washcloth as if trying to erase a blemish that wouldn't come out. In those specific locations she liked the feel of the suds on her skin; it was stimulating. She stared down at the teeny tawny colored wet hairs on her forearms as if each accelerated her pleasure points.

She closed her eyes and meditated in the cold water, her reflection, a black ocean of nothingness. Finishing her shower she dressed.

She smelled like her fruity and floral self today in her white short-sleeve chiffon-fabric blouse and black slacks. She'd slept alone in her father's summer house waiting for him to fly into Lagos since yesterday, since the incident.

She knew she had to get back to the States to conduct her business that was long overdue. She knew she could have left after talking to the authorities, but decided to stay in Lagos a little longer to have a powwow with her father. He'd want to know what had been her purpose in the building.

She admitted to herself and herself only that she had a virtuous time with Harris and his quest. Like a rollercoaster, the tension of death that surrounded her was disturbing, but enticing. Only once in her life she'd been to an amusement park and could remember the excitement of the different rides.

That was parallel to how she felt about Aaron betraying her, a building collapsing, high speed car pursuits, and being chased around the world by a lunatic. Where the rides had tracks, seatbelts, and handles, her safety-net was Harris. An amusement park full of thrills once was enough for her, as was this quest.

It was time to go back to the production side of the world, back to the sophistication of commerce, if I want to call it civilized, back to the burden of no love life in sight, reality. Most of all, back to the questions at hand that needed answers. She felt her father was the man to resolve them, so she waited here in Ikoyi-Lagos, Banana Island.

Her father's summer house secluded but on the residential side of the island had five rooms on the second floor customized for visiting associate businessmen and diplomats.

Chelsea stayed in the most feminine room she could find. Rosewood ceiling and walls, tan furniture, and multi-colored pillows was about as womanish as she was going to get around here, Chelsea realized. This being her favorite room, it still had that boyish look of two 38" model sailboats on shelves on both sides of a 46" hanging plasma television.

It was time. *My father should be finished with his hour meeting with his two best friends, my step-uncles, behemoth tycoons, and a politician.*

As she walked down the rosewood stairs in the enclosed rose garden she could see everyone in the glass living room shaking hands, ready to depart. Besides the bedrooms, most of the house was made of glass with juvenile five foot palm trees that surrounded the eight acres of land.

At the bottom of the stairs, a portion of the glass wall automatically moved aside. She then walked in.

The lavish living room consisted of two huge tan couches in the center back to back packed with pillows and two large stylish mirror topped end-tables in front of each couch.

The guys moved around the furniture, making their way toward the wall where she stood.

"Nzingha, it's good to see you," Morris said. They embraced each other and kissed on the cheek. He was dressed in an expensive well fit suit and tie as always, Chelsea noticed. "I haven't seen you in almost three months. Looking as pretty as ever."

Chelsea couldn't help but blush.

She got the same hospitality from Scott who was in a nifty suit right behind Morris.

"Hello, Nzingha," Scott said. "Your father and I are busy, so whatever you have to do, I'd say take your time, but hurry up."

"You guys being around him so much, it would take a miracle if I could steal a few minutes of his time," Chelsea said with a smile.

"Nzingha, don't listen to him," Morris said, looking into her eyes. "Take all the time you need."

"May I?" Chelsea asked in what she called her innocent young daughter voice.

"Sweet kid," Morris said, caressed the dimple on her cheek, and moved past her through the automatic sliding door.

"Don't go flying off to America so fast," Scott said, pointing his finger at her in a reprimanding way. "Like your father, we have a few things to discuss, too." He smiled as he followed Morris out.

She held a shy grin until the last person came to the door. She gave the politician a blank look, not knowing him like she had known Morris and Scott.

The official was an elder man dressed in full West African garb of a black kufi, dashiki, and sokoto. "Madam, Chelsea, you will not remember me," the man said, trying his hardest to speak proper English. She sensed the stress in his voice. "We met some years ago at a fundraising—"

"Femi Fawehinmi, it's nice to meet you again," Chelsea spoke, pronouncing every syllable of the Yoruba tongue. She didn't know the man, but registered his name from memory.

The surprised man smiled and bowed once at Chelsea, then at Xavier. "Truly, sir, you have an amazing daughter," Femi said in Yoruba. "She has the mind of a camel, and camels never forget injuries."

Xavier gave the man a nod and watched him shake Chelsea's hand and leave through the glass door.

Alone at last, her father must be saying, Chelsea guessed. Well, she was saying it anyway.

She moved hastily across the living room and gave her father a hug for about three minutes. She wrapped her arms around the brown three piece suit he wore to where she was rubbing his back. Her head was no longer buried in his chest as it had been in her younger years; now it lay on his shoulders and hollow of his neck.

She had felt more comfortable to lay her head on his chest, for she would have felt safer. As the years went by she would try and crouch down to hug him, trying not to grow up and face the world. The taller she got, the more she knew there was a terrifying world out there full of creepy people and menacing things.

She wanted to hug her father and never let go. She imbibed his smell his touch. As she squeezed him tightly, he kissed her on her warm forehead and she closed her eyes wishing he'd rock her to sleep.

"Look at that," Xavier said, still in an embrace with her. "The thermostat just dropped to sixty. The house knows you're here."

Chelsea smirked. They kissed each other on the cheek, then she grabbed Xavier's hand, leading him through sliding doors to a wooden walkway outside. The boardwalk led to a massive sundeck and pool area. Chelsea and Xavier sat under a blue canopy that shielded them from the continuing mist of a sun-shower.

Though it was eighty degrees, the cool breeze from the finishing storm was agreeable to her, for now. She glanced up at swirling clouds fighting to show the blues of the sky as the sun dipped beams onto the earth, mimicking a light show rumba or flicking flashlight.

"Sir, I want to get away from the house and technology for a minute and embrace nature and you," Chelsea spoke, sitting across from her stepdad at a white round table.

"Of course," Xavier said, waved his hand, and the butler from a bar in the glass kitchen responded.

On a tray he brought out two glasses and a glass bottle of water with the clear label, Veen, vertically embossed on it.

"Thanks, Yakubu," Chelsea said, remembering his name, though she hadn't seen the butler in some months.

He also looked surprised she knew his name and bowed at her greeting.

"I see you came prepared," Chelsea said to her father as the steward retreated to the kitchen.

She poured the water from the bottle, filling both glasses.

"Always," Xavier responded, picking up his glass, and sipped the crystal clear liquid. "Prepared nice and cold, too.

"So I hear you caused some hassle at the building."

He got right into it—good, Chelsea contemplated. "Yes, sir, and solved our company employee assassin case that's been ongoing for some years," she spoke. "Though thought dead by many, she's been arrested and will soon stand trial here and assumably the States."

"So I've heard."

"It's been rumored she's been affiliated with the Nigerian secret brigade. Of course, the SMB has denied her employment. Maybe she'll give up names of her cohorts if she knows she'll spend the rest of her life in jail."

"Maybe," Xavier said with not much confidence in his voice. "But agents like that never give up anything."

"Sir, with all due respect, I know you know the answers to my questions. Who's Lilith Chelsea and whose remains are in the jar in your vaulted octacube?" She took a couple of swallows of her water as Xavier sat back and took a deep breath.

"There's no short story to this," Xavier began, making himself more comfortable in his seat. "I never knew about your true family when you asked in your younger years. Then, when I did find out years later, there was a time when you didn't want to know about your past, so I never mentioned it. In those years I took it upon myself to find out, and lucky I did because a year after, the orphanage closed down.

"Lily Chelsea, her birth name, is plausibly your sister. The orphanage in America had records of your names, but not your mothers. At the time I adopted you, I had no knowledge you had any siblings. That's about all the records showed.

"When I went back to the orphanage I was burdened with rumors. Rumors had it that some unknown Algerian woman dropped twin infants off in 1974, one named Lily, the other you. The woman claimed she was raped and that the babies would be a disgrace to her family."

Chelsea realized, as she stared at the pool, Xavier had stopped talking for a few seconds.

"Are you alright? Do you want me to go on?" he asked and touched her forearm.

"Um, yes, of course," she responded. "Trying to take everything in is all. For forty years I never cared about my nationality, though today it seems to mean everything. All those years people have asked. I just ask them, what do they think I look like. Some kind of Brazilian chick, they would say." Chelsea and Xavier chuckled. "Until today I pretty much believed that.

"I was wondering, sir, why the twins weren't kept together. Usually twins are kept together."

"Who knows, it could have been a mistake, or just down right doing what they wanted to do, not following the correct procedures. All I know is Isela and I, my lady friend at the time, saw you and fell in love."

Chelsea's blush came back and she put her warm hand on top of his. His hand, though, seemed cold to her.

"And the jar and remains; what's that about?" she asked.

Xavier smiled. "Much easier story to tell. Inside the rhombicuboctahedron, what you called a octacube, is as you saw, a jar. The jar is an authentic three thousand, Before the Common Era, year-old relic, as is the mummy inside with a scroll. That scroll reads, if I could remember, *from her is the race of women and female kind of her is the deadly race and tribe of women who live amongst mortal men.*

"I won it at an auction in France. Experts say the Greeks believed it was the actual jar Pandora opened. All of which is my collection of artifacts, rare and expensive. Where do you think you get your desire to collect things, like your ancient assortment of books? In this case, like father, like daughter. You have your safety measures, I have mine, but on a more drastic, grander scale.

"The Atlas, the triangular trading system, and urns with your sister's name in which I changed from Lily to Lilith are just mere allegories. All trumped-up propaganda for fools looking for fortune and glory of things unreal and unheard of. I've fashioned this legend for more then forty years."

"I have to say you had me fooled."

"I would have thought no one could ever fool you, my dear lady. You could have called me, though. There's dangerous security systems set up down there. You could've got hurt. How did you come across the vaults anyway?"

"Just like you said, sir," Chelsea said, rolling her eyes. "I was in search of things that never existed. Following some agent's wild story about a solar-powered weapon."

"The same American spy who was killed or the one who got away?"

Chelsea hesitated for a second, looked up at the clouds, then answered. "Yeah, yeah … the American spy who was killed."

"I sense a touch of fondness," Xavier said with worry in his voice. "It's the thing that fools most. You're going to have to be more careful, my dear.

"The agent was creepy anyway. Authorities found a rabbit's foot, mojo, and The Monkey's Paw story book in his pockets. A bit over superstitious, I think. You're usually meticulous; what happened?"

"There's no short way to tell the story. Let's go back inside. I can feel the humidity rising."

Xavier smirked as they stood with their drinks in hand. Chelsea laid her head on his shoulder and he put his arm around her waist as they slowly walked back to the compound.

She dare not mention Harris. To her father and the rest of the Nigerian authorities, Harris was always going to be a rival secret agent even in his so-called retirement. She told her father about most of her adventures minus Harris and his dying father. She told him the security at the building were mistaken that she was with the agent that escaped. She said she only pretended to like him so he wouldn't hurt her. He managed to kill the superstitious agent she thought she cared for.

Well, she felt she didn't fib; maybe told a white lie—a sin of omission.

His dying father. That reminded her she had to get back to the States to keep a promise.

What am I thinking? Why am I even protecting this man who had put me through an exploration in vain? Deep inside she felt for the first time Harris was sincere, and she honored genuineness. She had a lot to ponder on her trip back to the United States.

The concept of a twin sister was curious and bizarre at the same time as was her life for the past couple of days.

Her father said he looked up Lily Chelsea for some years and hadn't come up with anything. *He also said he was on that case about the assassin Suraksha and look who found her. Or did she find me?*

He said he didn't know if Lily was dead or alive, but again she was free to search. *Nah, not interested. What's done is done. Maybe in some years I will. Nah, I'm way too old to think about acquainting myself with some mystery sister. Besides, Lily could be in Algeria with her mother for all anybody knew. My mother.*

I have the wealth and resources; maybe I'll go to Algeria and look Lily up one day. Nah ... I'm not even truly sure I'm Algerian. It was only gossip. Could I build off a rumor?

CHAPTER 31

IT ALL HIT HIM ABRUPTLY, such as life, he believed. There were whispers of turning off the life support systems Taffy was hooked up to in the Intensive Care Unit.

The doctors said he was not only brain dead, but his organs were failing. The only things keeping him alive were machines. They said if by some miracle he did wake up, he'd already suffered massive brain damage and doubtlessly wouldn't know who he was. He wouldn't speak or move. He'd be a vegetable, if he wasn't now.

With no biological children, and divorced wives deceased, Harris was legally next of kin. Taffy also put in his will that he'd be in charge of ending life-support if it came to that. He then mused about Chelsea and her Project Elf invention.

Could this creation bring Taffy from the severe dilapidated state he was in to where he had his wits about him? If so, then it could prove immortality. If this drug cured him entirely, then when will he expire? Never?

I supposed humans would live like gods. I'd emphasize like, because if Taffy died instantly, there was no bringing him back from the dead, unless Chelsea had that worked out, too, somewhere secretly. The world would have less offspring because of the longevity of life, overpopulation.

So many issues with the PE project. He thought about himself. *Was it egotistical that I want my father to live eternally or myself for that matter?*

Someone might say if God wanted man to live forever, he'd design him that way. I'd say, if I invented a way to live forever, why'd God give me the blueprint? Or why did God give it to Nzingha, an agnostic who was skeptical of the Almighty? For some reason he thought of the song "Forever Young" *by Alphaville.*

He had to contact Chelsea today and discuss using Taffy as a prototype towards PE. *What most likely would come up in their conversation would have been this quest that wasn't fully successful. Hey, I'm only human, lady; now can we talk about immortality?* He laughed at his thoughts as he moved in the lower level basements of the George Bush Center for Intelligence in Fairfax County, VA.

He followed John into the crime laboratory this Saturday in anticipation of the results of the finger. He had to wait three days for the forensic technician, Melvin's, analysis. John claimed he and Melvin had done a lot of favors for each other. Harris felt Melvin should be trustworthy enough for the task. If John was right or not about the trust of his friend, Harris understood he was going to have to take the chance.

John told him, Melvin was ecstatic about the results and wanted to know where the bone was found. John said, "Melvin used the word, *unimaginable.* He never used that word before." Harris guessed John felt it was efficient Melvin explain what he meant and examined in person. It was also best, Harris supposed, he as well come in and say where he found the digit.

The well lit white laboratory gave the impression of a considerable university science lab. Everyone moved about in white lab jackets and aprons occupied in studying whatever their chore required. There were gas and weapon test chambers. The place was organized in hanging signs that read analytical, serology, latent print, and AFIS sections. Yellow biohazardous signs also hung here and there.

On many counters Harris noticed state of the art video and still photography equipment, argon-ion laser, optical and stereomicroscopes with fiber-optic illumination digital imaging pick-up. *Don't forget your average racks of test tubs. Ah, good old Langley.*

Melvin Liu, his nametag read, had guided John and Harris into a secluded corner of the room by a table full of protection gear. Melvin took off his blue gloves and put his red adaptation goggles on the top of his head.

"Matt, this is Melvin," John said. "Melvin, Matt, the agent who provided you with that specimen." Harris and Melvin shook hands.

Taking a vial from the front of his smock pocket, Melvin handed it to Harris. Harris held it up, looking at the finger inside.

"I'd put that away if I were you," Melvin suggested and adjusted his bifocals.

Harris put the vial into his pocket.

"What's the deal, Melvin?" Harris asked. "Give it to me straight. How recent or ancient is the bone?"

Melvin glanced at John, then spoke in a whisper. "Stop me if I say something you don't understand and I'll try and break it down in layman's terms the best I can. Follow me."

Harris nodded for him to go on.

"The DNA from the piece of index finger you gave me isn't normal in any way, shape, or form. I'll start from the unusual to the impractical. I believe it feasibly belongs to a female in her teens. The genealogical ancestry is North African, Tuareg, or Berber in its purest form, no mixing.

"What's unbelievable is that this person shares only ninety-nine point five percent of the DNA of modern humans. We only have seen this in Neanderthals who died out some twenty thousand years ago. Now, because the finger of this person you found died about twenty to twenty-five years ago, it's not ancient at all. I also notice what type of blood flowed, which makes sense when dealing with a species like Neanderthals.

"There's a warm blood cyclical vasodilation and vasoconstriction of the peripheral capillaries. The only people on earth who have that are Mongoloids—Eskimos.

"This gets even crazier when I couldn't figure out what the other five percent of the DNA sequence was. It's some kind of biochemical compound I've never seen before. Imaginably this person was some kind of single cross biological hybrid experiment, if that makes any sense."

"I think I follow you," Harris said. "This person might have been an experiment like the hoopla on Plum Island. Blood adaption to the cold, Neanderthal-like DNA, and unknown proteins all sounds interesting.

"Let me ask you, Melvin, what do you think this is? When you say hybrid, I think of two distinctive beings mating. What has mated here?"

"The structure of the finger doesn't appear like a Neanderthal's at all, but much like humans of today. Which makes sense in a way because, though most humans today still have Neanderthal DNA in them, Africans don't have any Neanderthal genes in them. This person is purely African.

"It's that five percent of unknown proteins that's mindboggling and will need further study. Yes, I'd say this was some kind of experimentation, some kind of human chimera, transhuman or some would vow it to be a mating of human and an exobiology substance."

Everyone looked at each other in silence for a few seconds as if wondering what to say next.

"I still have a few pieces of the finger in test tubes," Melvin spoke. "Do you want them back or may I hold them for more conjecturing?"

"Hold them," Harris said. "I'd hold off on telling anybody about this, and if you can truly keep a secret, I might have a treat for you, like more fresh evidence of this DNA to examine."

"Agreed," Melvin said, and John nodded. "So where the hell did you get this? Could there be more people like this?"

"I nabbed it out of someone's safe from a full skeleton stuffed in Pandora's actual ancient jar," Harris said.

Melvin stared at Harris, waiting for him to laugh but no laugh came. "No, really?" Melvin asked.

"You wanted the truth, Melvin," Harris said with a smirk. "Or do you want me to lie to you?"

"Would it be possible to see this skeleton?"

"No, it got disposed of, and I think I know why. I may yet have more evidence for you, though."

The first thing that popped into Harris's psyche was Livenal and his first mission to Nigeria. His assembled team at the time found a project Livenal called Denisova. They said it had something to do with Neolithic man. He searched for the project in the mountains of Gotel in Adamawa and found an abandoned science lab.

Then he had to add Livenal's history of human cloning capabilities allegedly supposed to have been abandoned. Even with undercover agents, the U.S. central intelligence could explore but so much. Livenal could have done anything they wanted in Nigeria at any time. And he was sure the company did what they wanted; they all did.

A full collage was beginning to develop here, and Chelsea seemed to be the center focus. Chelsea's overheating spells—DNA from that finger that adapts to the cold which presumably belonged to Lilith Chelsea, Nzingha Chelsea's sister—abandoned human cloning lab owned by Livenal, Chelsea's stepfather—experimentations of a human hybrid, slices of unknown DNA—extraterrestrial.

Chelsea had told him a story early in his quest. Rumors swirled in Livenal of her stepfather's contact with an unidentified craft off the coast of Africa. This UFO incident theoretically started Livenal's science division.

Suppose the rumor was true, then all this would make sense. Chelsea, at birth, could have been implanted with a foreign gene and hadn't been told about it, giving birth to her science of metaphysics, antiparticles, ambient technology, and her best device, nanomedicine.

Clues had told, when he was searching for the Atlas, of energy being mapped in DNA. Imagine that, Taffy could have been right about an astrobiology presence. We were looking for little green or gray men and thrown off searching for weapons that didn't exist, *yet.*

The foreign substance all along could have been concealed in the DNA—Lilith's DNA and so Nzingha Chelsea's. *But how could she not know? Would she know? If it was in me, would I know if no one told me? The astonishing technology Chelsea fashioned was the five percent gene that made her brain work differently than other humans—the exobiological split that Xavier her stepfather was tampering with. The only impede to the human was overheating.*

He had to see Taffy one more time before seeing Chelsea in Ohio. He called Chelsea at Impending Towers and found out she was back to work as usual. She sounded delighted to hear from him and was even more overjoyed to talk about visiting his stepdad. He told her he'd meet her tomorrow and they agreed to discuss past events and promises at her house.

On his drive to Philadelphia, John had come through with his guarantee that he'd get to speak to the General. Harris spoke with the General on his cell phone, and soon many things became clear on where he stood with the CIA Director and the CGFSI.

TO prove all this, Harris thought, on his eight hour car trip to Columbus, OH this Sunday, he needed a drop of Chelsea's blood. He wondered how he was going to ask. *Hey, Nzingha, can I prick you?* Harris laughed at his own statement and knew that it was going to be an awkward situation. *Oh, and by the way, Ms. Alien, about curing my father...* Yeah, this is going to be odd. He figured he'd make it up as he went along. There were many ways to get DNA; a string of hair, a drinking glass. He was sure he'd find something.

On Harris's drive, General Anthony J. Powell listened to his story on the cell phone about searching for a mystery weapon that was never found and how the CGFSI did the same by sending their own agent.

An agent named Wild Mike had killed Sara, turned Brian, and in all probability killed Joseph, Harris explained. All this was for the cause of attaining information about a ghost product.

Powell said his story checked out with some bureaucrats he talked to. *Powell never called the CGFSI by their names; it was always the bureaucrats this or that.*

Powell informed him that there might be three more stars on the CIA Memorial Wall because Brian didn't make it. "He was found with his brains blown out in a hotel in England," Powell explained. "The Director is pretty pissed and indecisive if these operatives deserve the wall. They weren't on any mission he officially assigned. I told that bastard, what assignments has he ever officially assigned. You got things pretty riled up at Langley.

"The bureaucrats want you to stay on vacation on a no harm, no foul pass. I'd take their advice, son. These people are nasty folk. I like you, son."

Powell made it clear to Harris that he didn't need to talk to the Director for he'd explain the situation. "It's the least I could do for the son of Taffy," Powell said. Harris's only response was thanks.

Harris knew what Powell meant when the CGFSI said no harm, no foul. "Go about your way, Matt," they were saying. "We lost a man and you lost a couple of people. Don't pursue this quest any further or seek revenge because you're not going to like the outcome."

He sighed, knowing they were right about the threat they could be. They had plenty of assassins like Wild Mike at their disposal.

They had confiscated Taffy's notes and there was nothing he could do about it, but they missed the most important thing his notes led to—the half index finger in his possession and perhaps walking living proof of a weapon; Chelsea.

CHAPTER 32

ARRIVING IN COLUMBUS this late afternoon, he noticed the sun still hung tough in the western sky.

Chelsea's home appeared and smelled different on this visit. The aura of the white rectangular structure with many arches mounted on a hill engulfed by pistachio trees seemed miniature and familiar where before it was large and unknown. He felt as if he'd known her bodyguards for a considerable time. Daniel, the bald guy whose left arm was in a sling, appeared to be a good friend where before he was an enemy. Considering he had failed at his job protecting Chelsea, it was a wonder she didn't get rid of him.

As Chelsea guided Harris to her bedroom, he discerned the house had a summer fresh, clean linen aroma. He didn't know why his senses were heightened. *Oh, what was that? Peach blossom.*

He felt his senses were keener because he knew Chelsea was something more than human and quite tangibly an experiment or the creature from outer space he and Taffy had been looking for all along. He looked at her differently, more in a scrutinizing way; a way that he never looked at a human before. It was extraordinary.

"You seem a little uneasy today," Chelsea spoke. "Don't worry, my father won't come after you. He thinks you're dead and that my wittiness has triumphed on our little quest."

"Thanks, the best solution I guess," Harris responded. "My worry is you. I was praying that you were mentally okay. Watching people die is never easy. I'm sorry I've put you on such a—"

She put her pointer finger to his lips. "I'm fine. I go where I want, and you did tell me to stay in the hotel. I'm fine. I wouldn't be where I am if I had such a weak stomach."

Chelsea's lilac-scented, beige bedroom, wool carpet under her queen-size bed with large oil painting over her headboard looked unusual. It was the huge plants in the four corners of the room, he grasped, that's what he hadn't noticed before.

As she sat on her bed made of black satin sheets, he sat next to her. He couldn't help but notice she looked tantalizing in her blouse and slacks matching the shade of her bedspread.

Her beauty hadn't changed, so he had to control himself. She wasn't human. He needed a sample of her blood, a hair follicle on the bed, something. The place was tidy. He couldn't see any hairbrushes or combs.

"Could you believe," Chelsea spoke, "after the NPF incarcerated Suraksha at the Obelisk Building, there was a jailbreak just yesterday and forty prisoners escaped, one of them being she. All the prisoners were rounded up and accounted for except her. She has more lives than a cat. That's the Nigerian Police Force for ya."

"Escaping two exploding buildings and jail," Harris spoke inquisitively. "She had help."

"Yeah, you think so? That means more players to this game."

Harris made a face like *don't be so naïve. That's not you, Nzingha.* "I assume you spoke to your father. Did he have any information about you ever having a sister or cousin?"

"Actually, finally we spoke face to face. Yes, Lilith Chelsea, whose real name is Lily Chelsea, is my sister. He explained in much detail that the skeleton and jar were relics he won at an auction in France. It's supposed to be authentic Greek art—Pandora's actual jar."

"Interesting. So if the skeleton inside the jar isn't your sister, who is?"

"He doesn't know, but said he found some evidence at the orphanage before it shut down stating Lily and I were dropped off by a woman from Algeria claiming she'd been raped. In her culture it's the highest disgrace for a woman, so she never claimed the twins."

"Twins," Harris repeated, surprised. "Really? Tell me more."

"That's it; he doesn't know anything about Lily's whereabouts. He says that's all he knows, and that's just a rumor, the part where the orphanage claims who my mother is. But it all makes sense because of her culture, the embarrassment of rape, her dropping us off like that."

Chelsea seemed to have a sorrowful gleam in her eye for a second, Harris noticed.

Wow, she really believed the story, Harris thought. She was already calling some lady her mother. The pieces were falling into place too easy now. Her father, Xavier, was clearly fabricating a story. Harris pondered on how he was going to unravel the truth here; he needed more proof, her DNA.

Evidence wasn't absent here. But when the facts present itself, how would he give this type of truth? *Slow and easy, of course, when dealing with family issues.* He wasn't going to give Nzingha whom has been in the desert for many days—a desert of lies—a whole bunch of water all at once, that water being the truth. She'd just choke. He'll let her sip it first. And these lies had to be years in the making.

"So where did the name Lilith Chelsea come from?" Harris asked.

"The name came from my father, maybe in remembrance of my sister, altered in a fictional quest brought on by years of his eccentric antics, I believe. He's a big believer in lost ancient stories, like me and my biblical paraphernalia."

I'll bet, Harris thought. *There were a lot of half truths running around.*

"There are two other things I looked into right away when I got back to the States," Chelsea said with joy. "Remember that hologram of the Cygnus constellation, the six planets, and one of them called Kepler twenty-two B?"

Harris motioned with his head for her to go on.

"Well, I looked it up online and found Kepler twenty-two B is a real planet that orbits a star like ours some six hundred light years away in the Kepler twenty-two system in its Goldilocks zone … you know, habitable zone."

Harris bowed that he understood.

"It was interesting to me," Chelsea continued, "that I looked everywhere and couldn't find those other five planets in that system. It's like they don't exist. Or they don't exist yet, where scientists haven't discovered them or their keeping the planets a secret. My father though has it on the hologram like he knows they exist. Maybe just more of his antics."

Harris made a face like maybe after all he didn't understand.

"I know this might not make any sense but Kepler twenty-two was peculiar to me," Chelsea said. "Anyway moving on, the next weird thing was Aaron has gone missing. Remember the guy who—"

Harris interrupted her by tapping the back of his head.

"Yeah," Chelsea continued. "No one has seen nor heard from him for weeks since we last saw him. Friends have issued a missing persons report. Detectives have checked his house and haven't come up with any leads to his whereabouts. They said it seemed clean of any foul play. He hadn't contacted the job to find out if he was fired or tried cleaning out his desk or anything."

"Consider him dead," Harris suggested. "That assassin we encountered would have differently seen to that when Aaron came up empty without the Atlas. I'm sorry."

"Wow, he was a traitor but I never meant for this to …"

Harris put his hand on her back and rubbed it. "I'm sorry about all this, I truly am," Harris said. "I asked a lot of you bringing you along on this mission of my selfish—"

"Matt, I've learned a lot on this mission, seen a lot. Things I would've never known if I didn't go along. You don't have to apologize. Matter of fact I want to express my gratitude and give you back a gift.

"It's back to business now. Many politicians and legislators don't want to see PE come in full fruition. I want to give this gift to your father undetected by them …"

He saw that she noticed it was he who had that mournful twinkle in the eye now. He put his head down, not looking at her, and whispered, "I decided to take him off the machines the other day before I came here."

"No … but … I thought," Chelsea also whispered. "I could have …"

"It's hard to explain, but I made a decision after a day long debate with myself. Your project is young in its development and my father had too much heart, lung, and brain damage. I just didn't want him to be a walking vegetable, a zombie. I believe in your technology, but sometimes God's will is better. I mean, who wants to live forever? I don't believe things were made to last forever, everything ages, rocks age, even stars die. It's the natural order of things. The universe is eventually going to die. Do you want to be around when it happens? Should you be around?"

Harris knew she knew he asked questions not to be answered, but thought about. She lowered her head.

"So much death seems to surround you," Chelsea said. "No life."

"I didn't even get to talk to him in his last days," Harris said and felt a ball grow in his throat. He remembered feeling like this when he was seven years old and he was told his biological parents were never coming back. Like ... like, crying. He held back the tears and swallowed, trying to get rid of the soreness in his throat.

This all happened so abruptly, such as life. "I didn't get to tell him about the results of *his* mission, *his* quest. I think humans somehow are blessed with death so we can learn form it. I don't know if what I'm saying to you makes any sense." His voice cracked and he got up to leave. "I have to go."

He had abandoned the idea of grabbing Chelsea's DNA. He could get it some other time some other way. His only thoughts were of burying Taffy, and he couldn't let this woman see him cry.

Chelsea stood and blocked his path to the door.

What the hell is she doing he thought.

"I'm sorry about your father," she said. "I know he was a great man. I can't begin to imagine what you've been going through and have gone through in his last days. I just want to say I'm deeply sorry for not believing you in the beginning."

"It's alright, you really didn't know," Harris said, closing his eyes knowing they were watery; he had to get out of there. He then started blinking terribly, holding back ... "I wouldn't trust anything out of my mouth either after what I've done to you in the past."

Chelsea lifted his chin with her forefinger and steadily opening his eyes though watery he looked into hers.

He wondered what she was thinking as he looked into the black of her pupils. *What was back there in that hybrid brain?* Her eyes fixed on him seemed creepy. Her irises flickered in the dim glow of the room, shifting from murky emerald to dark jade green. *Some say the eyes are the window to the soul.*

She moved her head closer to kiss him, but he moved his head, backing away concurrently.

He couldn't do this; not right now, not knowing what he knew about her.

She let him walk another step toward the door, then she got aggressive. She grabbed him by the arm and spun him back around to where they were facing each other again. Her hands grabbed firmly onto his waist. He could feel her tiny fingers squeezing his sides through his blue shirt. It was as if she was trying to tickle him.

"I said I was sorry," she said, gazing up into his eyes again.

"Sorry about what? I accepted your apology. You don't …"

She leaned her head up to kiss him and he resisted again, backing away for a second time, but it was too late, her lips had found his. Her left hand clutched the collar of his shirt while her right hand snaked to his back, locking him to her like a squirrel on a tree, for a stronger kiss.

Her lips being soft and elastic, it was hard to refrain from sucking on them. Her tongue had a life of its own, different from the way she was moving her head. She moved her head gradually from side to side as her tongue went into his mouth like a probe searching for something, anything. It was tough for him now to repel her advances as he tongue kissed her.

He saw that she knew he was falling in line with her program, and she unhurriedly moved backwards toward her bed.

What in God's name was he doing? he wondered. He was here to get DNA, not mate with it. He saw the bed as a crude oil abyss in which this creature was about to devour him in, never to return from its lair.

Though this could work to his favor. If he could prick her while she was distracted in this sexual tirade maybe he could get a good blood sample. Even a better idea, he could bite her by mistake, then smear the blood onto his shirt. *She did smell good and certainly would taste good, too.*

They plopped back onto the bed at first in a perpendicular position, never taking a break from making smacking noises from salivary lips and tongue on tongue and lips.

She slowly and easily straddled him so that they faced each other where his legs were behind her at the edge of the bed, his feet planted on the floor, and her legs were folded, kneeling on the bed as she sat on his lap. He thought of it as a cuddled partnered yoga exercise.

He lost himself for a minute in her exotic desires. *Well, make that a few minutes.* Her hands caressed his back and head, moving her extremely warm fingers around bit by bit, as if trying to figure out every muscle and feature inside his shirt.

He could feel her body's warmth; it came hot but cozy, considering the cold room. He could feel her soft breast on his chest as she pressed against him.

He nibbled on her right ear and cheek as he little by little stroked her silky hair with one hand, running his fingers through her scalp. His other hand found its way in the back of her shirt and fondled her smooth warm back like a doctor inspecting someone's spine. Leisurely, up and down, his hand went, exploring her shoulder blades, the thin fabric of her bra strap, to the start of the arc of her soft buttocks.

Like a piece of candy, he sucked on her neck. *She smelled like jasmine and tasted like ... like ... mmm, honey with the flavor of vanilla.* Her creamy coffee complexion, so perfect, so unblemished, brought him back to the mission at hand. She seemed too flawless.

Two buttons on the front of her blouse somehow unfastened and her shirt dropped just enough to reveal the top of her burnished chest.

Harris contemplated biting into her neck like a vampire. He shoved his mouth and nose into her warm, extremely warm, shoulders at the collar bone, licking her.

Their eyes closed, she rubbed her smooth face with his. He heard her softly croon as he sucked on her sternomastoid muscle, moving to and fro caressing it with his tongue. She tasted so good he almost didn't see her as an individual and fought the urge to bite into her like food on a hot dinner plate.

As she slightly dipped her head back with mouth ajar, he kissed more on her throat. Feeling the veins in her neck with his lips, he could almost sense the vibration of her blood flowing. They both now were breathing irregularly. He imagined the sound of her heart beating as she squeezed him tighter in their embrace.

This was the time where the vampire couldn't take it anymore. His brown eyes turned red and his canines magically grew sharper. Her floral aroma, smooth latte skin the taste of honey, and her petite hourglass body overwhelmed and consumed him. The way she rubbed against his body just made him want to detonate. Her folded legs wrapped around his waist, squeezing him. He was seconds from biting into her.

He abruptly ceased and felt he came to his senses and an idea. He put his head down into her bosom innocently as if she was the mother and he was the child being cradled and rocked to sleep.

No doubt this took all his strength because Chelsea's extraordinary, sweltering, body warmth, smell, and shapely curves, were extremely intoxicating. Breathe, he said to himself, lightly perspiring, breathe— think about why you came here.

A memory had grabbed him from the past, a recollection of how he could attain her DNA. *Now why didn't I think of that before?* he speculated. It could have saved him this trip.

He had to go back to a hotel here in Ohio he was still paying for since the beginning of his, convincing Chelsea of the quest. There, he already had her DNA. *When all is lost, revert back to the drawing board and I might find some answers.* All along, the resolution was in his face. For some reason he needed a moment like this to figure it out.

"I'm sorry," Harris said. "I feel I may never see you again. Basically I can't promise you any type of relationship or this ever developing into anything. The truth is, I respect you more than most women—well, more than all the women I've met."

Chelsea ogled him for a few seconds, moving her eyes slowly back and forth. He watched her examine him almost as if she was trying *not* to understand. At first for a split second he noticed she showed a disgruntle expression, like *how dare you stop me in the middle of…*

The next second she swallowed, caught her breath, and succumbed like putting water on a fire, like a cold shower. Her eyes seconds ago wild, now lowered as well as her head on his shoulder. "You don't have to explain. I get it," Chelsea spoke in a low voice. "You're too honest, Matt." She smiled, showing her dimples that reminded him of peaches. "I like that. I do hope I'll see you again, though, at least one more time. Maybe by then you'll decide if you want to date me or not." She giggled.

Harris smiled.

"There's an event coming up in three weeks," Chelsea explained. "I was wondering if you'd be my escort at the grand opening of a museum in Harlem."

"Sure, I could do that," Harris said. "After all, I'm retired."

They both laughed, and for some strange reason for a moment he saw Chelsea as human again.

"And this time let's not say hope," he spoke. "Yes, you'll see me again. I'll make it my business to come, God willing."

Chelsea smiled. He liked when she smiled; it made her look adorable, intoxicating—human. He kissed her on her exceptionally warm widow's peak.

CHAPTER 33

DREAMS, WHISPERS FROM THE SOUL, Chelsea deliberated. Then what were her dreams about? Her dream last night was no nightmare, just bewildering. She couldn't ask scientists in onerirology, for they still didn't fully understand the meaning of visions.

She was lost in a labyrinth of ice tunnels. Gradually she made it out as if guided by an unseen energy. She was directed into the night of a snow desert world. The coldest, driest, windiest wasteland as usual viewed by her mind's eye had gone on forever.

The full moon lit the snow in a ghostly glow. Something else caught her attention in the night sky, something she'd never physically seen before.

Many long, some thick, some thin, trails of gleaming clouds went on thousands of miles across the heavens. They ranged from the colors of green, brownish-red, and blue. They danced and flickered as if the clouds themselves were on fire. The Cree, Native Americans, called them "Dance of Spirits;" scientists call them aurora.

Chelsea felt funny dreaming about such things, being that she never saw southern or northern lights. The occasional times at night she had sailed as far north as the Labrador Sea she'd not seen the light show. Bad timing, she presumed. All her hallucinations and nightmares were of people and places she'd never been. *How could this be?*

Her focus swung to Harris. How could he have rejected her sexual advances so easy? Arousing men had never been a problem to her and that didn't mean she had to flirt. All she had to do was be in the presence of men and she turned heads, touch them on the arm when she talked to them. Harris had somehow built a resistance to her. She wondered was he gay, and she didn't mean happy. Was he teasing her? His life's job was of deceit, so she questioned how sincere he was.

She concentrated deeper about the situation. She was snarled in lust instead of consideration. His stepfather had just passed away, so that could have changed his sexual attitude, though she was trying to comfort him.

She would have, could have, saved his father with her PE technology. PE was her creation of everlasting life like the tree in the middle of the lake in a dream she once had.

Harris chose God and religion over knowledge, and the consequence was death. Harris, to her, had figured death wasn't the greatest loss in life. He probably believed the greatest loss in life was his spirit dying while he was still alive. So he pulled the plug on his stepfather.

On the other hand her own viewpoints brought her to a different conclusion about life. She theorized; though no one can confidently say they'll live tomorrow, PE is for the idealist who wanted to die young as late as possible. She felt even though his father could have been cured practically brain dead, some life is better than death only because it's less boring. Some may laugh out loud at this, but she was serious. This was something she would have never discussed with Harris.

She wondered, did destiny play a role in finding out about her sister? She always chose plausible knowledge over believing in Heaven and Hell.

Harris was a CIA agent. *A retired agent, but could he ever really quit? Does the idea of agent and mogul marriage fit? The very sound of it doesn't fit.* She sure liked him, though.

Years were flying by and she wasn't getting any younger. Having a baby would grow more dangerous the older she got. Having a baby defined your womanhood; most women she knew seem to think.

How many relationships would she have to go through to get it right? Dating sucked when she had more money than most men. So if she was going to marry someone, she'd better get it right or she'll be like a Hollywood star, married three or four times.

She stared at the art on a lime gaiwan placed on the side shelf of her headboard.

Her recollections shifted toward frustration. She felt she needed a mate to share her plight, to share her plunder, to share her legacy. What was life without the next promising generation?

Then she dwelled on her saying of business before pleasure. She almost laughed out loud. Harris wasn't on any business trip; he wasn't even a businessman. He was a spy, an adventurer who brought her in on his voyage, so she could throw that business before pleasure bull out the window. What's wrong with me? she caterwauled subconsciously; he was the perfect candidate to at least try and date. But why didn't he want to date her?

She tried to meditate in her aggravation by channeling all her energy into the splendor of the Asian art on the gaiwan. It didn't work. She picked up the bowl and threw it across the room. *Isn't it always the one you hope for, the one you never get?*

THE sun was setting, giving the sky a warm royal to navy blue tint. Spain, the Dolce Sitges Resort, three men sat outside on a white couch in a lounge area around a small white cube end table its center lit by an orange glowing orb. Six other men in casual wear sat around them out of earshot at other couches with end tables lit with orbs, Castries's secret security Astor knew.

Ben Castries, the Chairman of the CGFSI, had personally called this meeting to give his solution to the problem and hear my excuses, Astor felt.

Astor believed he had to grovel. This man was consequently the most powerful man on earth, and Astor hated meeting him. He didn't know what to say, how to speak.

There's no easy way to converse with Castries. A man who was also Chairman of the Bilderberg Club, former vice-president of the European Commission, former member of the European Round Table of Industrialists, and at seventy-nine years old the Chairman and CEO of a worldwide conglomerate in oil and banking called Aeon.

He was the symbol of atlanticism as the US presidents were of democracy. He had the military, politics, and economics of Europe and North America in his pocket, and it was rumored that China owed him favors. He was a living god to men; the pharaoh of the western world.

Astor guessed he'd talk slow and candidly. Zamir spoke calm and frank as he always did without a care in the world, just like a Mossad agent. *Yeah, well, Zamir didn't have to deal with* Castries's *bullshit politics of worldly semantics,* Astor knew. All Zamir did, was do. Gave Zamir a mission, he got it done.

Zamir came to the meeting again in shirt and slacks where he came in a three piece suit like his boss, but that was Zamir. *Well, my job is more plotting and planning, a lot more sophisticated,* Astor felt. He had to explain his actions and goals, and projects of accomplishments and failures.

"Sir, an agent has fallen in Lagos," Zamir said as Castries sipped his white wine. "His last inquiry states that the Livenal Company doesn't possess a solar-powered weapon capable of harnessing the sun's capacity. There's no evidence of any such machine or substance that was ever started or pursued past and present.

"The Atlas was just a fabricated quest we believe to throw people off on a system they'd found in the Cygnus constellation. I think Livenal wants to boast that the planets are real, but don't have any proof."

"How much do they know about the system?" Castries asked in his Hungarian accent.

"They know about the five planets around Kepler twenty-two, including the recognized Kepler twenty-two B planet. How they attained knowledge of the six planets is unknown. Nigeria nor Livenal don't possess any telescope or technology to see those planets. Urban legend has it, they knew about these planets forty years ago under the project Pandora."

"How about the Chelsea Company?" Castries asked.

Zamir shook his head no and sipped his red wine.

Castries looked at Astor, smirked, sat back, and crossed his legs. "Please tell me, Astor," Castries asked. "These people don't know anything about the signals we've been receiving?"

Astor swallowed hard before responding. "Sir, our emissaries have reported that not only Livenal, but SETI, ESA, including the world, has never heard of such signals."

"Of course not. That would be impossible." Castries smiled. "Though some mole must have leaked information about Kepler or they're with us on our station on the Red Planet? I've been made to believe that's the only place clear signals can be picked up.

"Astor, check into Livenal more thoroughly. I want to know what they're doing every time they turn on their computers from business deals to smut. I need to know every time they take a dump what they write on the john walls."

"Right away, sir."

"We must take moving our world into a class I civilization slowly since harnessing power from stars is out of the question.

"How goes our plight in suppressing this new drug, PE?"

Astor knew the question was directed at him again when Castries asked, not looking his way. He watched the two guys sip their wine comfortably waiting for his answer.

"Sir, we have many bureaucrats, power brokers, and legislators on our side as usual. Soon you'll see more politicians and demonstrators protesting the drug, that's the little extra I put in for sureness. The masses will follow as always."

"Very good," Castries spoke. "In the end, as usual, it'll be distributed to the affluent. Has the project been secure? We don't need other countries outside our union getting their hands on this. I'd hate to order drastic measures to contain it. There's so much death when I give those orders. If I have to, I will. It would only be in accordance with the law of the Georgia Guidestones."

"As of now there's a tight lid on the project, restricted to Chelsea Industries and the DOE," Astor said. "Moles placed in Chelsea, of course."

"Very good," Castries said. "Sometime next month a meeting will be called at Bohemian Grove with the United States President and Great Britain Prime Minister to discuss the goal agenda for 2016. I do hope you'll be there, Mr. Cyril." Castries slurped more of his wine and looked at his watch.

Astor peeped Castries's smile. It was a grin that he was telling him more than asking. "Of course, sir," Astor responded.

God willing, Astor thought, and God desired it.

IT was a bright, clear, mid-sunny day as the Inspector General of the Marine Corps in full marine garb knelt in front of Harris who sat in a white chair on the huge green graveyard lawn.

Handing him a folded American flag, the marine spoke, "On behalf of the President of the United States, the Commandant of the Marine Corps, and a grateful nation, please accept this flag as a symbol of our appreciation ..."

General Anthony J. Powell, with a hand on Harris's shoulder, sat next to him.

About two hundred people surrounded Harris on this lawn at the Arlington National Cemetery. Senior officials from the Intelligence Community, White House, Pentagon, and members of Congress with their families were in the crowd.

Jeremy Taffy's memorial service had a military band, chaplain, and a performing drill team of armed honor guards. A seven man volley salute fired their rifles in the air and Taps was played. Men and women spoke their peace about how Taffy fought in the Korean and Vietnam wars, how he was a part of keeping the country safe, a true superhero.

Harris stared at the three flags held up into a clear sky by some servicemen. The red, white, and blue, the Maya blue with CIA emblem, and the FBI insignia, sapphire blue colored flags all represented Taffy as a whole. It was what Harris remembered of the old man that was full of wisdom.

He wondered, did he do the right thing by pulling the plug? He wondered would Taffy have wanted him to. He was a strong son of a bitch, but Harris was sure Taffy didn't want to become a vegetable.

It wouldn't have been Taffy to sit upright in his bed staring into space lifeless with no soul. Was that life or was that torture? Taffy used to say, "Old age is more than white hair and wrinkles. The truth isn't the weakening of the body, but the realness of the soul."

Harris felt he gave Taffy his last dying wish. He placed Lily's finger in the casket before it was permanently sealed. Proof of extraterrestrials or not—being that all this wasn't some hoax and just some earthly experiment—Taffy deserved it. It was Taffy's fight for the proof that Harris felt he won, so he gets the trophy. Besides, part of the trophy was living and breathing for further evidence to study its truths.

"God bless you and your family, and God bless the United States of America," the Inspector General said, and Harris accepted the triangle-folded blue with stars flag.

Harris cried, and through his tears he thought he saw Chelsea standing next to a tree in the distance. No, it was just some lady with short black hair in a black skirt suit. One of the congressmen's family members was all. He had to get Chelsea and the quest out of his head right now.

As some of his tears fell onto the flag, he realized his father figure, mentor, this legend, Jeremy Taffy, was gone.

EPILOGUE

IT WAS A SAD WEEK, Harris felt, after attending Sara Sanders' closed casket funeral. Joseph Healey was still missing, and Brian Glyn had an interment Harris dared not observe. He heard Brian's memorial service had the normal honors. Harris felt a traitor was always a traitor, and the Christians in Action were only saving face that their agents had done no wrong.

It was a depressing week—so much death. "So much death, no life." A familiar voice echoed in memory. His emotions swung from gloom to enthusiastic in finding out what Chelsea was.

His memories brought him back to the Doubletree Suites Hotel in downtown Columbus, OH where he had a room reserved for a month. He had a day left and made use of it to retrieve an important item. He didn't know why he didn't think of it before, but through the haste of guiding Chelsea out of the Oasis Club safely being his top priority he had forgotten the blood he wiped from her nose onto his sleeve.

If he remembered a day later housekeeping would have cleaned his shirt, contaminating the evidence.

There was his white Brioni shirt still on the couch, and there was the two tiny streaks of blood on the cuff—Chelsea's blood. It was almost as if faith knew he was going to need it.

Strange, Harris presumed, the smeared blood still had that electric crimson look like it hadn't dried. He wondered was it because of the fabric of his expensive shirt. He was going to find out in a few seconds as he got Melvin to see him again at the George Bush Center for Intelligence.

With his arms folded, he waited for the results. Harris gave Melvin the shirt a week earlier after leaving Chelsea's home. So again they stood in the unoccupied protection gear area of the crime laboratory.

Melvin handed the shirt back to him sealed in a plastic bag. It was clear Melvin was excited, but he muttered his every word, there were still many people in the room.

"Amazing, purely amazing," Melvin said. "Interesting, the DNA of the bone you gave me is a exact match of the blood on that shirt. What's interesting among many things is that the bone is about twenty years old where the blood stain is as fresh as a few hours ago. My presumption, the blood on the shirt belongs to a twin of the skeleton you found or it could be the same blood from the skeleton. The blood has elements in it that preserves its integrity."

"Really," Harris spoke, rubbing his chin. "Tell me, Melvin, the five percent of DNA that you couldn't figure out before; can you decipher it now that you have a fresher sample?"

"Yes, uh, somewhat," Melvin responded, making his voice lower where Harris had to bend so he could talk almost directly into his ear. "You may have to get a biochemist's second opinion, but see if you can follow me here.

"Life on Earth is based on twenty-six chemical elements. Ninety-five percent of this, life is built upon; six of these elements are familiar to you, like oxygen, hydrogen, and nitrogen.

"Five percent of this blood is of the rarest elements ever known on Earth and surely not sustainable in a human being, yet it's in this blood. It's like nothing I've seen before. These elements seem to continually keep the blood fresh even after it's exposed to an oxidized atmosphere. Basically it never dries, it never goes bad.

"It's why I thought five percent of it was unknown to me before. Now only three percent is unknown. At first for the finger I just used one standard periodic table. Looking deeper into newer developing tables I found in the blood's makeup elements like technetium, promethium, and iridium. These elements are mostly synthetically made, radioactive, and are found mostly in the core of stars.

"It's mindboggling that a human can produce this. This person must had been injected with the stuff. Then again, like I said, you might have to get a second opinion."

"Radioactive!" Harris said, not realizing he raised his voice a little.

"Yes, in the technetium, but not at high enough levels to do damage to the host or others."

"Yeah, but still," Harris said with worry in his voice.

"Hey, you're bombarded with radioactivity every time you walk out in the sun."

"So what do you need again," Harris asked, "to find out about the unknown three percent of this DNA?"

"A more up to date periodic table, if there is one," Melvin answered with not much zest.

"Do me a huge favor, Melvin. I haven't told my partner John about this. Do you think you could keep a lid on it for a while?"

"Sure, Matt, but you have to admit, this is a breakthrough of some kind of phenomena if this person is alive and walking. Whatever is going on I'd sure like to know what type of genes were created in this person. We're studying a new human species here. Someone's playing God with DNA."

"Yeah, tell me about it."

Harris had found the smoking gun to his quest. It was Chelsea herself. She was the anomaly. She was the weapon everyone was seeking. She was the hope left in Pandora's jar, the hope that mankind moved into a higher civilization. Everyone was looking for a solar-powered device to fire up their own sun. The map had led to Lily Chelsea and therefore Nzingha Chelsea, the weapon, the power, the DNA.

I get it, Harris considered. Xavier cloned twins some forty years ago disclosing his abandoned project inside them. Xavier concealed his project in plan sight.

Whoever wishes to keep a secret must first hide the fact that he possesses one, Harris measured.

Taffy's take on Xavier would be, a man is not what he thinks he is; he's what he hides.

However the true story went on how Nzingha Chelsea's sister died might remain a mystery, but the main elements of the existence of an experimentation was there.

Then to move on to the idea of extraterrestrial DNA, he wasn't sure and didn't rule that out either. Chelsea's DNA composition was off the recent periodic charts.

Chelsea was no doubt a great inventor of astronomical things. Floating cars, energy to last for centuries, moving things at speeds faster than light, and medicine to regenerate the body until it was whole again all sounded science fiction, Harris deemed, and it all came from just her. If that wasn't alien technology, I don't know what was.

Was it possible for one person to come up with all this in such a short time? This one person came up with this technology in a few years where the world couldn't figure it out in decades upon centuries or hadn't really came up with it at all. That song sprang in his head again, "Forever Young."

Then Chelsea had a human side to her in the way of relationships, business, and morals. She basically wanted what most humans wanted or at least strived for, minus a deity.

He'll be seeing her soon and wondered what he was going to say about the truth of her sister, Xavier, and her own DNA, for he now had proof of this quest's conclusion. It was supposed to be the CIA's motto "And ye shall know the truth and the truth shall make you free."

If Chelsea truly didn't know what she and her sister were, then he'd present the facts to her. He wondered how she was going to take it. *Would she believe me over her father?*

"Facts don't cease to exist because there ignored." Taffy would say. Harris wanted to tell Chelsea something else Taffy had told him many years ago. "I love you, kid; I would sooner have you hate me for telling you the truth than adore me for telling you lies."

No, maybe saying I love you might be too soon, he assumed, and so would the truth. Maybe he was just going to escort her to the grand opening of this museum and let nature take its course.

Maybe all this was one big practical joke and Chelsea was just some genius dreamer. She definitely represented the dreams of yesterday for the hope of today for the reality of tomorrow.

Through this quest he felt she secretly without so many words taught him to dream as if you'll live forever and live as if you'll die today. He felt it was a lesson not only for him but everyone. Listen to her business slogan, *never put off till tomorrow what you can do today.*

It was all about right timing. Time ripens all things and in time all things will be revealed. Harris felt time had ministered truth.

On another note "As tyme hem hurt, a tyme doth hem cure."

Ask, and it shall be given you; seek, and you
shall find, knock and it shall be opened

Matthew 7:7

Derrick John Wiggins who attended Lehman College has worked as a reprographics associate in Goldman Sachs, an investment banking firm and Paul Hastings a law firm.

He's also written a prequel thriller to Quest Pandora called Masters of Fire. You can see both trailers and place your comments at Youtube megadwiggins.